Bending at the Bow

Bending at the Bow

Marion Douglas

PRESS GANG PUBLISHERS

VANCOUVER

First Edition 1995

The Publisher acknowledges financial assistance from the Canada Council, the Book Publishing Industry Development Program of the Department of Canadian Heritage, and the Cultural Services Branch, Province of British Columbia.

The author wishes to acknowledge the Alberta Foundation for the Arts for assistance received during the writing of this book.

Canadian Cataloguing in Publication Data

Douglas, Marion K. (Marion Kay), 1952–
  Bending at the Bow

  ISBN 0-88974-051-0

  I. Title.
PS8557.0812B46 1995   C813'.54   C95-910661-8
PR9199.3.D68B46 1995

Edited by Nancy Pollak
Copy edited by Robin Van Heck
Cover and text design by Val Speidel
Cover art © 1995 by Sheila Norgate, *Broken Heart in Protective Custody*,
  mixed media on paper
Author photograph by Wendy Christiansen
Typeset in Weiss
Printed and bound in Canada by Best Book Manufacturers
Printed on acid-free paper ∞

Press Gang Publishers
101-225 East 17th Avenue
Vancouver, B.C. V5V 1A6 Canada

for Carla and Eric

Bending at the Bow

~

In thirty-seven years on this earth I have seen only two impossibly strange sights. Whether this should be considered luck or misfortune, I am not sure. The first involved Blodwen Scarfe, an acquaintance of my parents who, on Canada's one hundredth birthday, 1 July 1967, doused her hair with gasoline and set it ablaze. Burning like a match, she raced down a country hill on her bicycle and plunged headlong into the black water of what was known as the Little Mud River. I was standing nearby at the time, on the bank of that creek. I had celebrated my thirteenth birthday just ten days earlier.

The second strange sight I have seen often in the past year and a half, but it has not become any less outlandish with familiarity. I refer to the ashes I keep inside a white porcelain urn on my closet floor. These ashes once walked around in the form of Sylvie Rochon, my best friend, lover and companion of six years.

Recently, I have begun to see these two events — the near-suicide of Blodwen Scarfe and Sylvie's death — as a giant comb, parting my life, dividing it into this side and that, leaving me a narrow strip of white and perhaps dandruffy flesh to tromp up and down. And because I feel cramped with so little room to manoeuvre, I have felt it necessary once in a while to treat myself to the telling of lies. Lying is an indulgence, like buying new clothes or going to a movie, though generally more fulfilling. Crackling noises seem to occur behind my ears with each lie and, of course, there are the bruises. *Tell a lie and your heart gets a bruise.* That's what my grandmother Haggerty never missed an opportunity to say.

These injuries used to worry me. I no longer fret, though, because I have convinced myself that the heart, like the liver, can regenerate, creating new and innocent cells as needed. I imagine that by the time I go on one of my binges, my heart has restored itself and is an idiotically pink and expectant colour once again, prepared for an assault of purple and the darker greens.

The lies themselves are often very boring, having to do with events insignificant and banal, such as driving to Banff for the weekend, or going camping somewhere along the Forestry Trunk Road. I invent plans which then have to be disclosed to my neighbours so that . . . What? I myself am not sure. It is important to let them know when I will be away because there is Spike, my rabbit, to look in on and there are prowlers to think of. And there is the fact of being on the river bank, where you never know what manner of creature could haul up to shore. I watch my river bank closely, as do Ted and Maureen to the west of me and Edna and Isobel to the east, and even Ray, to the east of Edna and Isobel. River-watching is the thing to do for those housed along the banks of the Bow River.

"A cousin in Kamloops," began one of the lies I delivered this afternoon, watching my reflection in the car window as I hitched my sunglasses into my hair the way middle-class ladies will. "Andrea Haggerty," I went on. "She's a cousin on my mother's side. I haven't seen her since I was maybe fourteen. It's a tradition with all the girls on my mother's side to stay married for no more than five years at a time. Except for me, of course. I'm the one notable exception. But not Andrea. She's been married for two and a half years, which is about average."

Any kids?" Maureen wanted to know.

"One. A girl. I think her name is Madeline."

The lying details came to me without effort. There is of course no Madeline, neither am I related to an Andrea. The small amount of guilt I felt was assuaged by my belief that we do not necessarily pilot our own thoughts; often, it seems to me, they locate us or at least meet us halfway, rising up from some boggy site, a smelly hubbub impossible to ignore. My lies, unpremeditated as they usually were, could be thought of as transcendent.

"She must be just a baby," Maureen said.

"Well, actually, she's eight or nine," I said. "Andrea had her long before she got married. That's when the trouble began. It's the Haggerty nuptial curse."

What an incredible load of shit, I thought. My heart, which had begun the day the orangish-pink shade of a ripened mango, now floated in my chest the colour of an eggplant. I could see it clearly, jailed behind my rib cage, as I entered my car and the neighbours gathered round.

"Now Annie, you watch out for those logging trucks by Golden," Ray cautioned. "A buddy of mine got absolutely flattened like the coyote in those road runner cartoons. Nothing left for dental records." I tried not to be distracted by the white fleck of spit forming in the left corner of Ray's mouth.

Isobel shook her head and asked, "Is it really necessary to mention that sort of thing, Raymond?"

"Hey, it would've helped out my buddy."

Ted, arms folded, watched me. I had a feeling he might suspect my habit. Of the whole collection he knew me the best.

"Better go. See you Sunday," I returned his gaze with false confidence. "Thanks for watching the place. And Spike."

"Okay. Bye. No problem."

I drove off, leaving my house and my street and neighbours, all the visible details of my life, my single existence, which had begun to oppress me like an extra helping of gravity.

I need to do this, I told myself as I vanished from their sight. There were psychological luxuries, such as lottery fantasies and alcohol, and then there were necessities. I needed to lie, to go away leaving no truthful remains, to achieve escape velocity and float somewhere as in the space shuttle, away, above. To look out and see a blue and swirling atmosphere beneath which rotated my life and bungalow, my all too real and bodily history. To ride above the fact of Sylvie's ashes, lying below that precious atmosphere, beneath my roof, within my unlit closet.

～

And now for the truth.

I took the Trans-Canada Highway to the edge of the city, to the Calgary City Limits sign, at which point I turned around and headed back, taking Crowchild Trail south to Fiftieth Avenue. I travelled to its gravelly secluded end, to my workplace, the Calgary School (formerly "For the Deaf"). It was closed for the summer, but I had keys. I am an audiologist, equipped with my own office, and this was my specific destination.

The Calgary School (For the Deaf) is an old sandstone building, constructed in 1927 and added to and remodelled in various mismatched ways. Four years ago the Calgary School ceased to educate only the deaf and hard of hearing, hence the name change. Now all children in the area attend, along with numerous students with hearing impairments bused in from all over the city. Inside, it is like any school, except for the addition of some extra offices for the speech pathologists and me. But the original intention, to create an asylum on the edge of the city, remains unaltered, for although the city has grown, the Calgary School's location on the edge of a ravine, fortuitously near golf courses and undeveloped park land, has retained its remoteness.

Leaving my car in a nearby City Parks and Recreation lot, I skulked toward one of the school's side entrances. Armin, the custodian, was in his office listening to the radio and did not notice my furtive arrival. I knew well how to avoid him anyway: squirrel into the basement level as quickly as possible and take the very back, most derelict slate staircase up to the third floor. Once there, it was an easy walk to my office, which I unlocked and entered.

Relief. I felt rescued by my own disappearance. My heart's damage began to fade. Listening hard, I thought I could actually hear it spitting out those little bruise-marks like sunflower seeds, hear them hitting my window. In my audiologist's chair I sat, swivelling.

How long had it been? I didn't need a calendar to tally up the one year, six months and twenty-four days since Sylvie Rochon died. One is expected to get over such things, but on occasion one fails to do so. Or one does, but incorrectly, in a D-minus kind of way. The grade was handed out daily, it seemed.

I had never passed through the forecast stages of bereavement: the anger, denial turning into tears, and then the quiet acceptance, the little chat with God. Or, the hard moment of oneness with the earth, thinking of cheetahs as they hunt down gazelles, fawns dangling from the jaws of coyotes. *It is just the way of life.* No, for me there was just one long and gradually tapering stage — the stage of marvelling at the indifference of things. Sylvie's gloves, Sylvie's jars in the basement, Sylvie's map collection, Sylvie's Rocky Mountains, Sylvie's constellations. Not one of these seemed to have been altered by the loss of Sylvie Rochon. Only my interior shifted, huge tectonic plates on the loose, causing landslides at first but by now, I supposed, with most of their moving and uprising complete. I supposed now it was a steady process, one inch per year, forever.

Cause of death? A car accident. Some guy ran a red light. Well, not "some guy" — Wayne Abelard was his name. He was not drunk at the time of the accident; his defence was that he had worked all night at the Keating Carpet factory and had fallen asleep at the wheel. I do not know if this is true. I have never met Wayne Abelard, only thought about him as I run yellow lights or fail to merge properly. And at other times. Occasionally I speak his name out loud, in bed late at night or down by the river. It makes a clunking, gonging noise as it interacts with my mind: the noise of dumb, bad luck. Many times I have wished that his name could at least have been Peter instead of Wayne. I have wished a number of things about Wayne Abelard, in fact, wished his parents had not had sex on the night he was conceived or that Wayne senior had used a condom. Feckless wishes.

Swinging my chair around, I put my feet up on the window ledge and stared off into the blue, blue western sky. Once, it now seems long ago, after Sylvie and I had been living together for two or three years, I asked her what she would do if I died, got killed in a plane crash or ate some tainted oysters from off the coast of P.E.I. Sylvie, who could never be counted on to reply sensitively, answered with, "I guess I would take a lot of courses, like I used to before I met you. Evening courses. Course after course after course. I'd be known as the sad-eyed lady of continuing ed. Why? What would you do?"

"Well, I wouldn't take any courses, that's for sure. The opposite, probably. I'd stay inside and sit a lot, maybe stand around in a kind of daze. I think I'd use up lots of energy being resentful; I'm pretty good at that."

When Sylvie died, I remembered this prophesy and was true to it. Over the days and months I both stood and sat, looking at things, waiting for some transfiguration. I went out — I'm much too well trained ever to stop going to work — but I still managed to hate people for being alive. I imagined being cruel, slapping people's wasteful and pudgy faces or tripping them on the icy sidewalk and listening for their ugly, dry elbows to go crack on the cement.

After fourteen months of this, last March, I gave it up and took a course, the Sylvie Rochon Commemorative Yard and Garden Session was what I called it. At its conclusion I bought a product described as lawn aerator shoes, strap-on sandals with nail attachments that could easily have been designed as instruments of torture. I stomped around the yard in them, aerating my lawn, I supposed, and terrorizing Spike.

I also awarded myself a consolation prize: smoking. I had given up smoking years ago when I began to dream about my lungs filling with mucous nodules the size and colour of dandelions. Three cigarettes per day was my post-Sylvie ration. They have been, and continue to be, a great source of comfort.

I reached for my purse then, and violating a very significant rule, I opened my office window and lit up. The Calgary School was an uncompromisingly smoke-free environment. If Armin came along I would rapidly butt the thing and strenuously deny my guilt. Thus could I simultaneously develop unhealthy markings on both my heart and lungs.

So, you see, although more than a year and a half had elapsed since Sylvie's death, something was still wrong with my response to it. In fact, many things were wrong, I had to admit from my audiologist's chair. I was a liar with a bruised and dirty heart. Even my face, I suspected, had developed smudge marks. I wanted to hide my face. I had developed a clandestine relationship with life, or perhaps moreso with light. All of those days and nights of sorrow had brought me to an exile where I was simply alone, one who peeked out from between the slats of the venetian blinds, one who went to the movies unaccompanied. And for some reason, going out alone felt like a public and shameful admission, as if I were calling to other people in movie line-ups and so on, *Yoo-hoo, yoo-hoo*, gesticulating and making terribly indiscreet announcements about the condition of my underpants. Quite simply, I seemed to want a mate. I wanted a mate with me in all line-ups, all situations where inferences might be made regarding my desirability.

Oh, it's a sad commentary, I said to myself in my brother Grant's ominous voice, a sad commentary indeed.

By the river, in my bed, in theatre lobbies and in my audiologist's chair, I contemplated the lost integrity of my solitude. As a child, I never gave solitude a second thought; my body was mine and it would never have dreamed of hooking itself up with another for the purpose of pleasurable rubbing. Now I was a drifting piece of flesh. Without the anchor of a companion, lover, spouse, what have you, I wondered if someday I might find a part of myself washed up on the river bank.

And so at times it became apparent to me that I had to take a break and go into hiding, as I did today. Being in hiding was a relative condition, never noble but possibly just, possibly criminal, perhaps spiritual or maybe a trifle insane. Any number of conditions might motivate a hider, but not me, not this hider. I hid for no good reason except that instinct advised me now and again to hide out and instinct was not often wrong. Ask Spike, my rabbit. He hid often and effectively in his straw burrow. There was no reason, except his chromosomal recollection of the dangers of shadows, unfamiliar sounds, dogs, boots, and faces up close, too close.

I understand, Spike, I would say to him if he were here with me. I understood what drove him to hide from the watchers and the talkers. Retreat was the only option. Lucky for me I had this office and this sound booth. Such were the luxuries available to the trained audiologist.

❧

I first met Sylvie in February 1967, when I was twelve and she had just turned eleven. She was the daughter of the United Church minister, Reverend Philip Rochon and his wife, Daphne. There was also a fourteen-year-old son, Graham. The Rochon family had recently arrived from Burlington and was under close observation by everyone in my home town of Mesmer, Ontario. Sylvie and Graham were of particular interest, I suppose because the children of clerics arouse a certain prurient curiosity, being evidence that no matter how dogmatic or bloodless anyone may seem, no matter how dry and limp the handshake, there is always this fact: progeny. Sex has somehow been managed, the noisy pushing, the sweat, events completely out of control. We know, we have the results running around in Mesmer and elsewhere all over the globe.

Not that Reverend Rochon was of the effete and inexcitable class of clergy. He had a full head of curly, black hair, a hawkish nose and a wide mouth the ladies watched intently from their pews, moistening quietly. He was a locksmith, a sexual locksmith. I feel certain he took each and every one of those female minds and entered it. Reverend Rochon had that capacity because he spoke with both passion and intelligence. And he had those two beautiful children, with their blonde hair and eyes the grey and skeptical colour of a wolf, and Daphne, so lovely and restrained.

Of the Rochon family, it was Graham I spoke with first. I had decided to drop by after school to that house called the manse in order to get to know this Sylvie girl with the long hair, and as I approached, Graham appeared at the side door.

"Catechism class," he said. "Must be going. Must not be late for catechism class. Cataclysm class. Who made you? you might wonder. It wasn't your old man who did it, like you might have thought prior to catechism class. No, it was God. God made you. Simple, isn't it? Remember that."

Graham liked me from the start and I cannot say why. Maybe because I was the first kid to drop by the manse, Graham felt obliged to reward me with his most subversive thoughts.

"Do you know what I think?" he asked that afternoon. Hammering sounds came from within the house and a tired voice, "Sylvie, please not so loud."

"No, I don't," I finally answered, wanting him to get on

with it, somewhat amazed that he would actually await a response to what in Mesmer and environs was always a rhetorical question.

"I know you don't," he said, "so I'll tell you. I think that God died a long time ago and that he's out there now, just somersaulting through space, his big old pink ass just turning and falling. Of course, maybe it's not pink, I don't know, maybe I'm prejudiced. Doesn't matter. It's an ass and it's a big one. And the ironic thing is I don't think he's even going to roll by anywhere near earth. He's falling way out in some other galaxy. We don't even get to see the remains pass by, not here in Mesmer anyway. That's for sure. Anyway, gotta run."

It must have been the combination of the word "ironic" — a word I was unaccustomed to hearing peers use — and the fact I was entering the manse that caused me to anticipate mystery within. Indirect meanings, perhaps, things illuminated from behind, the enigma of the eclipsed? These were not to be. The manse was an ordinary house with ceiling lights which, even though it was late afternoon in winter, had not been switched on. From the kitchen, I could see the silhouette of Daphne, reclining on the living room couch. At the table stood Sylvie with a hammer. Everything was uniformly obscure and gloomy.

"My mother has a sinus headache. That's why the lights are off," Sylvie said. "I have to smash the ice and put it into this ice pack and she puts it on her sinuses." A whacking of ice inside a tea towel followed. "It'll just take a minute."

"Who is it?" came Daphne's voice.

"Somebody from school. What's your name?"

"Annie."

"It's Annie."

"Annie who?" asked Daphne.

Sylvie looked at me. "Clemens," I said.

"Pardon me?" came the voice from the couch.

"Clemens," Sylvie half shouted.

The ice pack having been filled and delivered, Sylvie motioned to me to be quiet and follow. Outside, she pulled a key from her pocket. "The Buick. I like to sit in the Buick and listen to the radio. I can even get Detroit sometimes, which is the only good thing I can say about Mesmer so far. We couldn't get Detroit in Burlington."

With the key turned to "Acc," Sylvie in the driver's seat and me in the passenger's, we listened to the radio. Sylvie told me two things that afternoon: that she sometimes pretended her parents were bank robbers and that her mother called her "Toots" instead of "Sylvie, dear." "Whenever she calls me 'Sylvie, dear' in that tired voice she always uses, I imagine she's saying 'Toots' but in a more energetic kind of voice," she said. The other piece of information she divulged was that she and Graham had keys for everything, the cars, the church and even their dad's study. Graham had had them cut at the hardware store. "Everybody trusts the minister's kids," Sylvie told me, "which they shouldn't, because Graham can lie like a rug."

Sylvie and I were childhood friends for six or seven months, until circumstances parted us. I lost touch with her not long after the Rochons left Mesmer. We wrote for a while, but the correspondence quickly petered out; Sylvie was never the letter-writing sort. I never forgot her, though; I somehow knew I shouldn't. Some people return, orbit by, and it's important that we be watching at the appropriate moment.

In the summer of 1984, seventeen years later, it happened — I ran into Sylvie at the Planetarium gift shop. She was shopping for a telescope, I for a gift for my nephew, my sister Lorna's son. Something about the way she moved caught my eye and I began to scrutinize, from the opposite side of a row of shelves, that narrow pale face. She was intently leafing through astronomy guides. On my side of the shelves I fumbled through paraphernalia, glow-in-the-dark stars and Mariner II pencil sharpeners before finally deciding to extend my neck, rest my chin next to an inflatable moon and whisper a tentative, "Sylvie?" If she only half heard the name, I reasoned, and it wasn't hers, there would be no response. But she looked up and there were those grey eyes again.

"Annie," she said, not questioningly but as a choice, decisively. *Red rover, red rover, let Annie come over.* Years and years fell away from me in an instant; I could almost hear them, that rolling sound of marbles on a slope.

We talked outside in the parking lot, her with a new telescope, me with a T-shirt, size 6X, bearing an image of our solar system. Sylvie didn't have a car; I offered her a ride, one of a series of offers I made that day. I offered to help her assemble the telescope and later, when darkness fell, I offered to kiss her. We never did look through the telescope; it spent the night on its lonely tripod and Sylvie spent the night with me. Less than two months later, she moved into my house. That was July 1984. She stayed until 18 January 1990 and not once during those six years did I tell gratuitous lies to my neighbours or drive to my sound booth for no good reason.

~

On this occasion, I had brought along a novel by Don Delillo and magazines, a *National Geographic* for browsing and the most recent issue of *Maclean's*, containing an article on the big bang theory. There had been a significant finding; this I knew from the headlines in the daily paper. From what little I had read, it seemed that some individual or group of individuals with an extraordinary set of telescopes and radio receivers had looked backward in time to the very moment the big bang itself had occurred, or perhaps circumstances immediately subsequent: the gargantuan hush, the enormous scattering. As the evening wore on, from the floor of my sound booth I mused on the clutter of sights the scientists would have had to pass en route to the big bang. I wondered whether they glanced briefly at Sylvie's automobile accident, stuck in the midst of the almost infinite conveyor belt of past events, between, let us say, some unfortunate woman's miscarriage and a child eating gravel.

The magazines and novel were meant to provide a diversion. The single tablet of Ativan I had brought along, however, was my comfort. Ativan was the trade name of the medication I took, as needed. My physician, Dr. Panesh, called Ativan a sedative; I preferred to think of it as a *nerve pill.* To think of it as such was more honest, I believed. To think, *I should take a nerve pill now,* rather than, *I need a sedative,* might lighten or even erase one of my false heart's skid marks.

Life is filled with minor reprisals, I concluded, hurling the Ativan to the back of my throat, washing it down with a swig of bottled water. "Nerve pill" was a phrase I had learned during the time I spent right after high school working in a TV dinner factory not far from Mesmer. It was a modern, industrial imperative that all the ladies in the employ of that manufacturer were prescribed nerve pills to help them out. The forelady let me know early on in my two months there that if necessary she could get me some, an offer I found appalling. My father had worked for twenty-five years in a pharmaceutical plant, developing rashes, polyps, even breasts after a period of working on the birth control line. I was certainly not in need of anything like a nerve pill. Nor was I like the other ladies, whom I secretly condemned for their hair nets and the plans they crossed off one by one: *we've got the washer and dryer set, now we'll be getting the dining room redone.* For me, it was only a summer job. My blood stream ran red and clear of pharmaceutical toxins. Now, years later, I was one of those women, I had nerve pills. They were a help, I am unashamed to say. They helped slow the approach of all the hauntings I sought to escape in the sound booth. Slow, but not entirely prevent.

The beauty of the sound booth was its absolute poverty of sound and sight. It was almost hermetically sealed, like most things nowadays, ever since the Tylenol poisonings; not even memory seemed capable of insinuating itself into my white and private territory. Once I had swallowed my nerve pill, sleep was an easy slide into the underworld. What could not be kept out of the sound booth, however much pharmaceutical help I enjoyed, was imagination. My imagination had an almost bacterial ability to take hold and grow. Thus some time in the night, as the Calgary School creaked and groaned above its ravine overlooking the Elbow River, the pale and relentless circumstances of my life caught up with me again.

Here they come, I said to myself from the twilight world of half-sleep, like a big herd of snails, snails under water, stretched out and swinging their antennae from side to side. They knew where I was; they thought it amusing that I thought they didn't. Up from the river they came, along the hardwood floors they slid, implacable, hundreds of thousands of snails. They gave off an unearthly smell of marsh and singed hair, like the smell of Blodwen Scarfe the night she set herself on fire. Escape down the hallway was impossible. Stepping on those snails would make a sickening sound, like breaking teeth, or dreams of breaking teeth. That was when I woke up, for good.

By six a.m. I had invented a convincing explanation for my untimely return home. "It was the clutch," I said aloud in my office. I'd tell Maureen and Ted and Edna and Isobel that's why I came back so soon. The car started to act up just before Revelstoke, so I turned around and came home before it went completely. Of course, Ray would want to take a look at it, but I would deal with that problem when it arose. One more yarn at this stage in the game would hardly make a difference to my disfigured heart.

~

Half an hour later, I sat in my back yard waiting for the sun to rise, reluctant to enter my house just yet. From the river came soft, gurgling noises, the river where I would be obliged to dump Sylvie's ashes one day soon. During our discussion about death, Sylvie had told me her preference was to be cremated, then dumped into the Bow River. "Not me," I said. "I'd rather be buried. There's always the off chance we might rise again. You never know." Whenever I made this sort of comment, Sylvie's face assumed the same expression as when she sniffed at refrigerated leftovers. But as for the Bow River and her ashes, like a fool, I promised. I simply have not yet been able to follow through. There is a coziness in having those flakes of Sylvie nearby, they give off a bit of warmth at night. And the river is so cold.

I often sit outside in the early morning; I like that time of day. It is a seam, a connecting point between yesterday and today, a place to sit and think without the endless intrusion of words. In the early morning, thoughts seemed to form on the inside of my skull. Like drops of water condensing on a window pane, they eventually ran downward, using themselves up in their brief tracks and ending vaguely, of too little substance for gravity to get a good hold on. This morning a collection of small, convex images gazed back at me: the car's dash board, Ted and Maureen, headlights, my own face talking, as I happily made up stories. And then Alexa, the usher who left.

I had met Alexa at a theatre grandly named Proof of Life on Earth, a place I had convinced myself, in a moment of right thinking, I should volunteer in order to meet new people. Completely against my nature, I had made a contract with myself to persevere for three months. The psychologist at the Calgary School, a very earnest woman named Harriett Dafoe, encouraged me and assisted in drafting the contract. And as a result of my contract with myself, I met Alexa Stewart, another volunteer but with a different motive, namely to work her way into the world of theatre. We ushered together every other Friday night for eight weeks and I began to like her. Alexa could tell stories intimate in detail and style. She told stories that suggested I was her first choice of audience, and I noticed that indeed, Alexa did not tell her stories to Steve, the box office man, or Bonnie, another usher, whose nervous laughter was more a shaking than a sound.

Alexa told me about her brother, Andrew, who liked to buy a new suit then go out shoplifting. And stories about her sisters: Colleen, the physiotherapist who insisted her daughter refer to her runners as "gross motor shoes"; Fiona, the dentist, the nervous one, prone to anxiety attacks while driving. Occasionally, Fiona called Alexa from roadside phone booths, convinced she had forgotten how to drive or that she couldn't trust her arms to obey her. "My arms want me to drive into Eaton's," she said once to Alexa from a phone somewhere in Vancouver.

There are minor thrills on this earth, little trophies we find now and again, like a fifty-dollar bill on the street.

Alexa's attention was one of these. Way inside my skull, beyond those semicircular canals, farther in, in the more glandular areas, there was occurring, I knew, a thrill response to Alexa. And that's what held my attention that morning, sitting on the seam between the twelfth and thirteenth days of August 1991.

I wonder what she's doing right now, I thought. I wonder if she's up; maybe she hasn't been to bed yet. Maybe she's having difficulties with an Instant Teller. She spoke of Instant Tellers often, of getting twenties from them as if they were kindly, compliant robots. She liked to keep track of her finances in terms of twenties, how many twenties into overdraft she was. Alexa was often into overdraft.

As I entered a stupor of pleasant conjecture, out of their yard and the early morning came Edna and Isobel. My neighbours had a sixth sense about my whereabouts, I was convinced, and since Sylvie's death had made it their business to fuss over me. I seemed to emit a type of siren noise that attracted them, especially when I was in my back yard, brooding or daydreaming, no matter what the hour of the day.

Edna and Isobel always appeared as a pair. Edna was forgetful and sometimes walked along the Bow, never far, maybe past ten or twelve houses, to where the river bends. The problem was that she would wander into yards, touch barbecues or swing sets that did not belong to her. People became quite alarmed. So Isobel was always close by, watching Edna for *signs*.

"You're back," cried Isobel, reining me in from my reverie. "Thank goodness it's you. Edna got me up, said

she was sure there was somebody in your yard. We almost
called Ted, then decided we'd check things out for ourselves. Of course, I don't know what we would have done
if there'd actually been a prowler. My karate's a bit rusty."

"Anyway, are you all right, dear?" Isobel asked me. "Are
you certain you should be out-of-doors at this time in just
a sweater?" Nursely behaviour was second nature to Isobel;
she had worked at the San, as had Edna, for years. Originally for the tubercular, then for the insane, the San, as it
was called by everyone, now stood grand and empty on
the other side of the river.

"I'm fine, Isobel, fine," I said. "My clutch started to act
up before I got to Revelstoke, so I decided to come home."
Sometimes, I admit, I lack the stomach to revisit my lies
and embellish them as needed; on those occasions I cast
all manner of bait to my audience, flattering comments,
juicy bits of gossip, whatever might be most distracting.
"And do you know what?" I asked. "I love it when you say
out-of-doors. Will you say it again for me? No one says
out-of-doors any more except you and Edna."

"Out-of-doors. There, I've said it. Don't say I never did
anything for you," Isobel said. "Now, here's a blanket. I
brought it along because I thought it might come in
handy for subduing that prowler. Put it around your shoulders and get warmed up."

A flock of geese flew by without honking, so low the
beating of their wings could be heard, strong beats that
could scrape your skin right off if they happened to dip
down into the yard.

"Well, there *they* go," said Edna, as if those particular

geese were acquaintances of hers. "You know," she went on, "I just realized now, I've always thought that, because they fly in a *v*, geese must somehow know our alphabet. Isn't that crazy?"

Isobel's response was a careful "Hmmm."

"Well, naturally," Edna said, "if someone had asked me, 'Do geese know our alphabet?' I would have answered no. But a part of one's mind can't help thinking otherwise."

"I suppose so, Edna," Isobel said, shooting a knowing look my way. I did not like to return Isobel's archness, had no wish to indulge in conspiratorial eyebrow activity with her where Edna was concerned, so I donned a neutral expression, the face of a referee, perfected for these occasions. In return for my effort at neutrality, Isobel started to leave, saying, "Well, if you're all right then, Annie, I'm going back to bed. Edna, are you coming?"

"No, I think I'll stay with Annie for a while."

Another look from Isobel, like a dart past my head. *"Don't let her out of your sight.*

The geese returned, having circled around and charted a course in their cryptic goosely minds. This time, Edna did not comment. From where she sat in the rickety lawn chair next to me though, I thought I heard something. Whether it was the fabric of her dress rustling or a quiet sigh I could not be certain.

~

Alexa Stewart was indeed awake, had not been to sleep at all and, yes, had gone to an Instant Teller yesterday evening to obtain money for gas, leaving her bank balance at a chilling –$120. Eighty dollars of overdraft protection left, four thin twenties. To Alexa, overdraft protection did not really feel like protection. No, to her it felt more like a walk-in freezer. Those negative numbers made her feel surrounded by frozen cuts of meat, stacks of ice-cold patties. Time to go and talk to the loans people, she thought, or else walk deeper into the big freezer, way inside with the hanging sides of beef.

Alexa was moving her possessions out of Janet Sainsbury's apartment and into her own. She had spent the entire night driving back and forth from the south of the city to its centre, had even crossed paths with Annie Clemens on one of her trips, unbeknownst to both of them. *Head light burnt out,* Annie had thought reflexively, on her way home, when Alexa sped demonically south. Now, finally, as dawn arrived, Alexa was moving her last cargo, the aquariums and fish. She had already made several trips to move buckets of aquarium water, which had sloshed wildly in the back seat and trunk. This did not matter; it was important to preserve the nitrogen balance for the fish. A sudden change would kill them. For this last trip the three tanks rode on the back seat, while on the floor and in the front sat numerous baggies filled with individual fish and a big puff of Alexa's own exhaled breath.

Alexa herself felt as displaced as she was certain her fish did. Poor little pisces. "Are you okay?" she asked and in response heard in the voice of Janet Sainsbury, *Your fish don't think. When you imagine your fish to be sharing your experience, that's called anthropomorphism.*

Janet, Alexa thought, how would *you* or anyone know how my fish are or are not feeling? Their transparent worlds are riding on an unfamiliar and, worse yet, plaid car upholstery, enough to make any creature ill at ease. Enough to make anyone thrash about and lurch suicidally against plastic walls. I'd like to see you imprisoned in an ocean of plaid.

At an intersection, Alexa turned on the interior light and began rooting through the glove box for any small relic of Janet that might have been left behind. Bingo. A bunch of red Cineplex pens bound together with an elastic. Thirty-four bucks an hour and she still felt entitled to steal their pens, Alexa thought, leaping out of the car and placing the bundle behind the rear tire nearest her.

Oh Grampa, kindly dead Grampa Hansen, Alexa thought, if you knew that your little orange Pinto were being used in this manner. Wherever you are, don't watch, okay. Just don't watch. Continue to play bridge — don't look down.

Then, with no other cars in sight, Alexa began leisurely to rock her car back and forth over the pens. Cases and contents were crushed, leaving a maroon inkblot strewn with vicious needles of red plastic. Alexa stepped out onto the street, admired the effects of her vengeance, and drove off.

Yes, yes, yes! thought Alexa. How satisfying, how intensely satisfying, and this is just the beginning of the greatest revenge play ever written. The heater blasted hot air to keep the fish warm and Alexa began to sweat. She drove faster, wanting to get the fish out of their plastic bags, wanting to get things arranged, wanting to get the telephone connected so that she could begin to leave sinister messages on Janet's answering machine.

Janet had diligently coached Alexa in the benefits of what she called positive imaging, but Alexa had been a recalcitrant student. She felt she had a natural bent for negative imaging. She could not stop herself, as she drove the final few blocks along Seventeenth Avenue, from picturing Janet, reclining with her cat, Diva, on the burgundy-coloured leather couch while Alexa hurled the last of her possessions — a few cassette tapes — into a cardboard box. Effortlessly, Alexa imagined that couch transforming itself into a huge rat-shaped clot of blood, into which she watched Janet slowly sink. Only Diva would be allowed to jump free, escaping with bloodied paws which would leave maddening but rather pretty prints all over the pale grey carpet.

Gratified, Alexa stopped her car in front of her new home, a three-storey walkup called the Daiquiri. Alexa liked the name. It had an unapologetically tawdry quality that would have given Janet the shivers. "Well, little pisces," she said to her fish, "let's get you off this plaid landscape and into your tanks. And I'll get into my tank. Life begins again, here at the Daiquiri."

~

T his fact of having met Sylvie so long ago and then become lovers in adulthood has affected time strangely, folded it up like a piece of paper, pleated it so that certain days touch that otherwise would not. Time is curved, scientists say. "Curved, isn't that a lovely word," Edna had commented one day. "An old Chinese fellow at the San once complimented me on my curved hair. He meant curly, but that's how it was translated in his mind." Perhaps time is in fact *curly*. At any rate, tracing the curves and curls of time has returned Miss Philippa Lynch to my mind.

Miss Lynch was a music teacher, an itinerant who came to Mesmer School in a little red car. She had long and spectacular scars up both arms, like the suture marks children draw on witches and monsters. The scars were from a car accident, and Miss Lynch's nerves were shot as a result of this mishap; she had a right to be nervous, everyone said. And because the adults believed that Miss Lynch had every right to be nervous, they helped her out. They made way.

On Fridays, Miss Lynch appeared at our school in her thin, beige and freckled body. During music class, if a map or blind snapped up unexpectedly, Miss Lynch would leap from the piano bench and scream. Stifled laughter would follow, though not from me. I found Miss Lynch fascinating, viewing her with the same lascivious interest I did dirty jokes. An adult who was terrified by small events, jumping and screaming, made for a lurid show.

Sylvie had not been at Mesmer School long enough to appreciate Miss Lynch's remarkable qualities. I can think of no motive for what I did other than that I wanted Sylvie to share in my knowledge of this unusual adult, to see Miss Lynch jump up and scream in genuine terror. I wanted Sylvie to see how shot full of fear older flesh could become.

Early on in our acquaintanceship we were sitting in the Buick one Saturday afternoon when we saw Miss Lynch enter the church through the side door. Apparently she was needed to play the organ that week, as she occasionally was, and intended to practice.

"Let's go in," I said. "I want to show you something."

Through the side door we went and down into the always-unlit room called the parlour, farther down into the kitchen and then the Sunday school with its concrete floor and white curtains over high basement windows. Sylvie followed behind me, with her wolf-eyes. We had to get into the balcony without Miss Lynch's knowledge. Up the stairs at the front of the church, four flights handily located in the foyer, and we were in the balcony, looking down at Miss Lynch, who had her back to us, arranging sheets of music.

The balcony had a bit of a rake to it, and curtains that were always drawn to the sides. But the best thing about the balcony was the board nailed along the base of the railing to discourage small children from wriggling between the slats. This board provided about ten inches of hiding space for anyone choosing to lie perfectly flat on the balcony floor.

"I need a hymnbook," I whispered to Sylvie. She grabbed one from a pew.

"Now, we just have to hide here behind this board. You lie down and I'll lie down behind you." Sylvie shrugged and complied. I took my position, propped up on my left elbow.

"What now?" Sylvie wanted to know.

"Just watch Miss Lynch," I instructed, and taking the hymnbook, instead of merely dropping it as I had planned, I heaved it high up into the nave, where it brushed against a light fixture before descending. With a supernatural thump, it landed on a pew. Miss Lynch screamed, jumped up and screamed again. We ducked.

"She has bad nerves," I explained to Sylvie. "She's afraid of everything."

"Wow, is she ever."

I had hoped Sylvie would not laugh and she did not. She displayed an appropriate amount of awe, which pleased me. We stayed for a while, hidden, listening to Miss Lynch, as she eventually returned to the organ and began playing. She never needed much time to regain her composure, proving, I guess, that Miss Lynch's fear was a reflex beyond her control and not a dread that sent her skittering through the streets at night, looking for some other place to be.

~

Something many people, except we audiologists and certain other lab-coated groups, do not know is that the main function of the ear is to maintain equilibrium. Hearing is important only to the so-called higher forms of vertebrates. But we all need balance, both the sort that keeps us standing up straight and the sort that keeps us from running off the rails. To keep us from falling over, we have the fluid in the inner ear. And to keep us on those mental rails, we have the inner monologue, a ceaseless dictatorial blathering pulling us toward right action and away from madness. From what reservoir of noise this inner chatter comes from, no one knows, but come it does. There is no stopping any of the sequels to the big bang, especially this one. It is inevitable, therefore, that embarrassing and puerile questions will be posed from time to time by the inner ear — hairless, breastless questions that gawk out from between our more reasonable thoughts. Questions such as: Who is my best friend?

Holidays encourage such thinking; summer holidays practically demand it. As I washed my car one August afternoon, dreading the return to work, I scrubbed my way toward balance with that very question.

Most recently, I decided, my best friend had been Monica. Monica moved to Vancouver last spring, making best friendship an impossibility. Even here in Calgary, she was a difficult best friend, much of the time preferring silence and solitude to companionship. Monica always chose to live in apartment buildings, at least fifteen stories above the pavement; she liked to remove herself from the activity closest to the surface of the earth.

Nevertheless, she and Sylvie and I nearly always shared Thanksgiving and Christmas; we shared those large rhythms, the big seasonal amplitudes, the ones that create particularly loud silences for the lonely and alone. After eating turkey or ham and drinking too much wine, Monica would abruptly say, "Okay, I'm going now," and be out the door as if on a mission, as if about to sign up for some duty the rest of us were too cowardly to face.

Monica was a unique best friend, the only friend I have ever had who owned a gun. It was a shotgun, purchased from the Canadian Tire store. She got a licence, learned how to shoot (at the Calgary Rifle Range), then bought a box of shells, the kind found in ditches and fields, empty of their shot, festive in colour. A little larger, I once told her, and they could be used as patio lights.

Monica bought the gun because she thought she wanted to kill her grandmother, a reprehensible motive but maybe not as bad as it sounds. I met this grandmother at Monica's apartment when I dropped by one day. She smoked American cigarettes and had a tarry smell to her; I couldn't help but be reminded of the roofing gang my brother Grant worked with for a couple of summers. The grandmother's name was Margaret Platt. She did not speak to me the day I met her, only sat at the kitchen table ordering Monica to do this and that. "Make some more coffee, Nicky. Empty the ashtray will you, pet?"

Of course, these were not adequate reasons to kill a grandmother. Monica wanted to kill Margaret Platt because she had forced Monica's mother, pregnant at age fifteen, to marry Hugh Stanton, the father, "Thus ruining several lives for the long term," Monica said once, "instead of just inconveniencing one, her own, for the short term."

The marriage had been bad, very bad, with much misery, much fighting, a broken nose (Monica's mother's) and finally a divorce that left Monica and her mother on Margaret Platt's doorstep. Monica was then eight. She lived with her grandmother until she was sixteen. Hardly a day passed when Margaret Platt did not comment unfavourably on Monica's hair, teeth, skin, legs, voice, even her odour. "You have the strangest smell about you, child," she would say, "like cooked noodles. Just like cooked noodles, that starchy smell."

Monica bought the gun on a whim for her thirty-second birthday. She daydreamed about stalking her grandmother out on the prairie, tying her to the hood of her car and driving triumphantly back into town. But when this daydreaming turned to *bona fide* hatred, when she found herself believing she could actually pull a trigger and cause parts of Margaret Platt to sail across rooms and onto walls or innocent poplar trees, she decided she had better move to Vancouver.

I am the only person on earth who knows this about Monica; she never told Sylvie about either the gun or her plans. I am the only one who knows, a privilege, an incredible privilege, I admit: the entitlement of a best friend. I liken it to those wacky reports of the miraculous, profiles of the Virgin Mary found in a loaf of bread or desk ornaments shedding real tears on Easter morning. When I looked at Monica before she left, I saw what nobody else saw.

Outwardly, and in all other respects, Monica was engaging, even charming. She worked at Word House, the same bookstore as Sylvie, which is how we met. People fell for her. She read avidly to compensate for her lack of formal education. The only quality in Monica I found annoying was her tendency to overuse the word *"Zeitgeist."*

Someone with whom you share a secret, someone who annoys you only intermittently and for the length of time required to utter a two-syllable word: these are qualities needed in a best friend, I thought, putting away the hose and bucket. Soon after, as I drove off late on that Wednesday afternoon to the Crosstown Flea Market, I decided that the best candidate for the position would be Ted, my next-door neighbour and occasional confidante.

Ted and I did have a secret, though far more conventional than Monica's. A couple of years ago, when Maureen was in Edmonton at her mother's house and Sylvie had gone with her boss to a book fair in Victoria, Ted came over to spend an evening. We were watching television and some comment led to another, somewhat vaguely sexual, which resulted in a moment of rather sudden and hot kissing, as if we had both been waiting for this opportunity for months. In thinking it over afterward, I felt certain neither of us had. By the time we were lying down and reaching beneath shirts, I had decided no, better stop, much to Ted's relief. He told me that being compared to Sylvie took the lead out of his pencil anyway. We wound up lying on the couch together like a married couple, watching the late news, which is perhaps what we had wanted all along. Since that day, though, something dormant has existed between us, unspoken thoughts that have taken on the qualities of a low-lying vapour, denser than air.

Yes, Ted would be a most suitable best friend. As for minor annoyances, I could identify one soon enough, I decided, turning off of Sixteenth Avenue and into the flea market, "The Crosstown — Traders in Debris," as Sylvie referred to the place.

Well, it might only offer trade in debris but the Crosstown had become a sanctuary for me, the woman now unescorted through life. It was good for those without even a designated best friend, a spa of sorts, a seamy Club Med, organized as it was and entirely predictable with no explanations ever needed. Sylvie and I used to frequent restaurants and outdoor cafés, where the patrons sat with their large Kennedyesque smiles and healthy, wide jaws. I no longer appeared to fit in such places, although my jaw was just as healthy as it had always been. Even the ordinary shopping centres seemed too brightly lit and coupled. Couples, couples everywhere. The sticklebacks, I called those couples, because only I smugly knew how brief their life cycles would be, how transitory their silly mating behaviour.

Now, the Crosstown could be counted on for darkness and gloom at midday, none of those huge white sets of teeth grinning above cappuccino, never. No surprises at the flea market. I knew full well what to expect before I had even stepped inside: the entrepreneurial spirit hunkered down and intoxicated with caffeine, disappointed and slightly churlish vendors, the never-valued displayed in a renewed attempt at valuing. Old Avon containers shaped like boots or trains. Things. And I was right: today there was the usual panorama of that which was not worth pawning, dotted with the usual clientele, those who found comfort in scavenging. People who, like crayfish or shrimp, could skitter sideways with great and alarming speed for specific prey: plastic replicas of Popeye, crocheted tea cozies, oil cans, grease guns, thermometers, you name it. I found the specificity of individual searches amazing. Amidst all of this seemingly undifferentiated junk were the tracks and trails of many a predator.

Normally, I was not after anything at the Crosstown. What I sought was its musty and begrudging communion. But that day I had a material goal. I was there to buy a retractable clothesline housed in a red metal case. One of the vendors, a woman named Luella, specialized in enamel basins and crocks, old cookware, mortars and pestles and the occasional piece of Medalta. Last time I was there, she had also had the retractable clothesline, for indoor use, and I had wondered ever since why I hadn't bought it. My parents once owned an identical device, designed for mounting on the wall, similar to the pencil sharpeners found in schools. From the metal unit, a double strand of cord could be pulled and attached to a hook on another wall, creating two lines for laundry. Once the clothes had been taken off the line, the cord could be wound into the metal wall case again. This process of reeling in the cord had a parsimoniousness I found pleasing. I liked to draw things in and tuck them neatly away; in fact, an ideal world would most certainly include a host of retractable options, especially for any appliance involving string, rope or hoses. Sylvie and I were opposites in this regard. She would have preferred to leave everything dangling. From hazy vacation plans to rarely finished papier-mâché projects, nothing about Sylvie Rochon sugggested anal retentiveness.

Luckily, the clothesline was still there. "How much do you want for this?" I asked Luella.

"Give me five dollars," she said. "It's in the collectibles books now. You're not going to get it for a quarter."

"I know. I know. My parents had one back in the days before dryers," I said, handing her a five.

"Enjoy," Luella said flatly, adjusting her wares to fill up the space made by my purchase.

I dropped the clothesline into my bag and looked around some more, satisfied with this find and happy, almost happy. Well, not quite, happy would be too extreme. But thinking about installing my clothesline cheered me, and the detailed planning involved brought me dizzyingly close to a state of contentment.

I would put up the clothesline as soon as I got home, I thought, in the kitchen. I could hang up little things, socks and tea towels. I liked the smell of drying laundry, especially in rooms other than the bathroom. I liked the idea of moving around and ducking beneath wet laundry. I liked the concept of less technology, less machinery, less fabric softener. Then, no, wait a minute, I thought, that isn't me, that's Sylvie. It was Sylvie, not me, who liked the idea of less technology and less consumerism, Sylvie who could stomach the odour of pawn shops and thrift stores. I frequented the Crosstown only because the smell of tobacco had overpowered the distasteful aromas of cast-offs. I would never have noticed this retractable clothes-line, never have visited the Crosstown, had I not lived with Sylvie Rochon for so long. Eulogies of Sylvie at times became confused with my own identity. I tried to watch out for this delusional kind of thinking.

Standing for a moment then in that enormous hall of junk, I became conscious of breathing in breath, recently used breath, breath that had moved over and through tobacco and coffee and cake donuts, breath that had hovered above baskets of spark plugs and rusted hand tools, breath of Luella, breath of the man who sold the coconut-shell monkey heads. Breath of people who had not kissed or been kissed for the longest of times and did not care. I was mouth-to-mouth with all of them and the effect was not resuscitative.

Time to repair to the little coffee room, I decided, the coffee room which was usually more chokingly filled with grease and smoke than the sale area. I was soothed there by the presence of the Greek woman who sold desserts and an old man whose hearing aid crackled and hummed fitfully. I considered advising him to adjust his ear mould, but did not. Best just to fall into this place where there was no need to talk or move or think or be pleasant in any way, where I could belly right up to my solitude, look my matelessness square in the eye.

Outside, I could hear the faint whirring of the Trans-Canada Highway with its people and people and more people driving by. I wondered whether, if I sat there long enough, the whole day, all of Wednesday, would drive by. Or maybe the week, or better yet, possibly my entire future. I wondered how it would look and what kind of car it would be driving. Maybe it, my future, would look a little bit like Alexa Stewart, I thought. I had seen Alexa often in her car, leaving the theatre parking lot. I had even once contemplated, in the dead of last winter, grabbing onto Alexa's car and sliding my way over the icy streets to her house for the night, surprising her, rising up from her bumper, a daredevil lover. If I waited in that coffee shop long enough I decided, my future, like Alexa, might happen to drive by in a rusty orange Ford Pinto.

~

Not long after the flea market, Ted convinced me to attend a meeting at the home of a woman named Martha Rigg. The meeting had to do with Canadian nationalism. Once a month a group dedicated to protective tariffs and opposed to free trade convened at Martha's house.

"I've met Martha," I said to Ted. "Remember? At your place. She's the one I referred to as Tits Rigg."

"Why Tits? I guess you've never seen Martha in profile," Ted replied.

"I think it's because at the time I was reading some pulpy book on the stars and there was a piece on Diana Rigg, one of my childhood heroines. Remember? *The Avengers*? And I had read that Laurence Olivier used to call her Tits because she didn't wear a bra. I think I probably met Martha just minutes after reading that. But, you're right, Ted," I said, "if my memory serves me right, Martha is one of the skinniest people I've ever met. She was unlike anything you would expect of a person named Tits."

"I'd call Martha the Anti-Tits, if I called her anything at all," Ted said.

This was certainly true I thought, soon after, having been transported to Martha's house by Ted. Martha was nothing but skin and bones. Her torso was boyish and her limbs the sort from which, when extended, knee and elbow joints protruded as if some insane gardener (such as my great aunt Agnes, who managed to fill her toaster with soil and spinach seeds) had shoved gladiolus bulbs under the skin at each site. Martha had baked bread for the occasion and by the time we arrived, everyone was lining up, sawing off hunks and buttering while she watched, arms crossed over her tiny bosom and eyes crossed ever so slightly behind her round lenses. In the middle of her living room stood a very complex-looking sewing machine, around which everyone moved.

Once I had obtained my allotment of bread, I settled in to staring at Martha, remembering my real reason for so readily consenting to attend what would no doubt be a dry affair. There was something I knew about Martha, something Ted had told me after my introduction to her. Just like me, Martha had had death's googly-eyed face come right up close to her and exhale its stunning breath into her nostrils.

The story was that a few years ago Martha and her husband, a fellow named Mac (short for Malcolm), were travelling through Mexico when three men broke into their van and shot Mac dead right then and there in front of Martha. They took everything, cameras, money, cassette tapes, clothing, everything but Mac. Him they left with

Martha, to drive through desert and scorched hills with the van overheating and Martha stopping and leaning down close to Mac's mouth, listening for breathing, checking for a heartbeat, appreciating that he was dead over and over again. How she kept going, I do not know. Just to drive to the hospital when I got the call about Sylvie was all I could do. I remember feeling stuck inside a Hitchcock movie, as if birds were pulling my mind right out of my skull, pulling long strands of pinkish brain out through my ears so that less and less cortex was there, only enough to tell me to keep going, keep steering until I arrived.

I am not acquainted with many people who have known this type of violence, commonplace in other parts of the globe but not here in southern Alberta. Here, life seems to hold us in a glove; we are kept away from death, it is difficult to get a real feel for it. With Martha, I felt myself to be in the presence of a minor but still very uncanny contradiction, a small and ornamental burning bush, perhaps a lilac which burned without being consumed on a suburban lawn. I remember staring fixedly and rudely at Martha, who took no notice.

She took charge of the meeting, reviewing the effects of the Free Trade Agreement, delivering what sounded like a very prepared lecture. Then she moved to the subject of the North American Free Trade Agreement, intended to include Mexico. "Yes, Mexico," Martha said, pausing and accidentally knocking a remnant of striped fabric off her sewing machine table. It was the plan to involve Mexico that had got her interested in the Company of Canada again, convinced her of the need to act to prevent a new

North American order based on Canadian resources and Mexican labour.

People chewed softly on their lumps of bread as Martha spoke. They were a doughy group, really, I thought, myself included. What effect could this flabby little team of bread-eaters possibly have? And as Martha talked about the component assembly plants, *maquiladoras*, being built along the Mexico-U.S. border, open vats of toxic waste and three dollars for a fourteen-hour day, my concentration wavered and settled on Mac, whom I had never met, and on foggy myth-making about him, his final days in Mexico, and other final days, specifically Sylvie's. I spawned a vague resentment of the attentive lot of chewers surrounding me. In time, people broke spontaneously into groups, letter-writing groups and information-gathering groups. Ted and I were ushered into the kitchen.

"Look at this," Martha said, holding aloft a large rectangular template, a cardboard image of Canada with the single word SOLD suspended diagonally between the Yukon and southern Ontario. Beneath, cut-away letters created the message REALTOR OF THE YEAR: BRIAN MULRONEY, and below that, FREE TRADE ISN'T.

"Do you like it?" she asked.

Ted gave a somewhat doubtful nod of approval. I asked, "What subgroup are we, exactly?"

"Come outside with me," was Martha's answer.

We followed along out the side door, through a composty-smelling back porch and into the yard. An old VW beetle of indeterminate colour sat in the dark, hunched up close to the house, filling up a yard that appeared all tan-

gled and overhung. Martha grabbed a jagged piece of dry-
wall from somewhere, tacked on the template and leaned
it against a shed. Then, handing me a can of spray paint
from the hood of the VW, she said, "Here, do it, Anne"
(calling me Anne, not Annie). "Spray it. Let's see how this
baby looks. I've spent a lot of time on this, cutting with
my X-acto knife late at night."

"Me?" I asked.

"Sure. Why not?"

"Shouldn't someone who's been to more of these meetings, someone who's a card-carrying member, be doing
this?" I said.

"Don't even mention the others. They're way too cau-
tious for me. Ted here, he's my man."

"So, why doesn't Ted do the spraying?"

"Oh, for God's sake," Martha said, pulling the can from
my hand and spraying with the full-throttled hissing of
the annoyed. "There," she concluded, thumping the can
back onto the beetle. Martha removed the tacks, turned
on the back porch light and there was the image, red and
spattery but with pleasingly discrete edges. "What do you
think, Ted? You want to do a little tomcat work with me
again? A bit of nighttime spraying? We were a good team."

Ted? Spraying? Late at night? I am certain my face
spoke of utter stupefaction.

"I don't think so, Martha," he said. "Last time you wanted
to fool around with mailboxes. I don't want to take chances
with my employer's property. Canada Post probably
already has a dozen reasons to get rid of me, and besides,
I'm getting too old for that nighttime stuff."

"I don't mean mailboxes, Ted. I mean the marginal types of things, things nobody really owns, hoardings and underpasses. Secret places. We simply leave a little message, that's all. There's nothing illegal about communicating, is there? It's not nearly as subversive as cheating on your taxes. And anyway, I can't help myself, but I'm too chicken to do it on my own. I need a companion."

"Not this time," Ted said. "Maybe it's the recession. It kind of makes me want to stay inside and look at my one remaining Canada Savings Bond."

That's when I offered to go with Martha. "Once," I said, "for the ride, as a companion . . . your moll." And I laughed heartily at this but Martha did not. She leaned against the beetle and said, "Okay. Maybe you could test my hearing sometime too, see if it's as acute as it used to be. That's what you do, right?"

"That's what I do some of the time," I said.

On the way home, Ted tried to talk me out of joining in on Martha's projects. He had not anticipated this outcome; he had only wanted me to meet some new people. And I myself could not adequately explain why I would want to take part in Martha's graffiti war. I cannot say that I cared deeply about trade agreements. I could only conclude that Martha had something, an attraction, not physical but yet biological, as if she had been sprayed with pheromones, as if her lost dead lover had coated her with the same air-borne precariousness Sylvie shot all over me at the moment of her death.

~

As children, my brother and sister and I, like most of our friends, had our days spun out for us as if we were fish tugging at a reel, moving this way and that, but always at the mercy of the hook. Evening came and we were yanked back to shore and out of our medium, back into the slow-moving places of parents and teachers and relatives. Not Sylvie, though. She never bore that childish look of waiting around, of anticipating higher authority. That was what I liked about her from the start.

We took to walking home from school together and sitting in Daphne's Buick. The Buick, whenever it was there — Daphne was inclined to shopping trips to Toronto and London — was always parked on the street, usually near enough to the church's side door to allow us to observe all sorts of comings and goings. One of the church's most frequent visitors was Miss Philippa Lynch. Another regular, but less frequent, visitor was Blodwen Scarfe. Indeed, it was from the vantage point of Daphne Rochon's Buick that I first began to pay close attention to Blodwen Scarfe and her dresses and shoes and dark-haired beauty. She did not come into town much and had a reputation for being aloof. But, because of the charms and mystery of Blodwen Scarfe — the big tobogganing hill on her farm, the fact she was childless — she had never in my mind been one of the humdrum characters occupying the plodding landscape of the grownups. She was different. I remember in the chill of March, wiping the condensation from the Buick's window to watch how Blodwen walked to her car, opened the door and slid inside. She moved like a movie star. She moved, Sylvie said, like her Aunt Dolores who lived in Los Angeles and almost had a part in the movie *Lawrence of Arabia*.

I learned much valuable information in that Buick; I learned about Daphne's family. Sylvie told me her mother's family was rich, the source of countless gifts for Sylvie and Graham, and cars and coats and dresses for Daphne. They were the Fryes; they owned a lumber company near Ottawa and felt that Daphne had martyred herself, marrying Philip, a minister, and living like church mice. Daphne often developed headaches, especially when her family visited. She missed her friend Bea Rosenhagen, from Burlington. "Her daughter was my best friend, Lily Rosenhagen," Sylvie said. "Her dad was a minister, too. That's partly why she was my friend and her mom was my mom's friend. Anyway, her dad got moved too. He got moved away to some place I forget the name of. I don't even know if it has a name. All I know is he has two churches now and one is way out in the country, just on a hill, no town at all. That's a sign of trouble when you're a minister, Lily told me. Her dad got into trouble and that's why he got the church with no town. And I'm starting to wonder, now that I know how big Mesmer really is, if my dad is in some kind of trouble too."

"But what kind of trouble could he get into being a minister?" I asked. "It's not as if he's like the manager of the Pharmaceutical and has to worry about safety. Jamie Fisk's father got his hand crushed and the manager got into trouble. He's from the States." (Nation of origin was often offered as an explanation for the negligence of the manager of Epson Pharmaceutical.) "Anyway," I said, "what kind of safety problems are there in a church? Maybe a two-year-old might fall out of the balcony, but that wouldn't be your dad's fault."

"Yeah, maybe," Sylvie said.

Another time she told me not to listen to much that Graham said. "He used to see a doctor in Burlington," she said, "you know what I mean? For his head. Don't listen to what he says. It could be we got moved because of him. He says God is dead and the Holy Ghost is a country and western singer. He cut some guy's picture out of the paper and said, 'This is him, the Holy Ghost.' It was this guy all dressed in black and with wispy little whiskers. I think he's a little bit mental."

We used to imagine that the Buick could rise, move straight up and hover somewhere higher than the water tower, higher than the hooks used to yank us home. That's where we would practice kissing, up there above the ground where Sylvie could claim to see all of Mesmer, which would never, ever be the size of Burlington. Never. Practice kissing was a popular activity back in 1967. Done completely without feeling and in a perfunctory way, it was an exercise like penmanship for most, but not for me. After the kissing there was always a moment just like the moment when Sylvie and I met again in later life — an acrobatic kind of moment, as if both of us were dangling in that paradoxical place the eyes create, outside her, outside me, inside both of us.

⁓

I t was Isobel who had talked Edna into selling her house and moving in with her, a fact Edna reflected upon often, sometimes ruefully, other times with what she considered soppy gratitude. Three-and-a-half years of adjusting later, and they were still living in what seemed to both of them, at times, a foreign state of camaraderie. They had their differences, the most significant of which seemed to be physiological. Isobel was six feet tall; Edna, five-three. Isobel was hale and hearty; Edna not so. Ironically, though, it was Isobel who most often visited the doctor, or medic, as she called him. Prevention was her theme. She swam for exercise, stripped and strode about the locker room during the seniors' swim, making comments such as, "Well, you don't have to travel to Greece to see old ruins, do you?" Isobel felt a trifle sexy entertaining the other women this way, maybe because her body had remained spare and athletic, never gone to sag and cellulite like most of the rest.

Meantime, Edna sat at home reading novels.

Isobel did not like fiction, she wanted the facts, straight up, like her Scotch. And so she brought home gifts of information for Edna, books from the library on the constitutional debate, handouts from the provincial government on bulbs or pruning, and from the doctor's office, pamphlets on health-related topics — heart disease, osteoporosis, Alzheimer's and low-fat diets. Edna tried to appreciate Isobel's offerings, all except the pamphlets from the doctor: these she viewed as a complete and utter waste. "I'm a lost cause," she would say to Isobel. "I'm eighty-one. There's nothing to be done to prevent eighty-one. There, I've even made a jingle to stress my point."

But Isobel persisted and this caused Edna not irritation so much as heartache. She was hurt by these informative, almost cheery, reminders of her own collapse. Her only recourse was to get rid of them.

It was the blue leaflet on low-fat diets Edna was folding into a rudimentary boat and sending off down the Bow River. "One more bit of paper can't hurt the environment that much," she said to herself, then stood for a while on the bank, watching her little craft sail away.

~

I could see Edna from the weather-beaten deck on the back of my house, the place I often sat to smoke one of my treasured cigarettes. It was evening, well into Saturday night, with the sun sinking around nine o'clock as it does here in the late summer. Before coming outside, I had admired the shadows cast on my kitchen wall by the tea towel, the dish cloth and the pair of socks hanging from my newly installed clothesline. These shadows made me feel as if I lived in a crowded and pleasingly chaotic situation. At that moment, I would have liked to be a cherished matriarch, mother of ten, happily accepting my lot, which evidently the real Annie Clemens was unable to do.

The real Annie Clemens preferred to sit on her deck, blaming her body for its failure to attract a lover, contemplating her thirty-seven-year-old parts in the way that a cherished mother of ten would never have wasted her time doing.

"Hi, Edna," I called. She waved on her way back inside, did not veer westward for a visit.

Yes, Saturday night was the worst night of the week. Once darkness fell, it seemed to me the night itself rose out of the river like some sighted being with a powerful set of binoculars. To remain on the deck became a challenge because, I was convinced, Saturday night could see me — from its vantage point on the Bow River — in much the same way people saw accidents, moving along, passing by that which had barely been missed, with relief and horror. I had an out-of-placeness on Saturday night, like the purse on the sidewalk no one thought to give the lady in the ambulance.

Monica had written, saying once again "I love it here," leaving me a bit cranky. It? So Monica loved "it" in Vancouver. How like her to love the impersonal "it." What? Or whom, I wondered. Had she found any new friends in Vancouver? Anyone to replace me? I doubted it. No matter how hard she tried, she would always want to be living on fifteenth floors and so on, above it all. Although, I had to admit, she didn't try very hard.

I could not say that I loved it here. It was denser than it should be, harder to walk through most times. I had noticed this for quite some time: as a single person I walked differently from the sticklebacks. With Sylvie, I had glided along like them, unaware of my gait. Now it seemed I walked with more and more effort, particularly conscious of my feet, ankles and knees. Christ, I thought, even my joints no longer enjoyed the oblivion Sylvie's company provided.

I took a deep breath and contemplated calling on Ted and Maureen. From my deck, the back of Ted's head could be seen in his living room. There he is, I thought, my new best friend, watching television, thinking, moving thoughts around in his mind as if they were pieces of furniture. Let's try this here, how about that over there. He didn't like his work as a letter carrier; said often that you could train a seal to do his job in a week. I knew this dissatisfaction occupied him much of the time; he read the paper's classifieds, businesses for sale, talked about buying a refrigerator truck.

No, best not to disturb them, I thought. I was becoming familiar enough with my habits to know I would be compelled to tell at least one lie, provide an explanation for myself, something involving cancelled plans and allusions to a hearty pack of friends I felt I should possess. It was hardly worth the effort; and besides, lying to one's best friend undoubtedly turned the heart into one huge contusion.

What I could do was walk to the video store, I decided. I could certainly make it that far on my self-conscious legs. The video store could be counted on, I knew, like the diner of past years, the Mesmer Café, for a certain conviviality and brightness. No one spoke, necessarily, but all were engaged in an easy sort of hunt. No speech sound was required or expected, just the tranquil grazing of a few humans. And tranquil it always was.

Once inside the video store, ensnared by the aroma of stale bagged popcorn and whatever that odd, near-rancid smell mountains of videotape seem to exude, I had the strongest desire to lie down and simply wait out Saturday night. I felt a retreat could safely be undertaken in my video outlet. Face down on the blue carpeting with the marquee lights reflecting merrily on my blue sweatshirt was where I would be most camouflaged. The word "collapsible" entered my mind in much the same way words enter the minds of those whose hearing I test: it had simply been thrown to me by some phenomenon. Without Sylvie, without Monica, with only my neighbours and far-flung family, it occurred to me that collapsible might be what I had become. An object whose supports can snap out of a locked position and fold up or out, a card table or an ironing board, leaning against the wall or flat upon the floor. The video store folk could come and go as they pleased, stepping quietly around me, the collapsible woman, my eyes level with their shoes and pant cuffs. I ceased my search for a movie long enough to glance at the footwear and pant legs of those around me: flattened running shoes, cowboy boots, frayed fabric. I stooped to pick up a gum wrapper, imagining how it would offend my collapsed self.

Then I left. I did not want a movie after all. I wanted to clatter out of there on my stick legs, my ironing-board legs, so I could laugh for a moment. Ativan, of course, that was the correct answer. And homeward I went, travelling in my ever-so-slightly-too-large body, disappearing around the mountain ash on the corner of Bow Bottom Road and Bowness Road. I planned to take a whole tablet (only five left — God *damn* that Dr. Panesh) and go to sleep, and in the morning Sunday would sit where Saturday had stood. Sunday, calm and sleepy, its eyes little slits of indifference.

∾

Alexa Stewart had settled into the Daiquiri; she was familiar with its routines. Weekend nights, young men walked the halls, pissing near the fire extinguisher, leaving pools here and there. After, they liked to chat outside near the dumpster. Often they spoke of burning the place down. None of this disturbed Alexa in the least, primarily because it represented the kind of recklessness Janet Sainsbury would have found appalling. And if events had the capacity to appall Janet, they had the ability to inspire Alexa. Such was her anger with Janet.

Alexa's greatest joy, now that her telephone had been connected, was to call Janet and leave disturbing messages on the answering machine. These messages did not involve Alexa's voice; they were either mechanical or electrical. The first had been the cry of the hair dryer, set at hot and held close to the receiver for one minute. Alexa timed this carefully. The second message came from the coffee bean grinder as it tore apart coffee beans. These acts were metaphorically perfect, Alexa believed; nothing but small screaming household appliances could adequately express her rage. Another time she held the nutcracker close to the phone and cracked a walnut. Bits of dust and shell fell into the receiver. Unpacking filled Alexa with ideas for revenge; each kitchen utensil revealed its black side to her.

Other days, Alexa sat on her living room floor and cried because Janet did not return the calls, not even to say "Stop being infantile," or to exhale irritatedly through those nostrils of hers and say nothing.

Janet Sainsbury was one amazing woman, Alexa often thought, one amazing woman. Janet amazed herself and others with her ability to prompt sycophantic loyalty. This ability had even resulted in the birth of Janet's own small cult, the Eye of the Beholder, its growth and evolution chronicled by Janet and her video camera. Janet loved cameras, she was a projectionist by trade, she liked to keep track of events.

As for Janet's own evolution, her origins were shrouded in mystery. She was a bit like Stonehenge or DNA. Janet claimed to have divorced herself from her parents at age eighteen, to have lived on a women's commune in Italy, to have been in Israel during the Yom Kippur war. Oddly, no pictures existed to support any of these claims. Alexa had at times wondered if Janet were an ingenious pathological liar, an invention, somebody spliced together from images seen in photojournalism exhibits, *Time, Newsweek, Maclean's* and National Film Board documentaries.

"We painted the cars' headlights blue," Janet said once, "during the Yom Kippur war, for the brownouts," and Alexa's mind had created a picture of Janet, sitting snugly in a library in Saskatoon or maybe Winnipeg, reading a magazine and confusing its contents with her own life.

Impossible to know the whole truth about Janet Sainsbury, Alexa thought, but I think I likely know enough for this lifetime. I know she could intellectualize a bowl of rice or a key chain into something profound if it served her needs in any way. I know that she would seduce Brigitte

McTeer, my best friend, *and* her husband, Henry, and then try to explain it as a metaphor for her appetite for me. Another human being as a metaphor. Good try, Janet Sainsbury. Even I am not so egotistical as to believe that. Fuck off, Janet Sainsbury, Alexa thought. You can take your labia majora and your labia minora and you can piss on them. You *can* piss on them, can't you? Just like you, Janet Sainsbury.

Alexa went into the bedroom to watch her fish, her sedating little roommates. She loved her fish. Often, she could feel this love for her fish radiating out of her in ever-widening concentric hoops, hatched lines like those used in science texts to show the motion of particles, radioactivity, magnetism and so on. Standing close to the goldfish tank, Alexa expected to see a slight rippling of the water, a slight rippling from her love-power. The fish came close, hoping for food.

"You're aware that she's gone, aren't you?" Alexa said. "Silver dollars? You must notice the difference. That huge, vain ego is no more. You know, the one who once referred to you as 'Alexa's plebeian pastime.' She's out of the picture now. She must have been like a big, black mountain to you, always off in the distance with her depressing black clothes. I wonder if you had a name for her. Possibly Mount Etna. I hope you don't think something terrible has happened, something that has screwed up your fish cosmology, although that would certainly please Miss Etna, to think that an entire fish culture had lost one of its most important symbols because of her. No, let me assure you, she was just a person, just one person in a landscape of many." And Alexa sat down on the pile of quilts and blankets she called a bed and resolved that her next phone call would involve her kettle, which could steam and whistle in a hostile way.

~

From the kitchen window, I could see Ted in his yard. He did not yet know that he had become my best friend and I was unsure how to notify him. There were no greeting cards that seemed suitable.

I must say, I liked the look of his head in the after-work September sun. It was a large and friendly head, kisssable in fact, the sort of head you would want to kiss on its very top. Ted's large head was orchestrating the yanking up of the croquet wickets in preparation for lawn mowing and I thought it best not to disturb him. If I had any telepathic powers at all, I could surely throw my thoughts the fifty or so feet between my head and his without moving an inch. Thus would I talk to my best friend.

Ted, I thought with vigour, Ted, listen to me. Do you realize most people think it necessary to be a serial killer to lead a secretive double life? Most people, but not me. I have known for some time now that secretive double lives can be conducted in very ordinary ways. I learned this lesson five years ago when Sylvie and I went to Vancouver to spend Thanksgiving with Daphne and Philip. They are still living, by the way, in Vancouver. We drove out; the Tercel was just newly purchased and could at that time be counted on to overtake some cars — minis and the like.

It was my third trip to the Rochons, who had actually remembered me from Mesmer. They liked me; they approved of me. If their daughter had to be living with a woman, then, I guess they thought, what better sort, what more steady type, than a trained audiologist. Mr. and Mrs. Rochon had abandoned the idea of Sylvie finishing anything in the post-secondary department. Graham, on the other hand, had turned into a gynecologist with a beeper and a skeletal girlfriend named Oona who rarely spoke other than to comment on the quality of fabric in a shirt or dress.

As Ted dragged out the lawn mower from the carport, I intensified the power of my thinking; I was about to be faced with some noisy competition. Are you with me here, Ted? I asked. Are you? Give me a sign. He yanked on the starter.

By that day, Ted, that Thanksgiving, Daphne and Philip were both in their late fifties. Philip was still handsome and satisfied with himself, completed it seemed by what was his last and most important church. Daphne had changed, though. She no longer drove at all; ecological conscious- ness had brought a halt to that and her shopping sprees. Long walks were her solace, it seemed, and sitting on the sun porch. Sylvie worried that her mother had no interests, no pets, no hobbies. She gave large sums of money to a conservation fund. Several members of the congregation thought her a bit dotty, with her wild white hair.

But the thing was, Ted, Ted — check the gas tank, Ted, yes that's right — she told me that day about her secret life. "You mustn't tell Sylvie or Graham," she said, "certainly not Philip. You won't, will you? I just want someone to know I'm not as lifeless as I seem. But not them. I don't know why. Why is that, I wonder. You get used to your family thinking you're a certain way and you don't want to upset the apple cart."

We were making gravy. Everything else was done and Daphne had banished the others from the kitchen.

"I ride the buses," Daphne said with a look of triumph. That was her grand announcement. "I have always enjoyed movement," she said, as if this were a rather exclusive trait. "And I've struck up a few friendships on the buses. There are several people who never enter a church who know me now by name. Sometimes Elsie, she's one of them, and I get off in Chinatown and have coffee. And sometimes I go off to the Army and Navy store with a fellow named Stan. I help him make his shopping decisions. In the summer I've started going to Wreck Beach — don't *ever* tell them that. It's not easy getting down that cliff and back up. And I've met some people there, too. Or I might go all the way to Lighthouse Park and just sit. And once in a while I take a load of laundry to the laundromat because I like it there too. If they knew, they would think I was crazy, especially Graham. I'm not so sure about Sylvie. But I wanted somebody else to know that I do things. I do do things," she repeated and her eyes filled with tears.

Ted filled the lawn mower's gas tank from a red jerry can. I increased my powers of concentration, watching for signs of a response from him. Nothing.

Five minutes after Daphne's announcement we were

assembled at the table. Philip said grace, which Graham observed by running his hand through his hair in a manly display of impatience. As we ate, Sylvie told stories about her bookstore job and her night classes in German. Graham asked when she planned to return to school in a serious way and Sylvie asked, "What province is that in again, Graham?" Philip, who had become a little tipsy, made frequent comments of approval regarding food and family. And Daphne, I remember thinking, offering up the mashed potatoes and stuffing, unbeknownst to everyone, sat daydreaming about the Vancouver transit system.

And so, Ted, you see it is not necessary to be a child molester or a villain to lead a double life. There are the Daphnes, I suppose, and then there are others like myself, who at times appear to occupy some sort of second row of choices, hidden behind the first. Do you know what I mean? I furrowed my brow, tightened the muscles in my jaw in one final telepathic grunt and awaited a response. Ted yanked on the starter for the third time and the lawn mower ripped into life.

❧

Edna and Isobel. As autumn drew closer, rare were the opportunities for me to be alone in my yard for any time at all before they appeared from somewhere, the other side of their house, the front walk or the riverside. And more and more, I was reminded by them, in their billowy dresses and nylons, of the way long grass will blow in the wind, in waves, showing the side that does not see the light so much, that will change less in death. Edna and Isobel had become like predictions for me, like my own worries about lung cancer on the loose, walking and talking, even though, for the most part now, I was comfortable with their intrusions.

Edna and Isobel knew Sylvie very well. Edna had moved in with Isobel a couple of years after Sylvie moved in with me, and their relationship, all three, was easy, largely because of Sylvie's interest in their bobbles and knick-knacks from long ago. Edna and Isobel knew Sylvie could always be delighted with a jar or an old pitcher or a bit of green Depression glass, and Sylvie knew they would be interested in almost everything she had found in the pawn shops. I often felt excluded, awkwardly separate from their simple exchanges, their girlish hand-clappings and little cries of pleasure. I even used to make faces behind their backs, as a matter of fact, jealous of the attention paid some piece of crockery or a pickle dish from the thirties. Once, I purposely broke a jar they had all been admiring. I offered to take it inside then strode into the kitchen, climbed upon a chair and dropped the stupid thing on the tile floor. Smash. Everyone came running. I apologized, cried tears of remorse while laughing inwardly. Narrow brown bruises covered my heart, appeared like smelt in the waters of Lake Huron.

After Sylvie's death, I was ill at ease with Edna and Isobel, distant and resentful of their frequent visits. But eventually I decided if they were to be constantly in my yard, spreading onto my property like poplar roots, they would not be treated like guests or shown cake plates or spoken to in the manner of grandparents. They could be treated like contemporaries, like Monica; they could listen to me and I to them. Now, we say whatever we want. Where there was once an exchange of artifacts now there were words and sometimes plain old silence. And occasionally, like today, their old age ambled over and came up too close, scaring me a bit.

This morning I was positioned in the sun, in my lawn chair, with my back to the river and my third cup of coffee balanced on my knee. I was sitting with the blank-faced expression of a reptile, a reptile capable of drinking coffee, smoking and entertaining worries about its diminishing store of Ativan. I had just lit my second cigarette, having considered increasing my daily ration to five, when they appeared, nattering.

"We have still not tipped too far away from the sun's direct rays," Edna said. "They're still of some use to us. They haven't become ineffective yet. Do you hear that in the weather reports sometimes? Ineffective sunlight? I don't think that can be possible. Do you think that can ever be possible, Isobel?"

"They must mean ineffective in view of the plants, not effective in making them grow. I think that's their meaning," Isobel said. "And what about you, Annie? Basking in the ineffective sunlight? Soon be time for you to head back to work. Ten days until Labour Day, last time I counted."

"That's the figure I got too when I counted this morning. But I have to go back before Labour Day, the last three days of August. Summer's over as far as I'm concerned."

Edna bent down to talk to Spike in his chicken wire world and Isobel settled her six-foot body at the picnic table. Time was not only passing, I thought, it seemed to be approaching as well, from ordinates I had never imagined and on limbs old, bony and wrapped in cardigans. Was this, then, "it," I wondered? Monica's "it"? Was this the way "it" was supposed to be?

I remembered from childhood those hints, those prognostications of adulthood, at least the few most enduring and melodramatic warnings, frightening little telescopes through which I squinted at . . . a back yard with my elderly companions? An urn in my bedroom closet containing some ashen leftovers of the person I loved? Bits of carbon that could have been scraped off toast? No. No. Well, maybe.

There was the time Miss Stevenson caught her heel in the schoolroom floor's hot air vent, snapping it off. Everyone knew she drank too much, but what made matters worse was, she began to cry, telling us that what we now thought were problems were nothing, *nothing* compared to what we would face as adults. There would be unspeakable burdens for us to bear, she said.

And Mrs. Elford, hands trembling, her whole body vibrating after showing us the film on venereal disease. Any questions? she bravely asked. Who would dare?

And Miss Johannson, who told us all confidently that of the twenty-eight of us, within ten years one would be dead of cancer and another would likely have developed schizophrenia. Not to be so smart, she said to us.

These were the predictions; those were the soothsayers.

We were heading to a menacing future filled with viruses and insanity. And yet, none of these had come to pass, at least not in the way it had seemed they would, as a sudden unexpected losing of the foothold, a splashing in up to the neck in horrors so mature it would be too late even to scream for help. Only once, when I learned of Sylvie's accident, had I felt as I believe all of those teachers hoped I would someday feel.

"When you were young," I asked Isobel, "did your parents and teachers like to scare you with stories about how bad life could get? I had a teacher who used to read to us from some horrible manual — it had a red cover — statistics on schizophrenia and other mental diseases. It had an impact, I must admit. Obviously, I haven't forgotten so maybe she was experimenting with teaching techniques. Do you know what I'm talking about?"

"Oh yes," Isobel replied, "good God yes. My mother was the worst; that was her MO. Veiled references to what men wanted in marriage were her favourites. I was horrified on my wedding day. Of course, I soon got over my horror.

"We had the Depression, but nobody really knew that was coming. You know, the worst thing that ever came my way, that nobody, least of all my mother, ever warned me about was my first husband, Bert, leaving me. That was June of 1955. It certainly knocked the wind out of my sails. And speaking of sales, that was the reason — Waterless Cookware — door-to-door sales is how he met Helen Walsh.

"It was such a shock to my system I didn't know what to

do. I couldn't bring myself to eat or wash or anything. Luckily it happened after the kids were old enough to take care of themselves, otherwise the child welfare people would have gotten involved. As it was, it was just myself I decided to neglect. Eventually I took to my bed as all good housewives do from time to time, but I had a plan in mind. I am never without a plan, you see. I would stay there, I thought, until I went over the edge. I stayed and stayed for days, getting up to make tea and eat once in a while, waiting for Bert, looking out the window. All that happened was day, night, day, night, until finally one of the doctors from the San came in to look at me. I kept calling in sick, you see. Then I decided to use up all of my holiday time on this plan of mine.

"When the doctor got there, I asked him when I could expect to go crazy. I told him I wanted to and if it took more time I was willing to put it in. Imagine! When can I expect it to happen? I asked, and how exactly will I know when it's happening?" Here Isobel paused briefly to monitor her audience's appreciation. I hitched my eyes to hers with a wan smile. Edna, holding Spike, whispered briefly into his left ear. Satisfied, Isobel continued.

"I can still remember his answer. He said, 'You can lie there till the cows come home, Isobel, but you'll still be as sane as the day you were born.' He told me I didn't have the constitution for it, going off the deep end, that is; some did and others didn't and I was one of those that didn't. I could try as much as I wanted but my body would keep me afloat. Might as well try to sink a cork. And then he said, 'If you're interested in having a job tomorrow, I suggest you get out of that bed and be at the hospital in the morning.' So that was the end of that. Dr. Reid was his name. A little man, from Scotland. Thought he'd come to the end of the known universe when he stepped off the train in Calgary. Remember him, Edna? Dr. Reid?"

"Of course I remember him, Isobel. I remember all the people I don't like. I wonder why that is. I never liked Dr. Reid. He was arrogant and short, shorter than me even, under five feet, wouldn't you say, Isobel? Those qualities don't go well together. They clash, so to speak, like pink and orange.

"But if you want to talk about how things can go wrong, I'll fill you in on that. The last thing you expect," Edna said, "the last thing you expect," she repeated, her normally pale complexion turning pink with what seemed to be the effort involved in completing her thought, "is, oh, I don't know. Never mind. Let's go, Isobel. Annie must get tired of us, always in her yard. People are going to start to think she's got a big pair of lawn ornaments, except for the fact that we're not very ornamental."

And the two of them drifted back across the property line to their home. Hellos and good-byes rarely occurred because they would return, possibly in minutes.

Dr. Reid certainly was correct in his assessment of Isobel, I thought; she was born to be sane. I imagined the infant Isobel, slimy and new, looking out at the world and thinking, "So this is the place where the people live. Well, well, well."

And I realized I was much like Isobel. There was no slippery slope for me. The interior events happened as they should, as if some stern custodian oversaw the release of hormones and chemicals, opened doors and slammed them smartly shut, said, "You, you over there! What do you think you're doing?" Dr. Panesh was right to be suspicious about my requests for Ativan.

I could predict the arrival of my period to the hour. While others complained of migraines and allergies, I could offer only occasional tales of foot cramps. My body held no deliverance: it kept me sitting, standing, walking and talking. Soon it would have me conducting hearing tests and studying audiograms and fiddling with amplification systems; it would have me chat in the staff room with teachers and speech therapists. The only thing it might do to surprise me was this: one evening my body might take me down to the river bank and have me bay at the moon, have me howl the way the wolves did at the zoo. I had heard them in broad daylight. Howling for what? Even they did not know. For something that existed before the age of consonants, before the invention of lip to lip, tongue to teeth. Yes, some night I might give myself a little treat, walk down to the Bow and begin to howl for some assurance not even the wolves could remember.

~

Without warning, Sylvie's mother forbade us to sit in her car listening to the radio. She said her battery was wearing down, she had had it tested, and she needed to be able to count on her battery; those were her precise words, spoken in the quiet of the manse, a place always hushed like my grandparents' house, as if sounds were dampened by the accumulation of wasted time. Daphne was sitting in the living room, wearing a blue, satiny dress, seemingly doing nothing other than sitting and thinking, when she spoke to us on the subject of her car battery.

"I drove to Bea's last night, seventy miles on country roads and secondary highways to a little town called Arnold. By the way, Sylvie," Daphne said, "I have their mailing address, so you can write to Lily now if you want. Anyway, it was after two when I got home last night and as I was driving home I started to worry about the battery. What if it died on me? I even stopped the car along the side of the road and turned everything off to see what it would be like and the answer is daunting, I can say with certainty."

Here Sylvie caught my eye and mouthed the word "daunting," a reflex response to new vocabulary she had as a child.

"No light whatsoever," Daphne went on, crossing her legs, "except a little sliver of a moon and the stars and cold. April is no picnic around here. I can see why they call it the snow belt. The roadside had banks at least four feet high. And of course, once I had turned the car off I began to worry that it wouldn't start up again. Heaven knows why I turned it off. Don't breathe a word of this to your father, Sylvie."

Sylvie nodded, shook her head, then poked at the bowl of hard candies on the coffee table.

"And so, I had the battery checked today; it *is* low and since I plan to travel to Bea's every now and again, I'd rather it wasn't. And Sylvie, if you think Mesmer is small you should see Arnold. Anyway girls, my point is — no more car radio."

Sylvie and Graham always obeyed at home. This characteristic only became perverse when compared to their irreverence and opposition away from home. Graham was scheming and lewd, Sylvie moved about with silent disregard for convention. Forced out of the Buick, we moved farther afield for after-school fun, into the church. On occasion, the custodian was in, or one or two of the United Church Women, always in the basement, tending to whatever subterranean duties their offices involved. No one gave us a second thought, Sylvie being who she was.

On the day of the battery talk, we opted to hide out in the balcony again for a while. Pressed between the rear pew and the wall, Sylvie said "Nobody knows we're here. Nobody. We could die and nobody would know. Nobody ever sits up here except Graham. And if he found us, he'd probably just leave us or look up our dresses if that's what we happened to be wearing." And then she said, "Come here. I have to show you something."

We crawled out of our hiding place and slid along the back pew. Sylvie picked up a hymnbook and handed it to me. "Turn to page one hundred and fourteen," she instructed. I did. There, in the margin, was a pencil drawing of a boy bending over, exposing his asshole. Between his spread legs could be seen hanging a largish set of penis and balls. "These are supposed to be stink waves," Sylvie said, indicating some squiggly lines emanating from the circular anus.

"Now," she continued as we moved a few feet along the pew, "open this one to page one-fifty-seven."

Same drawing, more stink waves.

"I know everything Graham does," Sylvie announced, as if this were a great burden.

"How?"

"He tells me. He can't resist. He's a show-off. He'll probably go to jail someday because he'll rob a bank, then he'll have to call the police to tell them."

We walked back and forth between the pews until we reached the railing, the spot from which I had thrown the hymnbook. There, we sat on our haunches, peering through the slats. That was when we heard the side door of the church open and slam shut as it always did. Footsteps were followed by a tap-tap-tapping at the study door. No answer. Reverend Rochon was out. Then came more footsteps and the appearance of Blodwen Scarfe in the doorway behind the organ, to the left of the choir loft. The weather was still cool then and she wore short, fur-lined winter boots and a lambswool jacket. On her legs were dark silk stockings.

Blodwen walked past the organ, stood looking into the choir loft for a moment, then walked to the centre aisle where she turned full circle and said, "You're not here, are you?" For a moment, she appeared to be about to leave but reconsidered and instead climbed into the pulpit. Sylvie and I slithered farther down until almost prone but still able to watch Blodwen clutch the lectern, smile at her imaginary congregation and say, "world without end," emphasis on end, "world without end," emphasis on out, and finally, "I'd better go." And she left.

"Dad has to talk to a lot of people in his office," Sylvie said. "They all have problems. Even though she looks like my Aunt Dolores, she probably has problems. You kind of get so you can tell just by looking at them."

"No," I said, "not her. I don't think so. She's nice. She doesn't have problems."

Sylvie shrugged, handed me a Bible and said, "Take a look at page five hundred."

~

M y first day back at work, after two solid months of holidays, and I wondered why I couldn't be more grateful. The others seemed happy enough, the teachers and the speech therapists, Harriett Dafoe in her pastel fashions, and needless to say the principal, Sam Yeats, with his more-enormous-than-ever white eyebrows. They chatted and schmoozed while I sat in my third-floor office, avoiding the social conventions of the staff room. This did not matter; the audiologist was indulged. I could be as eccentric as I wanted. I could grow a goatee or develop any number of bizarre tics and mannerisms, as long as I continued to test ears and amplification equipment. I was completely free to sit in my office doing whatever I wanted, from mourning the passing of my vacation, to toying with my faintly masochistic tendencies. (I kept a thumb tack in my desk drawer to indulge this occasional need. Poking at the skin on my knuckles just enough to cause a bit of pain, not to draw blood, seemed a reasonable way to pass the time my first day back on the job.)

It occurred to me as I sat at my desk, jabbing with scientific curiosity at my skin, I could easily believe with the fervour of a Pentecostal that for every sin I had ever committed a punishment would have to be meted out. The sin I had in mind went back to a camping trip Sylvie and I took years ago. We had gone into the interior of British Columbia, the Kootenays. And by some coincidence, a Mediterranean-looking woman travelling in an old Mercedes settled into the same design of travel and camping as Sylvie and me. She had first appeared in Nakusp, then at Slocan Lake and a couple of days later, outside of Nelson. She chose campsites not far from ours, always sticking to her solitary pursuits of popping popcorn over her fire and smoking, smoking, smoking. Most noteworthy about her was her method of storage. Everything was stowed in plastic Safeway shopping bags, scores of them piled into her back seat. When we overtook her on the road, she appeared to be engaged in a long overdue trip to the dump. What's more, she had an unsettling habit of scratching her groin while waiting in line at the water pump, the most public gathering place for campers. And this was where the sin entered into the picture. Sylvie and I dubbed her the Contessa Candida. We laughed at her. Ha, ha, ha. We laughed and laughed. We watched for her on the road and chased after other older maroon-coloured and boxy cars, thinking we had found the Contessa and her bags of gear. Once we almost crashed into the rear end of a logging truck, so excited were we with our chase, so overcome with humour.

And this was the retribution. During the summer of 1991 I had been unable to embark upon a vacation by myself, unable to drive off or fly away without superimposing the face of the Contessa Candida upon my own. The grim-faced smoker. The itcher. These identities became mine. Just as well, then, to be back at work for the fifth year, for the fifth big loop around the sun and to be looking out from my window at the same type of weather once again, the same late August weather trend of three or four days of solid drizzle.

Okay, enough, I decided, putting away the tack in my desk drawer. The repetitive scale of it all reminded me of the McDonald's boast — over four billion served. Take action, I said to myself in the voice of Ellen Nestle, habitual screamer and third-grade teacher, whose classroom was much too close to my office. Do it! Call directory assistance, unite with the robotic voice and get Alexa Stewart's telephone number. Make a stab at changing this state of affairs, this circling around with your lies and sins and your dark and messy office, your visions of the Contessa digging at her crotch.

Alexa Stewart was indeed a listing, she was a new listing and this augured well, I thought. I was not ready yet to make the call, however. I needed to fuss with some papers and files before dialling, I decided, then found I was incapable of even that. So I sat, much like the Contessa used to watching her fire.

From my third-floor window I could see a portion of the grey asphalt playground, the fence to prevent children from scrambling down the bluff, a crawlspace beneath the fence, the Elbow River, the golf club, the Glenmore Reservoir, an occasional boat and the dark and heavy southern sky. *You're lucky to have this office*, I told myself, first in my mother's voice, then in the voice of Ellen Nestle, then my own. *Such a beautiful view,* I assured myself in all three voices, expecting to be calmed by this interior acoustic wizardry, but I was not. The rain picked up a bit. I looked at Alexa's number and wondered what I was doing, what words to think to describe my actions to myself.

I wanted to call Alexa; that was clear. I tried to think further but the words had difficulty locating me behind the rain, in my sleepy and cluttered office. Succour, I thought. I would like succour, the word sailing into my mind like an old-fashioned airplane, a glider perhaps. And companionship, yes, love perhaps and probably sex. Yes, likely I was after that most of all. I would like a long list of words, words that would take me back to where I was before I became this person who had been stripped lonely, this remote and hiding creature, one who might be approached with a short stick in the way my father once approached a snapping turtle to demonstrate the power of its jaws. Yes, I will call Alexa now, I decided. I will make a foray into that part of the universe most unlike the Crosstown Flea Market, where people chase one another in order to kiss them and hold them and be held. The place where we follow the footprints of someone whose face we happen to like to ridiculous and unsheltered places.

I dialled the number and immediately became a little dizzy, my inner ear clenching itself like a fist, nervously squishing fluids around. Was it correct to attempt to grope one's way into another's existence like this? Alexa answered, slapping a certain course of events into action. Outside my window, seagulls circled high above the empty playground.

I identified myself.

"Oh," said Alexa, "just a minute. Let me get a cigarette." There was a pause, then, "Sorry about that. Something about talking on the telephone. I like to get my mouth doing as many things as possible, you know, smoke, talk, maybe I should do some, I don't know, maybe some whistling too. It's the oral thing, I guess."

"I wish I could have a cigarette now too, but I'm at work and this is a smoke-free place, as they're called nowadays. Although, I did actually stick my head out the window to have a smoke once when I was alone here. I felt extremely evil."

"I wouldn't have thought you were a smoker."

"Well, I'm not really. Just three a day. (A lie. I *had* changed the amount to five.) But they're a very significant three."

"Smokers are fine with me. I like smokers. We have to stick together these days. We have to be brave, maybe even form secret societies with handshakes and passwords. We'd have to have names, you know, club names, something like Sportsman's Choice."

"Yes," I said, "or maybe House of Craven."

"Right. Right. Hasn't it always seemed strange to you that Craven is the name of a cigarette? Craven, isn't that a synonym for dog-breath or panting? Like you want something so badly your tongue is hanging out? Maybe 'slavering' is the word I'm thinking of here. Yes, House of Slavering. That's what I was thinking about."

I laughed, though I would rather not have wasted my time doing so; I wanted to forge ahead with my task. Little beads of sweat formed above my upper lip. I wondered if each bead were covered with a little cap of chalk dust, and on top of that even tinier particles, bits of age and fright, and then on top of those a teeny cap with a Munchian scream reflected in each.

Oh come on, I thought, taking my tack from its drawer again. This is not a moment of uttermost Norwegian despair; this is Alberta; this is a request for a date of some sort. I gave myself a quick poke.

"Would you like to get together some time?" I asked, "maybe come over to my house for dinner or a walk? I live on the river."

Without hesitation, Alexa accepted my invitation. We settled on Sunday afternoon and at that moment the bells began to ring.

"Can you hear that, Alexa? They're testing the bells before school starts. It's a bit like a psychiatric institution here, everything changes with the bell, everybody shuffles off to occupational or whatever."

She took down my address and after a few more pleasantries, the conversation ended. Sylvie, Sylvie, Sylvie, I asked the empty room, what *am* I doing? With a mighty heave, I opened the window of my office and took a deep breath of the damp air. Three more days and then we would have September. The seagulls dived and tore at a soggy bag of potato chips someone had dropped. I admired them and their honest, bird-eyed greed. Then I closed the window, having decided to get to work.

~

Friday night it was, no, actually Saturday morning, very early, around four. I lay on my back in the yard. The air was chilly and the grass wet. I turned my flashlight on and off again, pointing it to the sky, watching the weak beam disappear, having nothing to interact with. Annoying the way that happened.

I had read and re-read the *Maclean's* piece on the big bang. I understood there were microwaves known as cosmic background radiation still moving out there, relic radiation it was called, from the beginning of time. Could those microwaves have created sound? I wondered, then decided no, wrong frequencies for us and our hearing apparatus. More importantly, I had learned the universe most likely came to pass as a result of temperature fluctuations, very small, but enough to cause a bit of a stirring action so that the original seamless soup began to lump up in places.

Flicking the flashlight off and on, into the sky, onto Ted and Maureen Nixon's green ash, I wondered where Sylvie might be now on the microwave/lumping continuum. Only she would know, out there with her secret. No best friend for her, unless she'd found another bit of soup to chat with.

She *is* out there, I thought, looking over my shoulder for someone who might wish to argue this contention; Sylvie is out there somewhere. No matter how much a cultural materialist or secular humanist a person might be,

something formerly Sylvie Rochon is out there. It's a physical fact. Energy cannot be created or destroyed. Cannot.
Hear that word? Speak it in the manner of Ellen Nestle, I
told myself. Can not. It has the conviction of its sound,
beginning and ending with little explosions of the mouth,
little bangs in their own right. Cold comfort.

All right, all right, make up something, offer yourself
some impotent solace. Perhaps, I began the story, when
Sylvie died, somewhere in Calgary a firecracker exploded, a
little bang, insignificant but nevertheless setting off a chain
reaction, let's just say, a burned finger, a concerned mother,
a trip to a clinic, bandages, Ozonol, advice, and as that concerned mother and child were leaving the clinic, perhaps, it
is possible, Alexa Stewart was entering, having maybe an
ear infection or some need of medical attention, and as the
mother left and Alexa arrived, in the doorway, their shoulders touched, well no, their jackets or maybe sweaters,
because although it was winter, we were experiencing a chi-
nook and the weather was warm. And when their shoulders
touched, the bang became a rustling sound and some movement of Sylvie back to me began. In the form of Alexa.

Sorry, Alexa. My apologies.

Alexa. In less than forty-eight hours she would be here,
in this very yard. The possibilities presented by this fact
were a bit of a flashlight as well, shining here and there
inside my mind, brightening up those dark, wet corners,
places centipedes might hide out, scampering away at the
thought of Alexa Stewart.

I got myself up and went into the Nixons' yard, bringing Spike along on his leash. Ted and Maureen had gone

away with their children and the wiener dog, one last camping weekend, I supposed. In their yard, in the half-moon light, were the remains of Maureen's annuals, mostly shrivelled and brown except for the calendula and their hardy blossoms. Yellow by day, calling out for attention, their nighttime modesty struck me as melancholy. How they accepted the darkness, form without colour, without even a breath of protest. I examined the Nixons' croquet set, picked up a mallet and whacked off a blossom. Then I knocked a ball through the nearest wicket. Hardwood against hardwood, a rare sound, evocative of the cloistered or the privileged, nuns, the very rich. To belong to either group, I thought, to be able to purchase a new lover with my mutual funds. Or, to be in a position to ignore the whole issue.

I returned Spike to his cage and went inside. No Ativan tonight. I planned to sit up with Sylvie and await the morning, await Alexa's visit two days hence, await events other than this nighttime. My entire body was capable of involving itself in this waiting. If I could last until dawn, the appearance of the light was a great release for me, like the freeing of all the animals from the zoo, a stampede of creatures running their shadows down the side of Nose Hill. And not the pleasanter creatures either; no, the ones with raw, red backsides, cleft tongues or mushy invertebrate bodies. They were happy to be gone and I was happy to see them go. Because then I would sleep until noon.

∼

Sunday arrived, the Sunday of Labour Day weekend, the day of Alexa's visit. The morning passed uneventfully with house cleaning and puttering, but by noon I had begun to notice a change in the day. It was the minutes themselves; they began to protrude a bit and take on another dimension.

A math teacher at the Calgary School, a woman named Francesca Lieber, once explained to me the purpose of numbers: to manage the continuous, she said, to hack up the continuous into the discontinuous, take an endless low noise and cut it into blips. This is what numbers will achieve and so, I thought as I cleaned my house, will lust. Lust could separate moments, chunk them apart, give them a shape so as not to be lost in the huge old flats of remembrance. I became conscious that each of my preparatory acts had its own small measure of scandal. Would Alexa, or would she not, fall for all of this?

By one o'clock nothing remained to be done, so I sat outside and read and dozed off, and in so doing lost a portion of my confidence. It was gone when I woke up, gone like a spilled drink. All I could do was sit and wait until Alexa arrived, which she did at ten past two.

This is how it went.

I began by showing her through the house. Alexa wanted to see the basement — I thought this significant and encouraging — so we went downstairs and admired the jars, Sylvie's old jars, for a while. I pretended they were mine, not only the collection but also Sylvie's interest and all of the information on jars I had picked up from her. I did not wish to explain the life and hobbies of Sylvie Rochon at that time and I felt a strange comfort in kicking off this relationship with a sequence of inconsequential lies. Rising to the challenge, I chattered convincingly about my interest in glass, with details about Beaver jars and Crown jars and their respective worth.

Because I was talking rapidly and nervously, at one point I experienced a bit of a swoon beneath the bare light bulb, which I interpreted as desire. Attraction can create a feeling of vertigo which in turn leads to a delightful feeling of pre-destiny: I must do this. I must kiss this person on the lips because we are in the basement, the underpants of the house and she is wearing lipstick. But of course I did not. The woman had been in my house for no more than half an hour. It was not my intention to horrify her. Instead, I considered showing Alexa Sylvie's map collection and claiming ownership of it as well.

"My mother collects glass," Alexa said upstairs. "She would love to see those jars. Her things are in the living room, though, and I don't think there are any jars. It's all kind of frou-frou against one wall, the great wall of glass as my brother and I used to call it. We liked to jump up and down right in front of it when we were kids, when mom was out, trying to simulate earthquake conditions. We could really get things rattling."

I took Alexa into the bedroom, pulled open the bottom

drawer of Sylvie's old dresser, and announced with conviction, "And these are my maps."

"Iceland," Alexa said, picking up the very top map. "Did you go there?"

"No, no, just bought it at a junk store," and I recalled the day Sylvie bought it, along with some plastic toy soldiers. Afterward we had sat at a restaurant and positioned the soldiers on the place names we thought we would like to visit.

"Why don't we go outside and have some coffee?" I suggested quite appropriately, almost liltingly, as if I were someone who never lied or assumed the identity of a dead lover. One who disposed of ashes as requested.

We sat in my old lawn chairs and I told Alexa a bit about my job, after which she began to talk in earnest. For Alexa, I discovered, talking was a dramatic monologue.

"It sure must be different in schools now," Alexa began, "if people like you are around. I have such bad memories from elementary school because it took me so long to learn how to read. I just couldn't get it. And I got really hung up on how the *g*'s looked like little bugs. I would have to stop and look at each one.

"When I was in grade two, Miss Dillinger made me go to the front of the class. She introduced me with, 'Class, this is the way *not* to read.' I went to the front of the room, but I didn't read. I couldn't, after all, it wasn't like it was a strategic decision on my part. I just stood there. I think Miss Dillinger thought she had made her point."

Standing, walking to one of my sunflowers, extending it to its full height, returning, Alexa went on. "Anyway, I told my mother about this incident and as a result, in my mother's own non-linear way, she became very critical of Miss Dillinger's appearance, in particular her wardrobe. She would ask me as soon as I got home what Miss Dillinger was wearing. 'Was it one of those horrible plaid skirts again?' and my mom would lift her own dress to mid-kneecap length and ask 'To here?' Then say, 'Such a flattering length for the boxy figure.' I started to feel sorry for Miss Dillinger and a little bit guilty because my mother just could not bring herself to blame me for the fact that I wasn't as smart as my sisters. It was everyone else's fault, something the city of Edmonton had neglected to do, kind of in the same league as the problem with snow removal. And my teachers just couldn't believe it. I still think that's why Miss Vossler shook me. It just didn't compute in her mind that a sister of Fiona and Colleen Stewart would not be able to read by the third grade."

Alexa paused to light a cigarette with much dangling of bracelets. I watched for the lipstick on the filter; yes, there it was.

"So, after half a year of trying to get me to read it still hadn't happened, and one day in February — I remember it was before Valentine's Day because I could see the hearts on the bulletin board blurring — her frustration got the better of her and she shook me. You know, in the good old-fashioned way," and Alexa began throwing herself from side to side in the lawn chair by way of demonstrating. "Everything went flying, my pencil crayons and my ruler came flying out of my desk. I remember feeling so humiliated but at the same time wanting to make a performance out of it, which I did, started waving my arms and making faces. Miss Vossler shook harder and I performed harder. It was a kind of duel which ended up in me being suspended for three days."

Watching Alexa, listening and listening, I recalled how Sylvie used to sit in that very same chair, sit for long periods of time without saying a word.

"My mother had an appointment with the principal," Alexa said. "I don't know what went on, which is surprising because Mom usually told us kids everything, all the stuff we didn't want to know, such as how she was feeling about Dad and who she thought he was having an affair with. Fucking Vera Olafsen, we heard more about Vera Olafsen — anyway, I came back to school and through some miracle in my brain all of a sudden, by the end of grade three, I could read. It really was sudden, like learning how to ride a bike. Miss Vossler took all the credit. Then the next year Andrew entered grade one and I faded in significance because he was such a conduct problem."

Alexa's performance was beginning to make me feel plodding, slow in my thinking, a bit rusty. I toyed with the idea of arranging another visit to Dr. Panesh. Since she wouldn't give me any more Ativan, maybe I could get something to pep me up. I was unsure whether without chemical help I would have the energy to continue with this engagement, to even begin to undertake a relationship, friend, lover, whatever, with anyone so different from my drowsy self. To convince Alexa I was anything other than an appreciative audience, it was necessary to motivate myself with a breath so deep I imagined the force of it scooping small melon-ball shapes from the bottom of my tar-stained lungs.

"I work more with the teachers than the students at my school," I said. "There's a grade three class right across the hall from my office. The teacher's name is Mrs. Ellen Nestle. She's what's known as a screamer; maybe she's a bit like Miss Vossler was. She can't seem to tolerate certain things, like disorder or clatter or mistakes or bad posture. Every month she gives out a posture award; she's a bit of a throwback. We talk sometimes though, out in the hallway: the effects of proximity. We're friendly.

"One day I came across her in the hall, laughing a little to herself. I went to talk to her and she started to cry. I wasn't sure what to do; she's usually so abrasive. I came closer and she gestured for me to go away. Which I did. I retreated into my office and then sat there feeling guilty. There's a little window in my door so I peeked out a couple of times at her blowing her nose and wiping her eyes. I kept thinking I should be more aggressively helpful, the way the psychologist is when she's around. The way she says, 'Are you okay?' in this concerned voice that can pretty well make anybody talk."

"Oh yes, I know that voice," Alexa said. "It's the voice that's actually saying, 'You appear to be cracking up.' "

"Correct," I said. "Anyway, the third time I looked out, Ellen was gone, back in her room. I could hear her saying 'All right, grade three, let's get to work.' I returned to my desk and my sound booth feeling lazy and ineffective. I felt like a cow, to be perfectly honest. Not in the insulting

'God, what a cow' sense of the word, but like an animal. All I could be expected to do was look.

"Because I work with sound and words, I was kind of struck by the fact I made a decision not to use them to some good end. Do you know what I'm talking about?"

"Oh yeah," Alexa said, "sure. It's this sort of thing: 'What? Me help out? Sorry. I'm a Hereford. I'm a cow.' Yes, there's many a time I've played the role of the gentle, dumb Hereford, but I'm not so sure that's a bad thing. Like Van Morrison says, there's the inarticulate speech of the heart. It can't decipher itself for us any better than for the chickens and Herefords, maybe. That's the one thing Janet Sainsbury can't seem to understand — I'll tell you about her later, maybe. Not now. No. Not now.

"Anyway, maybe with your teacher it was just that she hadn't slept the night before or maybe it was just the whole big ball of wax that got her going so that everything came splattering out as with a cappuccino maker, just pssst." Alexa made a hissing noise, causing all the muscles in her neck to tighten into cords, then threw the dregs of her coffee onto the grass. "Sometimes that's just what has to happen; there's no alternative. Anyway, why don't we go for a walk along the river? Is that okay or will people sic their little inarticulate dogs on us?"

"I'll lock up the house," I said.

We walked along the Bow's edge for a while, then scrambled up the bank to the bicycle path. It was a breezy afternoon, almost fall and the leaves were yellowing. At Bowness Park, we looked in at Funland, which was closed, suspended in postures of giddy amusement, then sat down on one of the many riverside benches. Presently, Alexa asked, "So, what's this all about, you asking me over like this?"

I viewed this as a ritual type of question, requiring a ritual type of response: one must respect the appearance of things. One must invent some motive. I sat in thought, inspecting the vista across the river. The stately Georgian buildings of the San aroused in me a genteel sensibility, a commitment to the long-lost myth of gentlewomanly honour, having to do with hooped skirts, crinolines, waiting, the authentic and maddening type of lust.

"Well," I began, "I liked seeing you at the theatre. I missed you after I quit ushering." This seemed right, I thought, this seemed acceptable. "No reason, really, other than I like you." I realized this was unconvincing, pictured my face assuming the distant and inaccessible look of Ellen Nestle in the hallway. *It's nothing, nothing.*

"Are you seeing anyone?" Alexa asked.

"No. Are you?"

"Not now. I was living with a woman, the aforementioned Janet, but I moved out a while ago. We were crabby all the time. In the midst of it all, analyzing this and that, it seemed so complex, but now, looking back, all I can think of is the crabbiness. Getting home and looking for some reason to be pissed off — the laundry, the garbage, the dishes, anything would do. And she didn't want me going back to school for reasons I still don't understand. But the final blow occurred when she managed, in between all of her other activities, her tai chi lessons and her running and her many therapies and the little cult she's started up, to seduce my best friend and her husband. Charming, isn't it? It's so, I don't know, so *seventies*. The word 'swingers' comes to mind."

"What does she do?"

"Janet is a projectionist; that's the one thing I appreciate about her. Knowing Janet has allowed me to use that word from time to time. *And this is Janet Sainsbury, projectionist.* It sounds so psychological."

"She works in a movie theatre?"

"Yes indeed. Cineplex Odeon, downtown on Fifth Avenue, and she hates it, but that's her problem. Anyway, let's not talk about Janet. Let's please not talk about Janet because knowing her as I do, she is probably talking about Janet herself right now and encouraging whoever is with her, most likely my best friend Brigitte and her husband Henry, to talk about her too. Maybe all three are having a lively discussion about Janet. And three people on the face of the earth discussing Janet Sainsbury is enough, although not for her."

"Do you still see her? Do you talk?"

"We haven't spoken since I left. I've left a few messages on her machine — well, they're not actually messages."

"What are they?"

"They're nothing," Alexa said, "I just hang up."

She clearly wanted to change the topic and immediately began to tell more stories of her family life. Fiona, the dentist, had left a clinic and entered into a new and independent practice and this had precipitated her major panic attack at the corner of Broadway and Main, and

Colleen, the physiotherapist, was having problems with her husband and had recently said that she knew she should never have married someone with such low muscle tone.

"At least they both have good paying jobs," Alexa said. "Sometimes I think everything got used up, genetically speaking, by the time Andrew and I came along." Andrew had not made a success of things. He lived with his mother in Edmonton and moved in and out of business ventures with alacrity. "And it seems like I've been downwardly mobile ever since my first job at Harvey's," Alexa concluded.

I assured Alexa I had not descended from high-achieving stock, that I, a zealous audiologist, was considered the star. I told her about my sister, Lorna, the loans officer in an Ontario bank and my brother, Grant, in turf management. I described my mother, Sandra, expert on gladioli and popular fiction, and my father, George, recently retired from the pharmaceutical plant on the outskirts of town. "He even grew breasts once as a side-effect from making birth-control pills, " I said.

"You're kidding."

"No, it's a fact. He took it in stride though, with humour. Even borrowed my mom's bra once and walked into the living room wearing it. The boobs went away after a while. I think Epson stopped making that kind of pill. I should have gone to see them this summer, but I didn't."

The afternoon was almost over by the time we arrived back at my yard. There was a clammy-handed farewell, an exchange of phone numbers, with Alexa promising to call and me saying sure, okay, yeah, with as much indifference as I could muster. And once she had departed, I was relieved. Ah, the alchemy of solitude. What mysterious conjuror, I wondered, can change it from bliss to terror and back again? I fetched the urn and placed it on my coffee table. Sylvie. All I wanted was to sit in my armchair with you.

~

That very night Martha decided she wanted to go out with her paint and stencils and do some work. "Fine. That's just fine with me," I said, agreeing to accompany her on this late-night mission. I can sleep all day tomorrow, I realized, that's the way it should be on Labour Day. Stay up late, all night if need be, and sleep away the following day. And besides, after my afternoon with Alexa I was appreciative of a diversion that would prevent me from driving to her place and offering myself up to her, a largish gift dressed in fall colours.

Yes, I was smitten with Alexa and had already sprung a geyser of plans in my mind. Plans to drop by her apartment, plans to meet her at the university, plans, plans, plans, spreading outward from my hard skull, but in the soft and suckerish manner of an octopus. I knew I could easily become a danger to myself in this state. Better to go off with Martha, take precautions.

"Have a smoke while you wait for Martha," I said to

myself gently. No need to scream that instruction. Best not to drink, though, I decided, if planning to commit acts of hostility against the social order.

A papier-mâché calf, created by Sylvie some years ago, sat opposite me in its corner of the living room. I watched it as if it might come to life, make a move, even toted it into the centre of the room for improved viewing. It, of course, continued to stand in its attitude of near-grazing, head lowered with what appeared to be the intention of eating carpet.

Sylvie was very proud of her calf; she considered it to be near-to-perfect (said as one word) and in fact it was; the calf had turned out well, in proportion, in scale. Sylvie used to consider the calf to be her issue. After completing it, she declared that this was as close as she was going to get to her full fecundity — a phrase taken from her very religious Aunt Elaine. And so it was considered, in a joking way, her child, our child. I drew the line at giving it a name. I can't bear the naming of cars and other inanimate objects, though I was able to forgive Monica for calling her Dodge the Hard White Dart. But anonymity had not diminished the calf's identity or its presence: there it still stood, just as Sylvie had hoped, her lineage, possibly the end of the Rochon line, as Graham was unlikely to produce a legitimate child.

This calf was truly the only remaining article manufactured by Sylvie Rochon. How strange, I thought, that all of the work, all of the endless activity of hands and arms and legs and feet could result in this achievement: one paper-and-glue facsimile of a calf. Although it *was* near-to-perfect, and how many can lay claim to such a legacy?

I eventually fell asleep on the couch and was awakened by Martha at the door hours later. We took off, me barely awake, content to be carted around like a tool, a rake, some implement that would serve a purpose. Martha's car was filled with warmth and debris, the by-products of much eating and drinking and painting and cleaning. In the back seat were the paint and the template and boxes of cleansers and soap and rags, along with a vacuum cleaner and two buckets. "I clean houses," Martha said, "at night on weekends when the people are away. And also a couple of businesses. That's why I don't mind going out at night, all night for that matter. I'm a bit of a nocturnal, I guess you might say."

"That's too bad," I said.

"No, not at all. The world, and most people, come to think of it, look better at night. It's really an entirely different society at night, a different city, maybe even a different country. It's hard to tell in the dark."

"I suppose," I said, somewhat reluctant to disturb my sleepy state. But Martha was like an electric eel, hunched over the wheel giving off noise, static and light.

Awakening then, coming to life, I asked, "Aren't you afraid of doing this graffiti stuff? Haven't you ever been caught? And what happens if we do get caught, just by the way? Who pays?"

"In answer to your first question, no. Ditto to the second. As for what if, I don't think much of anything. Maybe a fine, which is all right with me. I would gladly pay it and view the payment as the equivalent of purchasing a licence to do this work. Why? You're not getting cold feet, are you? I hope not, because I was planning to have you do the actual painting."

"Oh, an initiation rite, I see."

"No, I just like the idea of driving. It's a get-away-car kind of thing for me. Ted painted too."

"I just can't believe Ted did this with you. What did Maureen think? She must have thought he was having an affair or something."

"No, no, not at all. In fact, Maureen was in favour of the whole thing. It was Ted who tired of it. I've actually thought of calling Maureen and asking her along. I may yet."

"Maureen?" I asked, dumbfounded.

"Sure, why not?" Martha responded, rolling down her window, hurling out the apple core she had been gnawing on and closing the window again, all with great speed and intensity.

"I can't picture Maureen defacing public property. It doesn't quite fit with what I know about her. She gardens and plays baseball and . . ."

Martha looked at me with amazement, as if I had revealed incredible gaps of knowledge, an ignorance of the days of the week, for example, or basic number facts.

"It's not defacing, what we're doing here, Anne."

"E," I said, "it's Ann-ie."

"Okay, okay, okay. It's not defacing. It's far from defacing. It's the opposite. It's the conferring of a face, if you ask me. It's the giving of a voice to an inert, passive object. A bridge becomes a talking bridge; an overpass speaks to the motorists."

"Sounds a bit like ventriloquism to me, manipulating dummies," I said. Then, "Do you mind if I smoke?" I asked. "This experience is for some reason triggering my need for tobacco." It was the next day, really. I could honestly begin my five.

"Go ahead," Martha said. "The ash tray's full of change so you'll have to use the window. Anyway, back to the topic. Nobody is manipulating anything any more than anyone else on this planet. We're just saying something by means of a can of spray paint. Vocal chords aren't the only way, you know. You know what strikes me some nights when I'm cleaning businesses? That all day in that place people have been talking and talking and there is absolutely nothing to show for it. Nothing. At least the air drops off a layer of dust. But talking? No sediment whatsoever. Talk just floats away and disappears. Where does it go? You should know that. Aren't you an ear doctor?"

"No, I'm an audiologist."

"Well, same thing."

"No, I'm afraid not."

"Well, still, you should have some idea of what I'm saying," Martha concluded, a trifle huffily.

We were headed south on Crowchild Trail. Martha appeared to have a destination in mind. What it was did not concern me, the assistant.

"I'm not an artist," Martha went on. "I can't do that sort of thing so I do this. I spray paint. It's not defacing, Annie. It's not."

"Okay, I hear you talking. I'm not saying I agree but I hear you talking."

"Good," she said. "Now, I'm going to pull over here at the Thirty-third Avenue overpass and you hop out and do it. The stencil's right there and the paint," she said, gesturing into the back seat. "And here," she added, "wear this," handing me a pilled, black acrylic toque.

"Are you serious?"

"Yes," Martha said with extreme earnestness. "You have to cover up your hair, wear a disguise. It's a part of the whole routine."

I put on the hat. With this unanticipated millinery turn of events, I was now uncertain whether I was the same person who had been sitting peacefully by the river a few hours earlier, or even if this were the same month or season.

The car came to a halt next to a set of concrete stairs and a sign reading "Pedestrian Crossing." The stairs looked very inviting to me, as if they led to a quiet neighbourhood of older bungalows filled with happily sleeping couples, wrapped in one another's flannel-covered arms. Probably not one urn in any of their closets. A scent of wood fire hung in the air.

Holding the stencil next to the hapless grey concrete of the overpass, I sprayed full blast for ten seconds, jumped back into the car and was driven away. I felt dizzy and light-headed, astonished that the legs I could see beneath me were my own.

"Good work," Martha said, "good work. God, I love this. I can't tell you how much I love this. Okay, the plan now is to hit those hoardings down at Macleod and Southland, then go to an all-night coffee place for a couple of hours and drive back at dawn to see how it looks.

That's the usual procedure." I was learning that Martha was definitely big on procedure.

"I'm not sure I can stay awake all night, Martha."

"Oh, come on. We'll go to that big truck stop off Blackfoot. I'll buy you breakfast and a half-dozen coffees."

We ate breakfast at the truck stop and Martha tried further to explain the motives for her behaviour. "I love this place," she said. "I love my country. I do. I simply do. That's why I do this. I don't think free trade with the U.S. is good and I think North American free trade will be even worse. We need to keep our country a country. Like Norway, for example. Ever been there?"

"No," I said, noticing a round white scar on the bridge of Martha's nose, as if someone had pushed a pencil eraser into her nose, leaving a permanent depression.

"Mac and I went there in 1980. They manufacture lots of their own goods. You turn over something like a Tupperware container, for example, and it says 'Made in Norway' on the bottom, except it's in Norwegian.

"I find it so comforting sometimes," Martha continued, "when I feel lonely, that all across this continent there are people who maybe once in a while think about Lester Pearson. Do you know what I mean? It's like all above the map there's this big shared memory bank. It's like we're all on one huge party line, in a way. I think it's great. I don't want Canada to melt away, into a pot."

I thought I could see tears forming in the corners of Martha's eyes. This astonished me, but I felt a need to offer some compassion. "You must be worried about Quebec," I offered, "the unity question."

"I try not to think about that one. I invoke the logic of Doris Day — *que sera, sera.* It seems the only solution."

I began to remember as I ate my eggs what it was I liked about Martha, the pheromones, the shared and sudden estrangement from love and a lover's life. I liked her all the more, suddenly, for her sentimental nationalism.

When we left for our tour back through downtown it was almost six in the morning. We drove past the empty grey erections of PetroCanada and Amoco to Crowchild Trail and the paintwork. Martha slowed down and there it was, the red splatter on concrete: REALTOR OF THE YEAR: BRIAN MULRONEY, and so on. Martha whooped "Yee-ha" and I felt a little gag of joy mixed with caffeine intoxication and fatigue. My reasons for feeling excited were rather pathetic, really. Nothing even remotely political. I was hoping to drive Alexa past that very spot. I was planning to say to her, "Look there. I did that." Planning to surprise her with my chicanery, my secret other self — the confident subversive, a false identity bruising my heart but possibly luring Alexa into my bed. That was what I expected from this event; that was how I thought it might make a difference.

~

Prior to moving to Mesmer, Sylvie had never lived in or near the countryside. The first few years of her life had been spent in Saskatoon, there had been a year in Winnipeg, then the Rochons moved to Burlington.

It came as quite a surprise to Sylvie that in Mesmer one could walk four blocks from the church and be in the stubble remains of a grain field. It came as even more of a surprise that all of the grain fields, if traversed in certain directions, led to farm buildings and houses where people lived. While out on our walks, Sylvie often made reference to Goldilocks and Snow White. She was convinced, I was certain, that talking bears or friendly dwarfish creatures inhabited the country homes we came across. Finally, I offered to take her to the home of Blodwen Scarfe to demonstrate to her the normal qualities of the rural populace.

Blodwen and her husband Edward lived a country block from the edge of town, but their house with its deep laneway was readily accessible via fields and fencerows. The Scarfe farm was known to many children because of the particularly steep tobogganing hill in their front field. We were allowed to slide down that hill to our hearts' content on winter days and no one ever disturbed us. Off in the distance the farmhouse sat, serene and hushed it always seemed. Blodwen and Edward had no children. They could not have children, I had heard, some delicate imperfection existed, some little knot, a tiny blockage. For me, however, the phrase "can't have children" always conjured up an image of a logjam of babies backed up inside Blodwen, a watery sack packed full of little bodies, incapable of being had.

Edward and Blodwen's place had an allure in the summer too, when the Little Mud River flowed along the base of the hill and the concession road adjacent to their land became a meeting place for kids on warm summer evenings. Somewhat baroque in design, the bridge was ornamented with concrete balls at its four corners. These gradually chipped away with year after year of frost and warmth. The hill, the bridge, the river, Blodwen, the sack of unborn babies — all these features in my mind made the Scarfe home the logical site for Sylvie's first real exposure to human beings living in the countryside.

It was spring, early May, the day I decided to take Sylvie there. A blue day it was and Sylvie was wearing the fake buckskin jacket she owned and I coveted. Before heading out into the country, we went to the post office, on my mother's instruction, to fetch the mail and there had the unlikely experience of seeing Miss Lynch. Unlikely, because she did not live in Mesmer, but in the larger town of Kingsley. She had bought some stamps and was preparing several large envelopes for mailing at the table in the outer room which housed the post boxes. Miss Lynch stood in such a position that her right arm was almost at my eye level when I stooped to open the box. I was able to look briefly, but with intense interest, at a long line of scar tissue, a sight which caused a reaction I still experience when aroused or excited: as if a marble were scooting down my throat and out a little chute, bang onto my breastbone.

After depositing the mail at my parents' house, we struck off along a laneway for tractors and farm implements, on property belonging to Art and Bertha Van Epp. I told Sylvie about their dog King, a friendly old black, bear-shaped dog who used to come into town on his own on Saturday nights, just to be friendly. One summer night he went into the funeral home, just padded right on into that place of red velvet curtains. When Mrs. Epp got cancer, so did King. That was the eerie part about King, or so everyone said. Mrs. Van Epp got better, though, and King had to be put down. Afterward, some people began to say King had been a kind of devil-dog, going into the funeral home like that, maybe somehow giving Mrs. Van Epp the cancer. How would a dog know to come into town on Saturday nights? they asked. As for the Van Epps, they were always silent on the subject; their English wasn't all that good. I don't think they knew how to articulate a defence for King. I told Sylvie I considered King to be probably the greatest dog I had ever known.

"How *did* he know to go into town on Saturday nights?" she wanted to know.

"I think the smell of French fries from the Dairy Bar," I said. "The smell of French fries is always strongest on Saturday nights."

Having cut across one of the Van Epp's fields, we were then on Scarfe property. I knew where we could cross the creek, where the rocks were large and close enough together to allow us to hop across. All that remained was to climb the hill.

A veranda wrapped itself around two sides of the Scarfe house. On this veranda sat numerous red clay pots of different dimensions containing seedlings. No animal life was to be seen anywhere. Blodwen and Edward did not care for cats or dogs and it seemed even most of the birds were taking a mid-afternoon siesta. Surrounding the house were several umbrella-shaped elms, all in various stages of dying. It was the era of Dutch elm disease.

By the time we reached the base of the veranda stairs,

we knew Blodwen and Edward were both inside. Easily heard through the screen door, the tone of their conversation stopped us short.

"You are not to do this anymore," Edward said. "I want it stopped."

"Oh, what harm does it do, Edward? There's no harm in it," we heard Blodwen reply.

"What harm does it do? I suppose it does no harm, unless you count the harm it does to me. Do you? Do you count that at all?"

"Oh, Edward."

And that was the last we heard. We dashed around to the side of the house, fearing at any moment Edward would emerge and find us eavesdropping. Behind the inadequate shelter of a lilac, we waited for some time, then, at my suggestion, we circled out behind the house, behind the barn and through the fields. I seem to recall telling Sylvie more stories about King as we made our uneasy trip home.

~

Alexa was ready to return to university, to the third year of a degree in English and drama. For the past four years she had longed to do this but had not and was now pleased that she could place most of the blame for this on Janet Sainsbury's shoulders. Janet had convinced Alexa learning was best accomplished outside of academic institutions. She had bought Alexa the collected works of Chekhov and compiled reading lists that made no sense to Alexa, thematically or style-wise. "I think you should read all of these before Christmas," Janet would say, handing over a list of titles that might include Kurt Vonnegut and Virginia Woolf. And there were the assignments: "I think we should spend the next month or two on *Twelfth Night*," or, "Be Malvolio tonight. Just be Malvolio. I'll film you."

And I always went right along with it all, Alexa thought, amazed. True amazement is to be had looking back on a part of your life that seems to have been lived only by the large and voluntary muscle groups, arms, legs, neck muscles, jaw, tongue, while the rest was lazing around on a mat someplace deep inside, in a corner on a mat, for God's sake, napping. That's where I've been for the past few years. And despite all of Janet's diligence with my so-called education, where am I? Nowhere. A part-time job at a toy store. An inventory of worthless possessions unless I counted each of my fish as a separate item with a bar code of its own.

Incredibly, though, Alexa had to admit, Janet was an easier person to live with during her controlling martinet era than as a new-age prophet, before becoming the Eye of the Eye of the Beholder. Alexa tried to recall when this metamorphosis had occurred, when Janet had ceased to be content with her life as a projectionist, and owner and trainer of Alexa Stewart. When had she decided she must be more than these, that it was necessary to be a guide, a visionary, a crazed and pompous signpost?

Alexa had a ready answer. She had asked herself this

question numerous times before. It had all begun when Janet fell on a patch of ice one evening while out for a run. The doctor had recommended physiotherapy for her wrist and shoulder and off to Arthur, Physical Therapist, Janet had gone. From Arthur, it had been just a trip across the hall to Phoebe, Past Lives Therapist, the one who convinced Janet it was possible to cross the International Date Line psychologically.

"Why is that such a big deal?" Alexa had asked. "Wouldn't memory just be another word for that, or daydreaming about the future?"

After Phoebe, there was the shaman Rosemary, who told Janet she possessed the equivalent of a pulsar of healing energy inside her, "like a rock, a very hot rock."

In response to this, Alexa had said, "You know, the Chinese have launched a satellite into space. Just into space. No particular destination, or if there is one, they're not saying. Arthur and Phoebe and Rosemary remind me of that satellite. Sputnik Random. Therapists on the loose. A bunch of loose therapists. What? Why? Where? These questions come to mind."

"Alexa, Alexa, Alexa," Janet had responded, shaking her head. Alexa knew what this headshaking implied: her irredeemable position on a plane somewhere far below Janet's.

Alexa had thought it would all pass but instead it had grown. Janet and Phoebe gave birth to the group known as the Eye, with Janet as the leader, or maximum leader, as Alexa took to calling her, after Manuel Noriega. Sometimes she just called her Manuel, as in, "Manuel, can you get me a towel?" Janet, of course, hated this name game, and that day had fiercely thrown the towel at Alexa. But it's not really possible to throw a towel with much effect. Alexa had laughed, Janet gone out, probably to see Brigitte and Henry.

I should have known, Alexa thought. What is it about power and sexual bloat? Give someone a leadership role and within days the admirers are lined up, pants at knee level. From the president of Panama to the chairperson of the tiniest Calgary community association, they were all members of the same club: The Association of Grand Fuckmasters. They really required a regulatory body to limit their activity. It should have been obvious to me when Janet invited Brigitte and Henry to one of the Eye's meetings, just out of the blue. Undoubtedly Janet had consciously intended to get them both undressed out there on Paradise Hill, indulge in three-way orgasms and then confess to Alexa. Janet always confessed: she hated deceit and so did the pagan goddesses who believed sexual repression could lead only to anger and skin disorders, it seemed. Janet's defence had included the query, "Do you want my eczema to flare completely out of control?"

"Well, yes," Alexa had answered, "if that's what it takes. I mean, I'd rather you had eczema than know you were screwing my best friend and her husband."

"So it's not *what* I do; it's that you *know* what I do."

"That's not what I meant."

"Alexa, we have a boundaries problem. Your self and my self."

Alexa had heard this talk of boundaries before. The vagueness of its meaning, the implication she was a formless, protoplasmic being because she could not tolerate

Janet's infidelities made her wild. "Oh shut up, Janet," Alexa had screamed, enunciating up in an urgent way, as if calling for deliverance from a deep and murky pit. And that was the night she decided to leave.

Since moving into the Daiquiri, Alexa had left fourteen non-verbal messages on Janet's answering machine and her only satisfaction had been derived from this outcome: often when she called now, Janet's answering machine was not turned on. Janet simply did not answer, or possibly she was out with Brigitte and Henry, or worse yet, in with them. Who could know? Alexa sometimes let the phone ring forty or fifty times before hanging up, her heart pounding with pleasure. "I understand revenge at last," Alexa thought. But the invariable sequel to this thought was always, "Well, I half-understand revenge at last," because part of her still hoped Janet would come to her senses.

Alexa wished lovers came with a guarantee that each individual would not take it upon him or herself to change from one form to another, to shrivel up like the meal-worms Alexa remembered from third-grade science and emerge as some unforeseen creature. Or perhaps a type of insurance that could be claimed in the event one's loved one stood up at a Billy Graham crusade and walked forward like a lamb, as Alexa's own sensible mother had done after her husband's death. At least with her, the lamb-life had been brief; she soon told the Billy Graham corporation to stop sending literature. Well, actually it was Andrew who told them over the phone it was too late, his mother had developed anthrax.

Janet might still be under warranty, Alexa thought, she

might call back any day now. Underneath it all, there lived a rational person somewhere, probably. *Unless all of that past life stuff was made up,* Alexa said to herself. All of Janet and any worries related to her were underwritten by this quiet haunt. Nevertheless, nevertheless (always said twice), in the event Janet did call, Alexa thought she would like to have a fresh and clever greeting on her answering machine. A reminder, something to hook Janet and fill her with regret. A passage from *Twelfth Night* would be just the thing.

Alexa did not like *Twelfth Night* all that much; she was sick to death of it, in fact. It was all the Shakespeare Janet knew because she had quit school after grade eleven and begun her unbelievable ramblings around the world. Little time to read, apparently. Janet hated to think Alexa would become familiar with and appreciate any piece of literature she had not. *Twelfth Night* became a funny sort of roadblock, like orange flashing lights in the middle of the night. Cops: No, you can't go any farther, lady. Sorry.

Alexa found the passage she needed. It was from the first act, the scene when Viola arrives with a message for Olivia. Alexa read through it a few times, practicing the Elizabethan lilt Janet loved so much. Kneeling next to the machine, Alexa read, " 'I heard you were saucy at my gates and allowed your approach rather to wonder at you than hear you. If you be not mad, be gone. If you have reason, be brief. Tis not that time of the moon with me to make on in so skipping a dialogue.' "

Her message continued, "No, really, you know I love a skipping dialogue as much as the next person and, tis not really that time of the moon with me, so go ahead, talk to me."

Alexa listened to the recording a couple of times. She was satisfied; it was good. Janet would like it despite herself. Then she sat on the floor, looked around her new home and cried. She was broke. There had been the damage deposit for the apartment, and texts and tuition. Slightly more than minimum wage from the toy store. The indignity of the training manual with its one-line directives, Maoist in both metre and authority: Increase sales through improved customer relations. No hope of a student loan. Canada Student Loans believed Alexa Stewart could have saved thousands of dollars over the past three years if she had only planned and been more like the student on the cover of the government brochure. This student wore a pair of black watch tartan trousers and a white turtle-neck sweater. She carried a microbiology text next to her mid-sized breasts. Everything about her spoke of freedom from overdraft; lack of experience with the big walk-in freezer of a minus-two-hundred-dollar bank balance.

"I hate you," Alexa said to the brochure, "I hate you.

"But, I like Annie, I like the possibility of a new girl-friend." And, she thought, blowing her nose and studying the living room ceiling, I like that smoke detector up there. No doubt it could be set off with a match. This too was a bonus. Its nasal shriek could be the next message to Janet, once she got out of bed with Brigitte and Henry and switched on the answering machine again.

Things were not so bad. She would call Annie soon, maybe this week. She would try not to worry about her finances. No matter how bad things got, she could always watch her fish. And her fish would always need her to bring them their frozen brine shrimp and blood worms.

⟿

I was afraid this would happen and it did. Once the weekend was over and I was back at work, I became what Harriett Dafoe, School Psychologist, would likely describe as clinically obsessed with Alexa. My anticipation of her call bordered on violent. The energy created by my expectations could easily have ignited any number of small fires any place my gaze vacantly landed while I waited. I was prepared to throw myself into passion, however brief, however meaningless.

At the same time, a small and rational portion of my mind, apparently having been chunked off from the rest of me, observed my actions with a combination of awe and bewilderment, much the same way I imagined Spike watched me from his rabbit land. This part of me wondered, among other things, how many people at work and elsewhere, in social circulation in general, carted around an enormous and red-faced inner life. Extravaganzas behind the eyes, ribald scenarios that made a body want to lie down in the hallway and rub itself, maybe even do so in the staff washroom, emerging all placated and prudent once again. Plenty, was my guess. Sam Yeats? Ellen Nestle? One never knew.

Tuesday and Wednesday I was radiant with the effects of my imagined future romance. I stayed late at school, going through my files, reading up on auditory processing, booking appointments, postponing the trip home and the inevitable joy of Alexa's call. I had a sensation of bouncing at the end of a diving board, ready to spring high up into the air, high above the pool, higher than was thought humanly possible. And once in the air, I would be able to execute amazing turns and somersaults, full gainers, both doubles and triples. I would have no fear. The pool sparkled below, warm and inviting and any minute now, any second, I felt confident I would enter the water and the big difference would begin.

By Thursday night there had been no call.

The shrinking, but still rational, part of my mind began to wonder how all this had come to pass, a person mournful and empty for almost two years, swelling up in an alarming and imaginary way, like a Mickey Mouse hot air balloon, foolish and engorged with the anticipation of possessing someone completely unknown to her. I was haunted by a certain Archie-and-Veronica type of reasoning that concluded if Alexa were going to call in order to get together on the weekend, she would have done so by Thursday. To leave it any longer would presume a lack of callers, dates, Reggies and so on, which would of course be the correct and unflattering presumption. I invoked the voice of Dr. Panesh to advise me: Briefly, she would say, as she began so many of her judgments, briefly, what you have is a surfeit of chaotic activity in your mind, symptomatic of your condition, your condition of being apart, snipped off from all of the world's intimate affairs, snipped off from the secret parallel life. All that is required for your recovery is a certain body, a pair of hands, lips, a voice.

Of course, she would never say any of that, just as she would never say, "Annie, I've decided to write you a prescription for Ativan with an infinite number of refills."

I stared long and hard at the telephone. Then, at five past ten, I dialled Alexa's number, thinking if the receiver were picked up, I would hang up immediately. It was not. Instead, there was the machine, all Shakespearean and clever, which afforded me some solace and provoked a tinge of annoyance. This was the voice of my deliverer, the voice that might make of me a stickleback.

I hung up the receiver and picked it up again. I touched the cord. I held it. I was reminded of a strange old friend of Edna's who was brought to visit one day, delivered by her proper and vivacious daughter, someone I actually recognized, a Liberal MLA from the southwest quadrant of the city. The old woman's name was Frieda.

Frieda had a purse full of history with her that afternoon. She showed Sylvie and me her things in the back yard: a pack of photographs, a baby spoon, a Zippo lighter, certain poems clipped from women's magazines. But most memorable had been the section of telephone cord she had snipped for herself before leaving her home for the last time. The telephone people had been upset, naturally, and so had her daughter, but they put it down to a lapse.

"I knew what I was doing, though," Frieda said, leaning her grey, curly hair close to me, smelling of fragrant shampoo. "His voice is still in this. My husband's voice. John. He's been dead for fifteen years but I have a bit of his voice trapped in here. I can hear it if I hold it up to my

ear." And she lifted the length of cord to her ear and
closed one eye. "Just everyday things he used to say.
'How's things, Frieda? How's things? So long. See you
soon.' That kind of thing. I can hear him as clear as a bell.
Listen," she said, "see if you can hear him."

I held the cord to my ear. "I can't really say I hear anything, Frieda."

"Well, at least you're honest. Most people aren't. I'm the
only one who can hear him; I'm his wife after all. Why
would he go talking to you?" The little brown eyes gave
nothing away. Was she genuine? Was she putting me on? I
never knew. I only knew for sure Alexa's voice, delivered
by tape-recorded message, was long gone from my telephone cord. Likewise Sylvie's, way more extinct than
Alexa's. I unplugged the phone and went outside for a
smoke, my sixth of the day. I accepted that I was on my
way to a slow, wheezing and deserved death by emphy-
sema or lung cancer. No matter.

On my back porch, however, the swollen portion of my
mind took over and I resumed pleasant musings on Alexa.
What had first attracted me to her was the shape of her
ears — they were just like Sylvie's. The form of the outer
ear (many people need to be informed by an audiologist
such as me) is incredibly varied and embryologically interesting. Originally, the outer ear is composed of six little
hillocks with plenty of potential for diversity, a diversity
largely missed by everyone except those of us who happen to be looking. Miraculously, Sylvie and Alexa wound
up with more or less the same ears.

This coincidence of ears led me to thinking about the

big bang theory again, and the big bang theorists and their alter-egos, the theologians. I understood some of these people were now seeing eye to eye on the origins of the universe. After all, if there was a big bang, there must have been a big banger, someone to push the detonator. The specifics on this individual or force remained vague, however. Was it conscious? Did it inhabit some form or was it ethereal? What were the creator's plans for the events subsequent to the big bang? How well thought out was this action? As well planned as, say, an undergraduate's term paper on the effect of rubella, namely hearing loss, in the fetus? Did the creator, I wanted to ask the theologians, did the creator tighten up that ball of matter so mightily and with such microscopically detailed forethought that fifteen billion years later the fact of the sameness of Sylvie Rochon and Alexa Stewart's ears could be said to be planned?

No answer came to me. I wandered into Edna and Isobel's yard to take a look at their bit of riverside. They were out, I knew: every Thursday evening they bought groceries. I stood on the grass, listening to my distended mind as it imagined kissing Alexa Stewart's ears and everything between them.

~

Thursdays, Ted and Maureen drove Edna and Isobel to the Co-op for their weekly shopping. Occasionally, Isobel ordered up a cab on Monday or Tuesday, but generally she held out until Thursday, even though not entirely comfortable with the arrangement. Isobel was still not accustomed to help in all of its forms and contingencies, but she balanced the books with Ted and Maureen by supplying them with bottles of wine brewed in her basement, also known as Isobel's Winery. In fact, as they drove home, she considered what she would give them next. A bottle or two of the burgundy, perhaps. Resolving this caused a smoothing out of Isobel's mental landscape. Until the wine was actually handed over, though, there would be a lump, an obligation. Isobel liked the landscape to be smooth, like the prairie. It was easy to keep herself one step ahead of Edna, cultivating and raking. Not so with the others, especially when one no longer drove and had helpful neighbours.

The car moved slowly along Bowness Road. Infrequent comments were offered up, lazily. "I see that place finally folded," Maureen said, gesturing toward a dress shop.

"It's all part of the economic recovery, Maureen," Ted said. "The politicians have assured us we have entered the recovery. We just can't see it or hear it or smell it. It's a bit like carbon monoxide."

"Let's not start talking about the politicians," Isobel said. "It gets me too cranky."

Travelling along at a slightly busier velocity than the others in that car was the worried mind of Edna Plummer. She had been confused at the supermarket. Or had she? She wasn't sure. She had gone off to get some orange juice and had found the cans of frozen juices, then set off to locate Isobel and the cart. Up and down the aisles she had gone, feeling panic rise in her throat and a cottony silence fill her mouth. She began to wonder if she hadn't wandered off to the Co-op alone, walked out the front door like someone sleepwalking. The juice cans were freezing her hands and she thought of dropping them into her purse, then feared she might appear to be nothing more than a loony old shoplifter. That was when Isobel appeared around the corner of the cereals aisle. Isobel did not comment; not much time had passed after all.

And now Edna was unsure how to assess the whole event. She only knew this as she rode in Ted and Maureen's back seat: worry could become so intense for her she was certain it changed her breath. It was very odd. Some days when she was particularly worried Edna liked to hold a mirror up to her mouth and exhale, anticipating a spray of something like teeny, tiny asteroids, salt and pepper bits of worry. Edna only ever did this when Isobel was not around.

I have to take some action, Edna thought. Action. She had used that word in a Scrabble game with Isobel the night before. And as she played, Edna had thought, my thinking is becoming more and more like a Scrabble game, individual words slowly forming themselves, letters grouping and re-grouping. Seemed one word now sufficed, she thought, where years ago she would have yammered on and on.

"Why don't we have the bonfire party this weekend?" Maureen asked as they turned onto Bow Bottom Road. The bonfire party was a tradition, instigated by Sylvie a few years back, but foregone last fall because Sylvie was no more and everyone felt awkward, and the fall had been cold and wet anyway.

"Definitely," Isobel said. "I vote to have it. In your yard, as usual, and we'll supply the wine."

So it was agreed. Ted would notify Annie, who was in, he observed, pulling up to Edna and Isobel's house. "I'll ask her right now," Ted said.

"I see Annie's in now," Edna announced. "Her car's here now."

"Ted just said that," Isobel said. "I *knew* you were day-dreaming again, Edna Plummer."

Edna did not respond. As the engine was shut off, Annie appeared from the back yard to help with the bags. Edna pulled herself heavily from the back seat. In her mind a word was taking shape out of a couple of o's and f's, arranging itself for Edna's benefit, and that word was "failproof."

~

I resisted the temptation to call Alexa that week. Instead, I called Martha on the weekend and arranged to get together with her. "It won't be much fun," Martha warned. "I'm working both nights. I have three houses I do almost every weekend. Actually, I call them contracts just to give myself a bit of a boost. You're welcome to come along," she said, dragging out the last syllable dubiously.

I lunged at the idea, lunged at it Friday night after work in my highly impractical linen suit, one of the many outfits I imagined had crashed into the pool of abandoned Alexa Stewart fantasies and now hung wet and wrinkled from my shoulders. I was prepared to settle for an evening of charring with Martha Rigg. It was a pleasing proposition and I drove the route to Martha's with some excitement, thinking I might ask to see a picture of Mac, planning to broach the topic of his death and Martha's competent management of it.

Martha was ready and waiting with her cleansers and buckets when I arrived. "Most of my clients have their own stuff but I like to bring my own so as to avoid the products with the most horrific poisons. In fact, sometimes I make my own out of baking soda but I won't go on about that because, believe it or not, I have been accused of being tedious in this regard. In a couple of regards, come to think of it. Anyway, I hope you're ready for a full night. I spend about four hours at each place, that includes time out for eating — I like my food — so we're not going to be back here until seven in the morning or thereabouts. How've you been, by the way?"

"Just fine, Martha. I drive past our little paint job every day on my way to work and I have to admit I get a bit of a charge out of it. I figure no one would suspect me, the mild-mannered audiologist in her yellow Tercel. They all think I'm preoccupied with speech bananas and the like when in fact subversion is on my mind."

"Subversion," Martha said, stowing her supplies in my trunk as I had volunteered to drive. "I told you, it's not subversion."

"I know. I know. I know. I haven't forgotten."

"And what in the heck is a speech banana? I trust it doesn't grow in bunches on a tree."

"No, it does not. It's a shape, a banana shape on an

audiogram, the zone where the speech sounds are represented. If you have hearing loss but it's in frequencies not located in the so-called speech banana, then it's not such a big deal. But if you have perfect hearing for bird calls and lousy hearing for speech, then you're in trouble."

"Hmm," Martha said. "I see. South, by the way, head south to Elbow Drive."

"I've been told," she went on, "that I have exceptional hearing. I can hear conversations through walls with ease. When I was in university, living in a dormitory, I became a bit of a celebrity because of my talent. People hired me to eavesdrop for them. At first I didn't mind, but after a while I decided to draw up a code of ethics, like no listening in on sex, which was one of my most frequent commissions at first, before I decided to get ethical. I'd be standing in some smelly little room with my ear to the wall and an audience of six or seven, me saying things like, 'Oh yes, oh harder, don't stop, Ian' to much approval. I can't believe I used to do that, although I was a bit of a nerd and I have to admit I basked in the attention."

Not long after, we were in the neighbourhood known as Elbow Park. "These people fly to Vancouver every weekend practically, or New York or Toronto, shopping, shopping, shopping. And while they're gone I arrive, their little dust fairy, and clean the place up. I used to know them quite well. The husband, David, was a friend of Mac's in university and we even used to see them socially sometimes. I think they're probably a bit embarrassed by the situation now, plus they likely think I've gone a bit crazy because I have political meetings at my house. And because

I quit my old job and like to stay up all night cleaning."

"What was your old job?" I asked. We were already inside the house and Martha had begun rapid organizational motions, cleansers on counter tops, buckets clattering. "Atlantic Bee mops are the best, bar none," she said, then, "Don't tell too many people, okay. I was a social worker, juvenile probation. But like I say, don't tell too many people. The world loves to hate a social worker. In fact, now that I think about it, I probably achieved my highest social standing ever back in university in my eavesdropping days. I never got paid; don't get me wrong."

Martha showed me around the place. It was austere, all the rooms having dark walls and stained grey hardwood floors. "And look at this," Martha said, turning on the dining room lights. "This furniture came from some now-dead emperor's place in China. Amazing, huh?"

I was led to the single-lane swimming pool in the basement before Martha began her cleaning. "Go for a swim," she said. "There are some of Catherine's suits in the bathroom or just go naked. That's what I usually do."

The place was truly fabulous. The walls of the room housing the pool were covered in tile frescoes, Japanese themes, huge blue tsunami waves about to crash. And amidst it all I swam, back and forth, back and forth. I could not recall having been that content for some time. Not since before Monica left; not since I didn't know when. Perhaps all that happiness required was to become unnecessarily rich, rich enough to buy pre-revolutionary Chinese furniture and hire tile fresco-makers and jet off to Toronto or New York every weekend of one's life. Maybe wealth would preclude the need to hide out in a sound booth, or permit the construction of one in the basement for recreational purposes only. With a pool like this, I thought, I could keep miles ahead of those little crustaceans of memory, or fear. Which were they? I was not really sure. I was only certain that that moment, swimming naked in the pool of strangers while the vacuum whined somewhere above me, was a good moment.

I think I was reminded of my childhood, although there certainly had never been a pool, just a little blow-up thing my brother and sister and I used to sit in, often in our baggy-assed underwear. Maybe it was the sound of the vacuum cleaner. That far-off motor noise could conjure up plenty of childhood images, Saturday morning cartoons, the pleasing passivity of being cared for, being vacuumed around. My mother used to vacuum often and with extreme vigour, moving her large-boned body through the house. She no longer moves as she once did: arthritis has slowed that body right down. Most days now she sits while my father vacuums with a cheery efficiency. He reminded me of a nurse the last time I visited, that paid determination to keep all forms of self-pity at bay.

Back and forth in that privileged trough of water I swam, pondering the meanings of the sound of the vacuum. Stopping at one end, I balanced on my elbows and began bicycling slowly.

The interesting thing about certain vibrations like the vacuum cleaner, the audiologist in me could not help thinking, is that the sound can bypass the ear altogether and pass through the skull, to be picked up by the organ of Corti and shunted along to the auditory cortex, which tries to make some sense of it all. Buzzings and whirrings. Not much to work with but sound, nevertheless.

I had an urge to call Martha right then and ask her a question: What do we tell ourselves nowadays when somebody dies? What did you tell yourself, Martha, when Mac died? What stories are available to us at this time? I'm not sure that what is located in the speech banana can do the trick. Those sounds have been damaged, it seems, cracked open, leaving the interstices between each sylla-ble filled with . . . What? Pictures, maybe, bits of video-tape. Or perhaps just quiet, empty space like that occu-pying Sylvie's urn. Or maybe buzzings and whirrings. Buzzings and whirrings weren't a bad beginning, I could settle for that, settle for the consolation of a far-off vac-uum. It was about as much as I required at that moment.

But the vacuum was turned off and the ensuing silence hit me then, like the tile wave, a hard and suffocating crack on the head. "Martha," I shouted, "come down here for a while and talk to me."

~

We did not return to the Scarfe farm for some time after our first visit. And we steered clear of the church for a while too; every time we went there, Graham seemed to be on the prowl. He was singularly anti-social and had not earned one friend in Mesmer by that time, unless I could be counted as a friend. He did make a point of speaking to me, but only to deliver opinions or information he believed would shock or astound. I developed a dead-pan response to everything he had to say, which, contrary to what one might think, only encouraged him.

Sylvie seemed to wish to avoid her own parents' home, so my parents' house became fashionable for a while. George and Sandra Clemens were not church-goers and had no interest in fawning over the minister's daughter, a state of affairs Sylvie found refreshing. And she was enchanted by the idea of a father who worked in a pill factory.

My father's career had begun by then to be a bit of an embarrassment to me: I made a point of telling Sylvie the main reason my dad worked at the Pharmaceutical was the pension plan. This motive, in my mind, differentiated George Clemens from other dads employed at the pill factory, dads who did not mow their lawns regularly, dads who walked away from car wrecks a little too often.

Sylvie was not at all concerned with why my father worked for Epson Pharmaceutical. What interested her were the loads of pill containers he brought home from work. We spent hours sifting through the gravel in the driveway, looking for congruent groups of pebbles with which to fill our vials. Our search for pillish stones even took us out of town to the quarry. Detailed descriptions of what types of poisons we were creating and their imagined and usually devastating effects on humans and insects filled our days. We even made up little labels and taped them onto the vials. Inspired by pharmaceutical pamphlets Dad brought home from work now and again, we made up trade names like "Vanquor" and "Trelevate." "Nervox," we dubbed one: "Guaranteed to make the user as nervous as Miss Philippa Lynch. Nervox will make *you* jump." It was a pleasant time.

In the midst of this period, Graham began to press us to come to the church with him: he had something to show us. Invariably, when Graham had "something to show us," Sylvie and I reacted with a mixture of contempt and curiosity. We never answered his first invitation, or the second, but by the third I am sure he knew we could be counted on. In the end, we were nothing short of sheeplike in our compliance.

This time it was Reverend Rochon's study. I asked him why it was he never got caught in there and he said, "In order to be caught, I would have to be doing something wrong, right? Does this look wrong?" he asked, pointing to a math text and notebook. "Dad said I could do my homework in here. I asked him if I could. All I had to say was 'This manse oppresses me,' and he said okay. I've figured out that if I ask for something and in the same breath use a certain kind of vocabulary I know he likes, I usually get my way. You should try it sometime, Sylvie. I mean it. Just use a word like 'oppressive' or 'enlightened.' I get them from the sermons. I'm making a list. Anyway, I've found something quite interesting, which I'll show you for a dollar or a promise of future enslavement."

"I don't have any money," I said. Sylvie stared coolly.

"Well, all right. Just remember you owe me. The next time I want some Alpha-Bits up in my room, Sylvie, you are my slave girl. Understand?"

"Graham," Sylvie said in a teacherly voice, as if to say his name, to label him as if he were a natural resource, a spice, a type of ore, would cause events to move along. Which it did.

Slowly and with what he no doubt thought was high drama, Graham opened the big bottom right-hand drawer of Reverend Rochon's desk, the one drawer large enough to contain files. Graham had obviously combed his way through this collection of documents and papers. From the very back of the drawer, he chose a file labelled "Misc.," looked at us with an expression of supreme satisfaction and announced, "Love letters."

"Who from?" I asked.

"Women you wouldn't know, mostly from Burlington. I think I've figured out who they are. There are three of them and usually they just signed with initials but once in a while they used their first names. When I first found them I got pretty excited; I thought there might be some real hot stuff but since there wasn't I decided I might as well show them to you two. One of them for sure is that Mrs. Lowell who was always hanging around so much. Her name was Carol, right? Well, I knew she had the hots for Dad and I was right. I really think I might be one of those psychic private investigators when I grow up because there isn't much I guess wrong, so it can't be just guesswork. Anyway, listen to this."

Graham proceeded to read excerpts from more than a dozen letters from the ladies of Burlington, a Carol, an Ainslie and one identified as dw, lower case, no periods. Hers were the most passionate and direct in style. Whereas the others made frequent references to overwhelming feelings of love — Carol made reference to "agape" (pronounced by Graham to rhyme with a grape) — dw concerned herself (assuming it was a her) with eros and its creative power. She wrote poetry filled with images of fertility and heat. One piece, titled "In the fullness of time," compared time to a juicy mango, and ended: "i eat of time's moist flesh. time drips down my chin. each second is twice drunk."

"Hmmm. I wonder how time could drip down your chin?" Graham asked, looking at me suggestively, as if I might read some sexual meaning into this, which I did not. Because I was a year older than Sylvie, I think Graham hoped he might occasionally be able to communicate with me, if only through beeps and flashes from his secret life of loneliness and horniness and snooping and searching. I must have recognized that in some unconscious way, because I laughed at his question and said, "Mmm, slurp, slurp, time tastes pretty good to me."

Sylvie, watching us both with horror, said, "I don't think Dad can help it if other women fall in love with him. He can't stop them from doing that or writing him letters. It's a free country, isn't it? And I don't think you should be looking through his desk. That's private stuff."

Beneath that cool exterior, Sylvie was a loyal daughter, a quality I was relieved to observe. Sometimes Graham's disdainful attitude bewildered me, made me want to run home and sit on my dad's lap. I never did, though.

"Do you not think I should be about my father's business?" Graham asked. This allusion was lost on me.

"No, I don't," Sylvie answered. And I had to agree. Although, I must say now, in fairness to Reverend Rochon, there was nothing in that file — and we looked through the entire thing that day, opening every envelope, every decorative piece of stationery — to suggest he had ever had any part in requiting the agape or lust of his devotees. And, come to think of it, nothing to suggest he had not, either.

~

Labour Day night, Ted fired up a load of wood in his yard. Edna and Isobel were there, and Ray, who all together with Maureen and the two kids, Julia and David, and even the wiener dog, and I stood, watching the fire rise from the brick fire pit. It was not yet dark, the setting sun illuminating the sides of things, making the trees seem lamp-lit. And although summer was still with us, the season had slipped away and those three-syllable words we reserve for autumn weather were in use. You know the ones — glorious, radiant, marvellous: words used more as we grow older. Words Edna used, Isobel not so much.

Part of the tradition was for Ted to worry every year about whether yard fires were legal and then to complain about the need to worry about such things. "The urban zoo," he'd say. "What is the state of affairs when you can't light a fire without fear of police intervention? Is it generally now believed that people don't know how to handle fire?" Ted asked. "Maybe that's true now. We've been living in captivity for so long, we've forgotten how to deal with the elements. I'm surprised our children survived, Maureen." That was how Ted would talk; Maureen was used to it. She liked to drink her drinks and reflect upon the year's gardening successes and failures.

"If we lived in the country," Ted said, "we could have one huge bonfire. One huge, mother of a bonfire."

From the garden, Maureen answered, "Every year you say that, Ted, and it's typical. You keep yourself gloomy by having great expectations. Now me, I would be content to have some Brussels sprouts that reached maturity instead of just a bunch of bug-eaten leaves. I really don't know why I bother. To call it a growing season in Alberta is really stretching things a bit. Either the season is too short or every year my vegetables are plagued with some kind of growth hormone deficiency." She began ripping bean stalks from the soil, handing them to the kids, who carried them to the fire pit, holding stems above the blaze and watching them smoulder. Isobel pitched in, yanking Swiss chard and spinach from the soil.

Twenty-four months ago, I thought, Sylvie was standing in this very yard with this exact group of people. Commemorative moments such as these came and went, small rain forests of memory offered up to me out of the blue. So many times I have wished for something more concrete than memory, a coin perhaps, a memorial gold coin featuring Sylvie Rochon at the fire pit of burning leaves and branches, her back to me in that old red plaid jacket she wore for yard work, the one that still smells of her. Once a week I bury my nose in that jacket, rationing my sniffs out of a fear the scent might be depleted by my consumption of it. I think smelling that jacket is the closest I ever get to praying for Sylvie because the scent of her, the leftover bits she sloughed off into that red fabric, can bring me to my knees.

Ted poked at the fire. Edna threw on some more wood and leaves, keeping a wary eye on Isobel in the garden.

"You're not happy with the scale of this blaze, are you, Ted?" Edna asked. "You want something bigger, don't you? A big leaping blaze. I know all about that. I've always liked the grand scale myself. That is one thing about working at the San. Did I say is? I meant, that *was* one thing about working at the San. Each morning you felt as if you were entering some grand old southern plantation farm, all those huge buildings with their columns and so on. And when we had a fire, like the fire we had every January, it was a big event. The fire itself, I mean, not the social affair. You really couldn't have called it a social affair. I don't know exactly what you would have called it. Anyway, it would be a tremendous blaze and very satisfying to watch. All the patients seemed to be calmed by it and the people who lived over here then, across the river, they'd stand on the banks and watch too. I never thought I'd be one of the people living on this side of the river. I really loved that fire and I think now it was simply because it was so very high. Huge. That's what you want sometimes from a fire, isn't that so, Ted?"

"That is exactly so, Edna. Exactly."

"Don't tell Isobel," Edna said, "but I'm going to scoot inside and grab a drink of water. I had a little bit of the wine and it's made me quite dry."

"I can get you a drink," Ted offered.

"No, no. Please. I like to take the opportunity every once in a while to do something completely on my own, even if it's only to walk such a tiny distance as to my own house to get a drink of water and maybe putter around for a minute or two. Isobel will not let me out of her sight. To be honest, there are times when I feel more like a pet than an old woman. Do you know what I mean? The kind of pet you need a fenced yard for.

"I sincerely hope," Edna went on, "that I never become like my dear friend Frieda. You met her once, I believe, Annie. She's in a home now and the last time I went to see her she was up on the third floor standing by the window, looking out onto the sidewalk. People were walking by and she said to me as we were watching the people, she said, 'Edna, how do those people get out there? How *do* they get out there?' You see, the doors are all locked because some of them wander and Frieda, she thinks there's some way to get out that other people are keeping a secret from her. It's funny to think about it, isn't it? That is what she will leave this world thinking. It reminded me of two people tunnelling toward each other and missing, not meeting, one up here and the other down below. Well, I'll take my leave now and go get a drink of water like other people do. I'll be back, don't worry. And don't anybody dare tell Isobel."

Edna walked across my lawn, stopping only to poke a finger into Spike's cage, then disappeared into her own yard. Ted and I watched the fire; to help with the garden work now would draw Isobel's attention to Edna's absence. Best to let her have her untended time. Through my open back door I could hear the telephone ringing, five or six times, then stopping abruptly in mid-ring. A fish jumped and splashed. "It wasn't for you," said Ted, in the direction of the Bow River.

~

I lay awake that night, thinking about the christly river and begging for sleep. I was afflicted with a hyperconsciousness of the Bow and all the cold-blooded life it carried, not to mention those things that had fallen in or been cast away or poured in and, worse yet, dissolved. To dump Sylvie into that when it was impossible to conceive of what might be wafting by at any moment? Impossible to imagine and I found myself trying not to, yet the closer to sleep I hovered, the brighter the imaginings became. Catfish. I could see catfish. Huge ones scouring the bottom, dozens of them, muttering in unison. What was their bubbly submarine chant? At first I could not make it out. Oh yes, of course. "We will eat anything. We will eat anything," was what they were saying. And in their indiscriminate scavenging, they had cut their lips and bellies and eaten remains capable of killing most forms of life. Poor things, really. They grew tumours on the outside, some as large as tennis balls. And their cuts never healed. If we happened to see these catfish walking along the sidewalk, walking upon tumours grown into the form of mushy paws, we would jump back and gasp.

Not yet. That had not happened yet in all the ecological mix-ups, all the motion from one state to another: Sylvie to dust, catfish to land rover.

I was awake enough to long for sleep, even among those catfish. I began to see sleep as an indigo blue place beyond a very narrow opening; if I could just get my shoulders through, the rest of me would follow, fast and slippery like a birth. I could leave the old carbuncular fish behind.

Something jangled. The fish? The fish were calling with a jangly, underwater ringing sound. No, no. It was the phone, the telephone. Almost two a.m. but I did not mind. With the receiver at my ear, I heard, "It's me, Alexa."

A-lex-a. These were wonderfully soothing sounds to me, the sounds of this name and that voice. I could see the cilia in my inner ear swaying just so, rocking. All the hair cells in my cochlear epithelium said thank you, thank you for calling, thank you.

～

The plan was made and followed: Alexa came by my house again, on Sunday afternoon. This meant exactly two weeks had passed since her first visit. Alexa barely seemed real to me by then, corporeal, that is; she seemed to have entered that expired and spectral world of past fantasy, peopled with imaginary figures who have lost their colour. But there she was in my kitchen again, talking and opening a bottle of red wine, with all of her colour and voice and motion. As I watched her I wondered what the likelihood of fantasy and reality coinciding was and how that felt: preposterously lucky, I concluded.

There had been traffic problems for Alexa.

"It's a favourite daydream of mine," she said, "while I'm driving, that cars could be manufactured of sponge instead of metal. The entire body could be sponge with some kind of lightweight engine so that when some dick-head is in your way, the solution would be to smash into him. The solution to red lights would be to run them and risk the possibility of a sponge pile-up. It would be great. It would be like driving around in a tampon. There would be light days and then, if it rained, there'd be your heavy days. In fact," she said, pulling the cork from the bottle, "for the truly organically inclined, the natural sponge car could also be used as a ready supply of tampons. Just rip off a corner. Just slowly use up your car. Just slowly, bit by bit, stuff it into your snatch." Alexa thumped the bottle onto the table and began looking for glasses.

"Up there," I said, "above the sink." Examining her closely for any small sign of vulnerability, I was pleased to discover a nervous pink blotch forming on her neck; it looked like an inverted map of Texas.

"I avoid driving as much as possible," I said. "I tend to agree with Prince Charles that cars are a bit of a blight, that all of life has become organized around them, although I don't know why I'm talking about Prince Charles — I read about him in the paper this morning, I guess that's why — I don't normally; I mean, decades could go by with nary a mention."

"Well, I like cars," Alexa said. "I can't fault them for any-thing. It's the people inside I have trouble with. Even

Prince Charles cuts people off, I bet, or revs his engine at stoplights once in a while."

I began to imagine Alexa developing a picture of me as a devoted monarchist, one who began crocheting Christmas gifts for the royal family in August. I imagined her sharing this image with the ex-girlfriend, Janet, who would laugh haughtily no doubt, her silhouette a delicate ha-ha-haing, flowing nicely into one of the more advanced tai chi positions. During the preceding weeks I had developed a picture of this Janet individual, a woman dressed in robes, thin, capable of running the New York Marathon, yet well acquainted with eastern philosophy and language. A Taoist, an accomplished acupuncturist, what have you. No energy at all was required to build upon this image, this elaborate and towering spectacle. In fact, during one brief out of control moment, I watched my inner screen with horror as this conception of Janet removed an exquisite antique bone chopstick from her draping sleeve and made numerous rapid stabbing motions toward my left breast.

Maybe just let Alexa talk, I thought, resisting an urge to cup my hand protectively over my breast. I have always been inept at this sport. My performance was much like it used to be in field hockey, standing on the sidelines, hoping not to get smashed in the shins by one of those God damned sticks. Sooner or later, I knew, the ball would come to me, regardless of my effort, followed by a herd of muscular and red-faced girls in full-cut kilts swinging wildly up at the back, revealing the underpants I loved to glimpse. The way those kilts would swing up, almost like waves cresting. Those were the habits that had brought me to this juncture, I concluded: standing on the sidelines, watching for the kilts to swing up, avoiding the sticks as much as possible.

As I contemplated kilts, Alexa began talking about her sister. Colleen had phoned Alexa to say her daughter, Victoria, had been tested and found to be gifted. "Her IQ is in the 'very superior' range. How is that possible?" Alexa asked. "Does that seem possible, that an IQ test can tell a three-year-old is gifted? The word even sounds, I don't know, all ribbons and bows. 'I am gifted, Mommy.' I don't think so," Alexa said, "the Stewarts aren't inclined that way."

I talked. I responded in some manner as I studied the half-moon smudge of lipstick on the rim of Alexa's wine glass. I would have liked to explain my fascination with lipstick to her. I would have liked to explain it to myself; it seemed purely Pavlovian. I began to salivate a bit, even thought I might bark, but instead I spoke calmly of what Harriett Dafoe had told me about intelligence tests. Time passed. A casual observer would not have guessed these two women were sniffing the air for messages, responding to one another's scent for obstinate and inexplicable reasons.

We decided to go outside and look at the river. The weather was warm still. "I can't bear to think of winter coming," Alexa said. "I have this hope for Canada," she went on, "you know, while everyone is worrying about national unity and the constitution, I think we should make a grab for some of the U.S. I'd like to see two breast-shaped chunks of land annexed, extending down to maybe Arizona in the west and Arkansas in the east. And when that happens, my plan is to move to one of the nipples, probably the western one, because I'm basically a cowgirl at heart."

I laughed and wondered how exactly I would ask her to spend the night: that was what I wanted. It hardly mattered that Alexa Stewart seemed incapable of looking directly into my eyes when speaking. Never mind that I could almost feel the breath of the field hockey girls as they herded past with their clubs.

Then I said, "I'd like to make a dedication. Because this is my house and it's on the river, I feel I have property rights over whatever portion of the river happens to be passing by at any given moment. So, I can dedicate a piece of the river to you. That piece right there. See? There it goes. It's yours. It's kind of a fleeting honour, I guess. Maybe a person becomes a bit delusional living on the river, delusions of grandeur. It's really only people like the Royal Family who made dedications. There I go bringing them up again. What is wrong with me?"

"I like that idea," Alexa said. "A little piece of river. Thank you."

That is when I kissed her. The moment seemed right and indeed it was because Alexa kissed right back with enough tongue to make the bony spaces behind my ears fill up as if small wings might pop out or a group of moths, the surprise of it all causing a gush in my underwear.

"Would you like to stay here tonight?" I asked, listening to these words I had spoken. They seemed misplaced, taken from some other time. I was reminded of a comment Edna had once made: "You don't often see ladies wearing feather hats anymore, do you?"

"I'll stay as long as we go right now, get undressed and into bed while there's still some wine in my arteries, because that's the scariest part for me. Once that's over with for the first time, then I don't feel so anxious." Disarmed by this confession, my heart pinkening then reddening by the sincerity of my fondness for her, we went to bed. At some point, Janet Sainsbury's chopstick fell from my breast maybe, her sleeve, someplace in between, to the floor, a faint little rat-a-tat-tat followed by a rolling away. Alexa was mine.

Not much later, it seemed, but it was. The red digits said four-sixteen a.m. Alexa was sleeping with her arms beneath her. I moved closer and placed a hand on her shoulder. Was this really someone else, someone so decidedly not Sylvie Rochon? The warm fleshy reality of it was absolute, and yet, in that dark hallway leading to sleep there was always time and opportunity for barter, a pawn shop dimly lit, and Sylvie was there of course and in my half-sleep I believed I had brought the right treasure. I could make a trade. Such a warming thought, even though some place in my mind said, *Chilly now, fall.* Outside the open window there was an absence of sound. Only the river could be heard, its voice nattering by, its hurried murmurings in the night sending out the most breakable of sound waves, filled with irregularities and yet a gathering quilt, sailing up and ballooning down upon the corners of the city. I love sleep, home of our separate intimacies.

~

I had been to the Mesmer United Church for social events, weddings, foul suppers and the like, but never to attend a Sunday service. It was Graham who talked me into going to Sunday school. "Why shouldn't you have to suffer as much as me and Sylvie?" he asked. "What do you do on Sunday mornings anyway? Watch Popeye cartoons?"

So I began attending from time to time, sat on the wooden chairs in the basement which, because it was a church, I assumed, had no basement scent. The man who ran the Sunday school services was called the superintendent, although I knew him as Harold Maltby, the mechanic from the Esso station. Here he was now in a black suit and white shirt, speaking from behind a lectern. I felt as if I had gone through the looking glass or happened upon a place where all things might become something entirely different from what they were in ordinary life. I wondered if Miss Lynch might stroll in, cocky, sexy and scarless. There was a sense of possibility present in every object in that church basement.

The very first time I went was called White Gift Sunday. I will never forget it. Each child was holding a round or rectangular package wrapped in white tissue paper. I was to learn they were cans and boxes of food, destined for a mission in Toronto. Suddenly, Toronto became a place where poor people opened white gifts and ate at last.

Harold spoke at length about the poor and the mission

while his restless audience shifted their chair legs on the concrete floor, each movement causing a migraine of noise which appeared not to disturb the speaker. As Harold spoke a benediction and some closing remarks, Graham, from the row behind, handed me a drawing. "Look at this," he said.

"What is it?" I whispered.

"Each of these is a galaxy," he said, pointing to various infinity-shaped sworls of pencil marking. "The Milky Way is not represented here. Now here," he said, indicating a small curve on the very edge of the page, "here we have God's big ass, like I have told you I believe, falling through space."

I turned around to look at him, wordlessly, then returned my gaze to Harold, the chameleon.

"You know it's true," Graham hissed in my ear with a provocative intensity. "Now watch Harold, Annie. Watch him."

A crush of children in the aisle succeeded Harold's closing thoughts, a horde of supplicants bent on escape. Harold, it seemed, wished to wrestle his thin body through this short throng so as to shake hands with his congregation on their way out. He moved with the impatience of someone trying to get through to the scene of an accident, wanting to bat away these people and their terrible disregard. Graham found this entertaining. By the time Harold had arrived at the foot of the basement stairs, half the children were gone. The only ones who took the time to shake his hand were the girls wearing hats. Although, I did, and my head was bare.

Outside, the adults were gathering, emptying the church, shaking hands with Reverend Rochon in the dignified and interested manner Harold Maltby must have hoped for. Blodwen Scarfe was there in a blue dress and shoes to match, looking beautiful I thought, looking just a tiny bit more awake than the rest. My mind flashed briefly to the Jehovah's Witnesses who came to our house with their publication *Awake*. I wondered if Blodwen had perhaps been the inspiration for their title.

I watched Blodwen, after Graham and Sylvie had been collected by Daphne, stood there in the spring sunlight and watched her nodding her head in agreement with someone, saw her lips moving, noticed her husband was not present. Then she moved away from the group and stood watching as well, just like me, with a curious expression on her face, almost fearful, as if these clusters of people might separate violently like atoms and send us all skyhigh in an enormous burst of renunciation.

Blodwen turned and walked away in the direction of the same country laneway Sylvie and I had taken to her house. Soon she was wobbling along on high heels which sank occasionally into the soft earth, reminding me of the way heat teeters above the black soil in spring in that part of the world.

Later that day, I asked my parents what they knew about Blodwen Scarfe. My mother, who stood ironing in her white short-sleeved blouse and black pants of a stretch-knit fabric, said, "I went to high school with Blodwen. She was a year older than me, so we didn't chum around together. I knew enough about her, though, to know that she was clever. Athletic, too. Always got the prizes, best student of the year and so on." Mom shook some water onto the shirt she was ironing from a bottle she used for that purpose. "It's my opinion that she's wasted her talents. She actually didn't even get her matriculation, she was so anxious to marry Edward, whatever for I can't imagine. Since then, she's withdrawn from the adult world; I know she puts up with you kids tobogganing and so on, but really . . . She's been approached to sit on the library board because she does read, but she declined." She handed me the shirt she had been working on: "Hang this on that chair back."

"Her sister Loretta was an accomplished skater and a swimmer, almost got to the Olympics once. She went to the University of Toronto on a scholarship and she's a professor of something now, as is her husband. I knew Loretta better, even though there was a bigger age difference between us, because Loretta was an extrovert and Blodwen is an introvert. There's nothing wrong with being an introvert, but Blodwen takes it too far. I'm surprised she's going to church now, to tell you the truth. You knew her, didn't you George?"

"Well, yes, I knew her a little," Dad said from the kitchen stool he liked to sit on, eating peanuts from the shell. "I always kind of liked Blodwen. She never seemed strange or anything to me, just happy to be on her own. Then she started going around with Edward. I probably haven't said more than twenty words to her in the last ten years. I think it's this whole kids thing that's mostly to blame for why she is the way she is."

"What do you mean?" I asked, hoping to have this mystery made clear to me at last.

"There's some problem," my mother said. "They can't have children."

This was hardly satisfactory, but I knew by my mother's tone of voice it was all the information I would receive. Images of the backlog of miniscule babies holed up in Blodwen's abdomen filled my mind one more time.

"Why don't they adopt a baby?" I asked.

"Well, I've heard," my mother answered, "that Edward's afraid to adopt because his brother adopted that Benny boy, who turned out to be retarded and goes to a special school in Kitchener. The impression I have of Blodwen is she wants to have her own children and that's all there is to it. Adoption wouldn't be the same. She has a romantic nature; she's not a particularly practical woman. She must be thirty-eight by now, wouldn't she be, George? You'd think she'd give it up. I don't understand how people can spend their lives spinning their wheels," Mom concluded, as she flung another shirt onto the ironing board and began to wet it down.

∾

Alexa came by the very next day, directly after her shift at the toy store, working with the fucking toy polloi, as she referred to her customers. Alexa loved to hear herself make such comments; she liked to say them once, then again with some variation in enunciation, then nod approvingly at herself and smile. "I shouldn't say that, about the toy polloi, I mean. It's elitist, really. It has to be. Janet Sainsbury coined it. You know, she never once came to see me at that store. In fact, she would never admit to her friends that I worked in a shopping mall on a part-time basis. What a cunt she is."

Sitting down, calming herself, then adopting a neutral expression, Alexa said, "Okay, that's enough. I'm done with that. Whoosh, it's out of my mind now. It's — you know all this ritual psychology stuff that's going on now? Janet's an expert in it all. Here's how it works.

"In your mind, place the bad thought on an assembly line in a wiener factory somewhere. Watch it travel along. Observe it being packaged up with eleven other wieners and disappearing. There it goes. There. I've purged myself of Janet."

And this seemed to be the truth, although I must admit an assembly line of my own was needed to carry away the bundles of suspicion I had instinctively manufactured, all bearing the label Janet Sainsbury. Never mind. Alexa's attention had become entirely my own, a rather wonderful situation because the attention of Alexa Stewart was about as pure as light, light that can embrace you and warm you when it is yours, and leaves you waving your arms in sudden and blind disbelief when it is taken away. Where is it? for God's sake, you want to say.

In a very short time, Alexa said, "Take off your clothes, honey." And I did.

And when Alexa left, as she did last night, late, because she had not fed her fish, or at least that is what she said, I was left here with my urn and my ashes — Sylvie, Sylvie, what can I say? — and the late-night digital glow of 3:13,

3:14, 3:15 and so on. The situation was a bit like the aftermath of a maelstrom. I half expected a reporter from the CBC to appear, or at least a curious meteorologist. Amazing how a tornado can leave certain objects, in this case everything but the bed, completely untouched. Here we have a cup exactly as it was left, even this vase and this funerary urn, untipped. Ah, the fury and the whimsy of nature.

The hour was certainly well past midnight and so I was justified in getting up and enjoying my first cigarette of September sixteenth. I was rather pleased with myself all in all, in particular with my knowledge of the big bang theory. I had used this to my advantage, I thought, to impress Alexa. I had told her, with confidence, that we now understood how lumps of matter had been formed from the original soupy chaos following the alleged bang. And from the lumps, I told her, had come all the elements on the periodic table, and from them . . . her, me, in short, an apparent order.

"And what about the non-lumpy things?" Alexa asked. "Like, let's say, revenge for example. Where does revenge come from?"

"I don't know about revenge," I said. "I don't seem to recall it from the periodic table; I don't remember a symbol for revenge. Rev? No, I don't believe it was there, so I don't really see how revenge could be involved in the big bang chain of events."

"Oh," Alexa said, "oh." And then she went on. "I really have to be honest," she said. "I really can't keep quiet. It's a family trait. Everyone in our house was always talking. If you were quiet, everybody became suspicious, they thought you were plotting. Talk equalled honesty in the Stewart household. Talk equalled nothing hidden here, no secrets, no surprises. It's the way I am. I must tell. So what I have to tell you is about Janet Sainsbury. I hate her. And because of that I've been doing some things that aren't very nice and I'm afraid it might escalate."

"Well?"

"Well, I leave anonymous and disturbing messages on her answering machine. Noises — you should be able to appreciate that, being an audiologist — like the smoke detector. For my last message I ground up some almonds in my coffee grinder while holding the telephone receiver close up to the noise. And, well, I feel as if I'm getting nowhere with this tactic and I'm worried that I'll have to do something else."

"Haven't you already, by getting involved with me?" I asked.

"I have to say, in all honesty, which is a phrase I hate, by the way, my cousin George uses it at least twice per sentence, in all honesty I would have to say that that may have been part of my initial motive. I've thought this through. But, no longer."

"No, of course not, now that we're into the third date or whatever you want to call it of our relationship or whatever this is and we've made a deep and lasting commitment," I said.

"No, no, no. I won't have you being sarcastic about this. At the very least, it's an attraction we have here and there's a certain wonderful simplicity to lust which is something I have to say I think men know more about than women.

Women muddy up the waters right away with feelings and analysis and long-term projections and it's, you know, one day you meet and a week later you're immersed in that person's way of life and taste in art and fridge magnets. I don't know. I would like it to be, just once, a pure little moment of lust. Just that."

"And what about Janet Sainsbury?"

"Oh, let's forget about her. I wanted you to know that I'm capable of actions that might be called borderline. In fact, my whole personality was once called that by a psychiatrist I saw in my last year of high school. Anyway, I'll probably go to see her one day soon because I can't stand to be ignored. I want you to be apprised of these facts, as they like to say in certain circles . . . apprised. That's what the secretary in the English department is always doing to me, apprising me. Sounds like, I don't know, getting your lid ripped off. Do you know what I am saying to you? I don't like to be dishonest. Janet Sainsbury is in my mind at times; she's writ large in there, as they say. She's the past, she's gone, but the past sometimes can't help itself, it's a bit of a groper, a bit of a *frottage* artist when it comes to the present."

And I said, and I think I meant this, "Lust is fine with me, if that's what it's going to be. I haven't had much lust recently so it's nice to have some around again. And in such a nice container. Nice container, nice label: Alexa Stewart. So, we'll have lust."

"Yeah," Alexa said, "we'll be guys. We'll be guys about this."

And then Alexa picked up the weekend *Globe* from the floor beside the bed and began to read. Fine. Lust it was and lust it would be, if I ever saw Alexa Stewart again. Not a bad deal. Sure, I'll take the lust, I decided, instrument of revenge or no. I was a satisfied person. I understood the big bang theory and I had performed rather excellently with Alexa, I thought, making her moan, making her say, don't stop, don't stop.

Something Sylvie swore me to secrecy on was her hard luck with orgasms. They didn't come easy to her. She had a fear of that much abandonment with another person in the room; she couldn't say why. For a while, I blamed it on her collecting of stuff, even got angry at her once when she came home with a bunch of pins from the Lake Placid Winter Olympics. I told her that if maybe she stopped hoarding things she might get lucky and have an orgasm. Her response? "Oh, go to hell. You know as well as I do if I didn't have all these things I'd probably never come, on my own or with you."

She was right. Somehow the logic fit. Sylvie Rochon was never much of a guy. She did not finish things. Not her car payments or her B.A. or any cleaning up or her lovemaking. Even her eating was incomplete; she liked to leave one little pile of mixed scraps on the side of the plate, a burial mound of protest. And then finally it was her life she failed to complete. I have often wondered if she even bothered to brake when she saw Wayne Abelard in his truck. Possibly not; she was likely preoccupied with the thought of locating a map of Sierra Leone to complete her Africa section.

Well, Alexa comes often and with alacrity, unless, of course, she's faking it.

~

ate afternoon Tuesday, and Isobel was on her way via
Calgary Transit to the pool for an adult swim session. She had long given up the idea of talking Edna
into coming with her. Edna could not see the connection
between mind and body, a fact Isobel found astonishing
considering that Edna, too, had worked at the San. They
had argued briefly after lunch about Isobel's theory on the
relationship between craziness and laziness, and then Isobel had left in a flurry of warnings and injunctions. "Edna,
please don't go for any walks. There's plenty you can do
here. If you feel restless, you could try the calisthenics."

"Yes, yes, I suppose I could," Edna had said. "And I
could also try eating the red wriggler worms from the
compost. There's no end of things I could *try*."

"Sarcasm is not good for the blood, I don't think, Edna.
But regardless of that, I'm off. See you later."

Edna watched her go from the front step. Very warm
for September, she thought, very warm.

Edna liked Isobel, even loved her occasionally, but most
times viewed her as a well-intentioned jailer. We have one
of those relationships, Edna thought, like the hostage
develops with the terrorist; there was a word for that, but
Edna realized the likelihood of her ever remembering it
was slim, very slim. She reckoned there were whole huge
warehouses of words and information she would never
locate again, never. As Isobel, the terrorist, rounded the

corner and disappeared, Edna, the hostage, went inside.

She had a plan in mind, a walk she was going to undertake, an independent walk to Bowness Park. This was an extraordinary goal for Edna but not as impossible as one might think: Edna had already developed the technology required to keep her steady on her course. What she had come up with were bits of paper, long narrow strips cut from Isobel's helpful literature. The paper used for these brochures tended to be coloured, most often yellow or blue, and sturdy. The strips Edna cut could be secured under a rock and easily seen from several paces. And Edna simply wrote over top of whatever advice the brochure offered, bits of her own, phrases such as "I am only out for a walk." Thus would she mark her route. And if stricken with that odd feeling of forgetting suddenly, everything, she need only consult the nearest marker.

It had happened again in the last little while, twice in fact. Just last Sunday at a coffee shop with Isobel and her friend Lois. Edna had gone to get herself a second cup and there, waiting in line, things had fallen away, a silent landslide of memory and moorings. Nothing and nobody looked familiar. And it *had* been a sensation in her mind — not her body, she wanted to tell Isobel, but her mind — from left to right like anesthesia, only through some miracle she was still standing. Then all was returned to her, came back like a movie projector being turned on, everything slurring back into action and clarity.

The other occasion was the last time she and Isobel had gone for a walk. The biggest challenge, Edna decided then, was to not let on, to Isobel or anyone else. Edna likened this to her own sudden nakedness on a busy street corner. It was the opposite effect of the emperor's new clothes. Edna Plummer's wardrobe was intact but that was about all she could count on for certain.

Since those two incidents, Edna had a definite feeling that time was running out. Looking around as she put on her red cardigan, however, she concluded that time looked exactly the same, no matter how depleted the supply. It gave no warning. Nevertheless, she thought, if she searched the place long enough she might locate her particular fund of time, her account, most likely in some place dark and cramped, behind a picture frame maybe. She thought of peeking behind that horrid brown painting of Isobel's, thought she might see some indicator back there, but changed her mind. Back to the task at hand.

Today would be the first of the trials. With the markers in her pocket, nothing could go terribly wrong. Just up the river bank a bit, then back. No more than twenty minutes in all. Just to feel this old body, Edna thought as she closed the door, striking out on its own.

~

Ted saw Edna going by from his carport. Through the open rear end of the structure he thought annually of converting to a garage, he watched her stoop down, walk a little farther, then stoop again. Collecting stones maybe. Normally, she was with Isobel, but not today. Ted began unravelling the hose and dragging it into the driveway.

He had been thinking since early afternoon about his father, about an event he remembered from at least ten years earlier, from the time not long after his dad had sold the farm and moved into town. There, not knowing what to do with himself, he had taken to frequent and somewhat desperate waterings of the lawn and driveway, scattering the Saskatchewan dust around as if this were an essential service, as if people were counting on him. One day Ted had driven up while his father was busy with his hose work and found himself suddenly and thoroughly angered by his dad's behaviour. He had sat in the truck, pissed off at his old man for no reason other than the look on his face. It was a vacant look, the look of looking for a magic cure, an antidote to all that was urban and stupefying.

Really, this business of watering down driveways was no more than an excuse for something else, to be outside looking for or at women, an excuse to be in the front yard holding a hose, a big pee-pee, yes, and shooting it wantonly. "Hey Dad, rein it in there," Ted had finally said that day long ago, striding by on his way into the new bungalow to discuss tree-planting with his mother.

Since his father's retirement, Ted had strongly resisted the notion of suburban yard activity, had even once said to Maureen, "Maureen, if you ever see me watering the driveway, I want you to run down to the Kellys' and get their buffalo gun and come back and shoot me." But today, during the final hot portion of his appointed rounds, Ted had gotten an urge to come home and do just that. Driveway-watering was a rite of passage he supposed, a tribal ritual it was time he endured. By the act of hosing down the driveway he could enter a new and yet venerable stage of life. He was eager to get at it. And the symbolism was not wasted on him. Twelve years married. That pretty well said it all. And to add to it, he had seen the car in Annie's driveway too, the other morning: the dark-haired one had spent the night. It was enough to stop you in your tracks, cause you to pick up a hose and commence to spray.

Flicking the nozzle of the hose up and down, Ted attempted to create waves, an airborne set of sine curves, then tried for a perfect lasso. "Need to get some hobbies, Pop," he had said to his dad later that day, "that hose stuff doesn't suit you." And what had his father gone and done? Got himself a job as the town meter reader. Not a lot different from being a letter carrier, Ted thought. And for a while he stood and watched, mesmerized by the heat and sun, as the water rolled down the driveway and into the gutter.

~

Along the riverside, Edna was already returning. She had not gone far. It was only the first trial, after all; next time she would go farther.

~

I had made a few notes at my kitchen table on the King James version of the creation story. In my reading on the big bang theory, I had learned that many theologians now accepted the creation story as a metaphor and, becoming curious about the specifics of this old tale, I looked it up in Genesis. According to the author, the order of events was as follows: day one, darkness and light; day two, firmament — whatever that might be; day three, plants; day four, sun and moon; day five, fish and fowl; day six, cattle and people; day seven, relaxation. There was no mention of day five-trillion-and-nine, conception of Wayne Abelard.

My first concern with this metaphor was for the plants. How had they managed to survive for the twenty-four hours they had pre-dated the sun? It seemed that they would all have been frozen stiff by day number four. Shouldn't a metaphor of such enduring significance at least be free of botanical impossibilities? What must the author of Genesis have been thinking, I wondered.

Then I moved to the garbage can, where I began prying bits of riverside mud from the soles of my shoes with fork tines. Behind me a row of socks and underwear hung from the flea market clothesline; I had done some hand laundry earlier, in the kitchen sink. My motive for all of this kitchen-based activity was to stay as close to the telephone as possible, in anticipation of a call from Alexa. But ultimately it was only Martha who called, offering another night of social disobedience but willing to compromise on details. "I'll make it a Friday night so you can sleep in," she said. "I'll even feed you dinner before we go. It won't be as risky this time. There's a place along one of the bike paths along Ninth Avenue, beneath the tracks. There won't be anyone around at three in the morning. I'm feeling like I have to get out and do something. I've been writing letters all week, which is all right, I do believe it has an impact, but not the same effect for me personally as a little graffiti." Without taking a breath, she asked, "You see what they're doing with the softwood tariffs now?"

"Martha, you forget who I am," I said. "Remember, I'm not Ted. I'm his neighbour. We have separate brains. I don't follow the trade agreements that closely, although I have to admit that since I've been hanging around with you, I do tend to notice some of those free trade pieces in the paper, but I think that's mostly because I like you, not that I care that much about these issues. Isn't everything owned by multinationals anyway? It's kind of come to pass like the Bahai were predicting back in the seventies, one big nation by the year 2000, only it's one big company."

"One big nation?" Martha repeated, incredulous. "Do you recall the former country of Yugoslavia? What about the soon-to-be-chopped up country of Canada?"

"Well, I meant economically. You know what I meant. Anyway, yes, I'll go with you on Friday, if I get dinner. Otherwise I won't. Don't harbour any illusions about my motives."

"Good, good. I'm not a vegetarian but I eat a lot of grains. Is that okay with you?"

"Grains are fine," I said. "Anything except millet. It can get kind of gluey."

"It's settled then. Be here by eight."

After hanging up I returned to picking mud off my shoes. I began to contemplate calling Alexa and leaving a message on her machine; she was probably at her toy store job or the university. My incentive, really, was to listen to Alexa's voice on the machine and hang up, but I resisted following through on this plan out of fear of being mistaken for Janet Sainsbury and thus inciting Alexa to greater acts of retribution. Difficult to predict what might come of a tape recording of a telephone receiver hanging up. The assumption the caller was Janet, increased need to speak with her, sudden car-trips late at night, with ensuing reconciliation and passionate, recalcitrant lovemaking. Or, fuelled need for more revenge, time spent with me viewed as balancing of the books. Who could tell?

By the time the late news was over, I had decided to call. There was the recording, then the beep. "Hi, Alexa," I said, "it's Annie here. How are you? Seems I've been thinking of you lots. How's school? Give me a call. Bye." I stood for a moment then, feeling garishly vulnerable, rather bright in my need of another, throbbing like an extraterrestrial whose blood system is illuminated and external, stitched onto the skin instead of hidden beneath it.

Maybe I should forget Alexa, I said out loud. Maybe I should forget Sylvie, too. This sentence was also spoken, given a chance to roam around my house, an eyeless old girl in slippers and not much else, not much resolve. Nevertheless, I hauled the urn from the closet, put on the shoes I had just cleaned and tromped to the river's edge. It's time I did this, I thought. Sylvie, it's time I at least let you get started on the evolutionary chain, get a toe-hold as some algae. But I did not take the lid off, just stood there and attempted to cry, but found I could not manage that either.

Ted's back screen door whoofed the way it does when

closing, and in less than a minute, there was Ted. He saw the urn, but did not query. Ted will not insist on knowing about the lesser incongruities; he'll simply pick up the slack by talking about himself, a quality I appreciate, truth be told.

"Well, I've decided that I definitely made a mistake when I didn't buy the farm from my old man. It's one of those big mistakes, the kind I'll be drinking myself into a stupor over when I'm sixty-five. The big kind, the kind you think about on your deathbed. Too late now. Plus I heard this week that Canada Post has bought some new seals from Barnum and Bailey. I guess the intensive week-long training program will have begun, now that they've all aced the civil service exam."

"You underestimate the importance of your job," I said. "Lots of people count on the letter carrier for human contact, especially old people. I don't think they'd get the same quality of conversation from a seal." And so my best friend and I stood and talked for a while, the way people do, filling up the surrounding air with little beats of sound, breathing out what might as well be notes on a harmonica, so little do they have to do with anything, so content do they make us feel.

◦◦◦

Martha prepared a dish called spicy Mexican lentils, raw hunks of cabbage with her own oily vegetable dip and more of the bread I had first sampled at the meeting. The meal left a volcanic heaviness in my stomach. Martha delivered a brief polemic on the virtues of buying goods made locally, or at the very least in Canada. During a lull, I excused myself, went to the bathroom and discovered my period had started. In the cabinet beneath the sink, I found a tampon, along with a bag of Famous Amos chocolate chip cookies, manufactured in California. Perversely, I admired Martha all the more for this deception. Why not cheat on ourselves? Why not imagine our brief little lives to be virtuous?

"I have something for you, by the way," Martha announced when I returned. "I've been reading Simone de Beauvoir. It's helped me to understand what's wrong with you."

"Fabulous," I said.

"I'm being serious, really. This is it. You're too stuck in your own subjective world. You need to involve yourself in projects that will help you to transcend this state of affairs, move beyond your own brainwaves. So I bought you something to help you out of this fix," Martha said, reaching behind her chair. "This." She held up a white plastic bag. "It's from Fabricland."

Inside were a pattern for sweat pants, a length of grey fleece, some elastic and a spool of thread. "It's everything you need to start sewing, except a machine, of course. I'll help you if you want."

"This is what Simone de Beauvoir advises? I thought she was an existentialist."

"She was, she was. Do you think sewing and existentialism are in some way mutually exclusive?"

"No, I guess not."

"It might seem silly," Martha said, "of course it seems silly because it's something we ladies do. But after Mac died, sewing is what I did. It's not so much for the final product as the process. Cutting up a big swatch of cloth and hooking the pieces together so they have a shape and a purpose. It kept me going. And I hadn't even read Simone de Beauvoir at the time. It was purely instinctive. Do you know how to sew? Do you have a machine?"

"Well, yes, the basics, home ec. But it's never gone well for me," I said. "Something about that tension, everything gets gnarled up on the back. And fabric stores intimidate me. I don't understand the procedure. Are you supposed to pick up the bolts of cloth or not?"

"Oh come on," Martha said, "there's nothing to it. You grab what you want and take it to the counter. Anyway, you don't have to go to the store. I've done that for you. And it's a very easy pattern. See, it says so, 'Very Easy.' "

"I appreciate the thought, Martha. I really do."

"As long as you don't just appreciate, my friend. As long as you do."

"Oh, I will, I will," I said, imagining the white plastic bag of cloth sitting for months, maybe even years, maybe the rest of my life, on the floor next to my chest of drawers.

A few hours later and we were driving east on Ninth Avenue, past the King Eddy and over the bridge. We parked the car at Fort Calgary; Martha had all the needed supplies in her backpack. "Let's walk along the bike path," she said, "just to the tracks. There's nobody around. Don't worry."

"I'm not worried this time, Martha, my cramps are too bad. Look at the moon up there. Do you think the women on Jupiter have three periods a month or what? You'd never think to look at the moon that it could have this effect on us, that it could pull blood from people just by sitting in the sky. I got my period at your house tonight; that's why I'm going on about this. I stole a tampon from you, by the way. Hope that's okay."

"Have you been eating every three hours?"

"No. Why? Should I? If I get really fat will my period stop?"

"No, no, no," Martha said. "It's the blood sugar level and PMS. It's supposed to be kept on an even keel to prevent PMS."

"I'm not that bothered by PMS. Or I have it all the time and don't notice."

We arrived at the Elbow River, so still, as if it had come to a halt and were contemplating changing direction. The underpass was not far off. Lights had been installed and were permanently on; too many homeless in this part of the city, a dark dry place would be dangerously inviting. Best to illuminate. As we drew closer, in fact, the brilliance of the lights was repellent. I wondered if we might not be thrown backwards by the strength of the wattage or destroyed the way insects can be by light. But no, we entered the little tunnel unchallenged.

"This looks like a good spot," said Martha. "Let's cover this up, whatever this is. Let's see, 'Metallica fucking, fucking rules,' " she read. "I think a nice map of Canada would be more suited to this space."

Martha fished out the stencil and held it against the concrete, then handed me the paint. I sprayed with abandon. Red streaks immediately began to drip from the forty-ninth parallel. Overhead, on the tracks, voices could be heard. "Wake up, everybody," one of them said. "Do you hear me?" he shouted. "Wake up ya bunch of fuckers."

"Can you shut him up?" a female voice asked.

"Shut up, Mike," said a third voice, male, tired.

"Wake up" was heard again, only quietly this time, conversationally, followed by the splattering of a stream of piss into the Elbow River.

"Let's go, Martha," I said. "I want to get out of here now."

"Oh come on. Why are you so afraid? They don't have any idea we're here. We know more than they do."

"It's just a survival instinct I have, Martha."

"Survival isn't all it's cracked up to be," Martha said. "It's not worth cutting everything short for. But let's go. I can see you've had enough."

We packed up everything and were ready to leave when Martha stooped down to examine the red image of Canada we were leaving behind. One streak of paint had congealed to a halt that would have been somewhere in Mexico had the map included all of North America. "You know," Martha said, "where that line of paint ends, I'll bet you that's almost exactly the place where Mac got blown away. Right there, just outside of a little place called Rodeo."

She pressed her index finger into the drop of paint, pulled it away, looked at the red then dabbed it on her wrist. "Let's go," she said.

~

It was me who suggested another trip to the Scarfe farm; Sylvie had lost interest in the species known as country folk. The quarry was her new love, a destination three miles out of town by bicycle, a place to look at rocks, work on a raft we planned to have finished by summer, and feel as if the place were ours, or primarily, hers, Sylvie's water hole; Graham knew nothing about it. It took the offer of a tour of the Pharmaceutical with my dad to lure Sylvie away from her plans for a day, but she bit and agreed upon one more visit to the house of Blodwen. I had no idea how I would ever fulfill my end of the bargain.

Everything was in leaf by then, filling out; we were heading toward those dawdling days of summer holidays, soon, soon, soon they would be right there, right outside the town limits of Mesmer. By the time we arrived at the stepping-stone bridge that day, we could hear Edward out on his tractor, singing, meaning Blodwen would be found alone. I remember enthusing about the neatness of the Scarfe farm to Sylvie, comparing it with my Uncle Albert's farm, for example, with its two big hounds and their bad smell, and the back entrance to the house strewn with bones and a wadded old blanket ideal for hounds to lie on and humans to trip over. The Scarfe place was a model, I assured Sylvie; most did not have flower boxes on the side porch; most did not have such persuading silence on the other side of the screen door.

Knock, knock, knock. "Mrs. Scarfe," I said. "Mrs. Scarfe!"

"Yes?" came the voice, then the body, Blodwen, tall and floral in nylons and sandals. I thought of pictures I had seen of Hawaii. Behind her stood an enormous potted plant, with leaves that resembled elephant ears. House-plants other than geraniums were uncommon in Mesmer.

"I'm Annie Clemens," I said, "and this is Sylvie Rochon. She's never been on a farm before. Her idea of the country is all from fairy tales. She used to live in Burlington. We were wondering if we could visit for a while."

"Oh, well, come in, of course, certainly, of course. I recognize Sylvie. Who doesn't recognize the minister's children? I suppose that's a bit of a curse for you. Come in, come in," she said, repositioning a bobby pin.

The kitchen was dark after the bright sunlight. We took off our shoes and walked on the cool linoleum, alternating green and white squares. I tried not to touch the white ones, telling myself that if I did Blodwen's plugged-up babies would never escape; as a child I liked to imagine myself the arbiter of others' fortunes in variations of step on a crack, break your mother's back. Blodwen, in particular, I seemed to want to tamper with.

"My father was a lawyer," Blodwen said, "*the* lawyer in Mesmer, and that had a funny effect on me. I always felt that way down deep inside I was looking for a law to break. I never found the right law, I guess. Or maybe I'm still looking," she said, laughing.

"Annie's father works at the pill factory," Sylvie said. "I'll be getting a tour there soon, with him. I can't wait. I've never been in any kind of a factory."

"Well, the city girl comes to the country to learn about agriculture *and* industry. Did you want to tour the house as well as the barn?"

"Sure," I said, eager to have some input into a conversation that appeared to be wrapping like a cat's cradle around Blodwen and Sylvie, leaving me standing outside the string, on a green square of linoleum. And besides, I did want to tour the house. Two-storey houses were very alluring to me, having always lived in a bungalow. Once in the upstairs of anyone's house, I anticipated sensational sights the ground floor could never offer — men in boxer shorts, women in half slips and brassieres.

We were shown the dining room and the living room with its baby grand piano, the pantry, three bedrooms upstairs and a fourth made up as a study for Blodwen. She had an electric typewriter and a cork board covered with letters and clippings. "I was up here when you knocked," Blodwen explained. "I spend a lot of time up here, too much time, actually, according to Edward. I like to write letters. I'm almost embarrassed to admit it but I have pen-pals, six of them. It sounds so childish, doesn't it? Two of them live in England, one in Australia and three in the U.S. They're my friends. I'm not very good at conversation but I can write letters. I guess that's odd. But enough, enough, Blodwen. These girls don't want to hear about your habits. Come here and I'll show you something," she said. And that is when she led us to a door at the end of the hallway that opened up onto a miraculous sight — a second flight of stairs.

"Come on, come on," Blodwen said, and we began our

descent. I was overcome by the improbability of it all, a secret set of stairs completely out of keeping with the rest of the house. Each step held some bit of clutter stacked on it and pushed to the side, this one a pile of *Ladies' Home Journals*, the next a collection of Edward's old shirts, shoes, a box of photos, and upon the very bottom step, a doll in a cap and diaper. We trotted by it all in single file, to arrive at a landing and a door which opened onto the kitchen, just behind and to the right of the wood stove.

Downstairs, we sat in the kitchen while Blodwen made tea and insisted on braiding Sylvie's hair before we visited the barn. "You don't want to get it all full of straw," she said. I distinctly recall becoming conscious of my own hair at that moment, as a heavy, brown and unbraidable pelt, the sort of hair that would be enhanced by the presence of straw; I was developing the lumpish sensation of the dark-haired girl, ignored. This had nothing to do with Blodwen or Sylvie, though, I realized; it was in the league of the inexplicable, like King and Mrs. Van Epp.

Blodwen asked Sylvie what life was like as the daughter of the United Church minister. Sylvie's response was typically unforthcoming. "It's okay," she said. "Sometimes you get the feeling people are staring at you. Graham hates it." Sylvie looked up at Blodwen and shrugged her shoulders inconclusively. "I don't *hate* it."

"Every once in a while," Blodwen said, "I get the feeling that I'd like to stand in front of a group of people and talk to them, but then I realize I don't want to talk to them so much as have them sit there and admire me. What a predicament. Too shy to be as vain as I'd like. Have you ever heard of such a thing? Edward would like me to get out more. Socialize, he says, socialize, as if it were just a matter of a command performance. And now he's made his plan to bring the mountains to Mohammed, as he says. I'd like to talk him out of it, but there's no talking Edward out of his plans. He wants to have a birthday party, on Dominion Day, Canada's one hundredth, you know, with fireworks and a big bonfire. I'm not so sure it's a good idea but I guess I'll have to go along with it. It's the sort of thing Edward would like to do more of. You two will have to promise that you'll come."

"Definitely," I answered, for both of us.

"All right," Blodwen said, "I'll show you the barn now. It's more or less empty except for the poultry. The cattle are all out. Although, there might be one in there, waiting for the breeder. Honestly, someday I think I'll write a play and call it "Waiting for the Breeder." That's what I just told my friend Yvonne from Massachusetts in a letter. I suppose I shouldn't talk to you girls that way. You'll have to pardon me."

All I remember of the barn was following Blodwen and Sylvie up one passageway and down the other, watching Blodwen in that fragrant place, against the whitewashed walls. Blodwen of the thick black hair, Blodwen of the lipstick, nylons and high heels every moment of the day. I believe I fell in love with Blodwen Scarfe that day, in the manner of someone close to thirteen years of age; that is, as an awareness of wanting to be the pail she picked up and placed upon a shelf, an awareness of the unacceptable greyness of my formerly white running shoes. I don't think Blodwen noticed the change in me; out in the yard, her final act before we left was to take a bobby pin from her hair and wordlessly secure a wisp from Sylvie's braid.

～

"Maybe you should come to my place. Maybe you should see it." Even on the phone Alexa tended to speak in a sideways kind of language, always on the diagonal, never direct. I still felt as if I hardly knew her, as if I owned only the edges of an unfinished map. To know another life: this is a slow and puzzling adventure, especially when that life is Alexa Stewart's. She was my new world; I had her to wonder about, to hold on to, to clutch like a meaty engorged thing, like I might have clutched my penis if I had had one, like Christopher Columbus probably clutched his from time to time in moments of mingled doubt and joy. Aah, if nothing else I have this.

Although I was far from being a stickleback, the possibility I might become one had wrought significant changes in me already. Alexa's presence in my life had resulted in a decreased need to scurry, to take myself to my sound booth, to want to escape or pretend. She had caused me to become smaller and more manageable, attractive even and at home on the earth again, as if my feet and the concrete now belonged together. I had decided, with some effort, that I was in love with her, and would have done whatever she asked, even though she asked in funny, oblique imperatives. So I answered, "Yes, I'll come over. I'd love to see where you live. When?"

"Right now, right now. Come to the Daiquiri, you know, Thirteenth Avenue and Fifth Street." Yes, I did know the location, because, needless to say, I had driven by the place at least a half a dozen times in order to pass through that cloud of electrons emitted by one's lover's dwelling.

Half an hour later, I was there. Appropriately, the entrance to the Daiquiri was littered with broken glass. I entered a rather grim hallway; faint ripping sounds rose from my shoes as I lifted them from the sugar-coated flooring. Before I had a chance to knock, Alexa flung open the door. "I know," she said, meaning "I know everything you're thinking about this place so don't begin to comment on the obvious." "There's no security system," she went on. "Guys are in and out of here all night. I hear them talking about burning the place down. It's funny how arson as a goal is so popular and also pretty much available to everyone, regardless of socioeconomic status, race or creed. A job might be beyond your reach, a steak dinner, university entrance, but not plans for a big arson job. This is a true democracy we live in here." Leading me to the kitchen window, Alexa said "They like to stand out here by the dumpster. I'm glad I'm on the second floor. Once in a while I light one of these," she said, holding up a pack of red firecrackers, "and throw it into the dumpster when they're not looking. They can never tell where it came from. Sometimes they get really scared."

"Aren't you worried they'll come back and break in and kill you?" I asked.

"Nah. They're too stoned to know what's going on.

Usually I just hear a chorus of 'What the fuck?' and I sit here in the dark and laugh. Anyway, there's a deadbolt on my door. The manager keeps saying he'll put in security doors but he never gets around to it. Anyway, this is my place. Kind of minimalist, isn't it?"

The kitchen was completely unadorned except for fridge and stove. In the living room were a tape player, several tapes strewn about the floor and a wicker chair. "Come and see my fish," Alexa said, taking me down a narrow dark passageway to her bedroom. There, three tanks sat illuminated and bubbling in the twilight. Over the window hung a piece of fabric, black background covered with red roses the size of softballs. "I spend most of my time here when I'm at home. When I'm not at the toy store or school or with you, I watch my fish. I love my fish," she said, nodding her head, "yes, I love them. They are the opposite of my family of origin. They never make any noise. They can't make any noise."

"These are the silver dollars," Alexa said, pointing out three flat and silvery fish. "They're very nervous, skittish one might say. And these are the neons. They get along with the silver dollars as long as they're jumbo-sized; smaller ones have vanished. And in this next tank we have the snails and the red caps — goldfish for luck. And finally, more tropicals in this tank, swordtails and these weird little guys are called puffers. They swim funny, sidewaysish.

"Do you know what the snails did last night?" Alexa asked, walking to the rose-covered fabric, looking out, keeping her back to me. "They had sex. Yes," she said, turning around, "it was a lot like the Clairol commercials of yore, slow motion toward each other. They were all kind of extended, as undressed as a snail can get, and then they did it. I really had a strong urge to reach in and flick their shells off so that they could really go at it. I thought maybe their little pink bodies might like to roll around the tank together, unshelled. It seemed like the shells were preventing them from having, you know, full-blown enjoyment. Full-blown enjoyment hardly ever seems to be part of the plan, does it?" she asked, actually looking me in the eye.

"Oh, I don't know," I said, "I've had some pretty full-blown enjoyment with you," wondering what she was meaning, feeling slight umbrage at this observation.

Alexa's eyes filled with tears then and she said, "I went to the food bank today. Yes, " she said, pacing around the bedroom, swinging her hair, "I had no money, hence no food, so I went there, filled out a few forms and came home with some groceries. Simple enough. It's just that I've never been in this situation before. I have a total of fifty-five cents; this is the extent of my wealth, including investment portfolio and et cetera, et cetera. It's not such a big deal, I've been telling myself. I'm poor now."

The tears were rolling down her cheeks but Alexa made no effort to wipe them away. I couldn't help thinking she likely would have been very pleased if I had produced a video camera and captured the moment on tape, *à la* Janet Sainsbury.

"I guess I'm part of this new trend I've heard about," she went on, sniffling. "It's called convivial poverty. It's a 'we're all in this together' kind of thing and I guess I'm at the vanguard. Or maybe I just think that. So I'm trying to be happy about this set of circumstances. I get six dollars an hour from the toy store and no student loan because I've been out of school for three years and they figure I've saved like the sensible person I am not. And I won't ask my mother for money. And I had to pay a damage deposit when I moved in here; that's a joke, I know. And I had to buy books. And my fish eat gourmet bloodworms and frozen Oregon brine shrimp because I'm an asshole and buy them this luxury line of food instead of the more economical flakes most fish are content with."

The pampered fish drifted in their tanks, orange and silver groupings of indifference.

"In the less convivial moments of my poverty," she continued, "I have realized that Janet Sainsbury was basically supporting me and I was barely conscious of that fact. When did rents go up so high? Oh, never mind. I'm being boring.

"I have some soup and some bread and coffee — I'm like a Russian now. I have the basics. I may go down to the butcher shop later in my cloth coat with my string bag and beg for a soup bone. Anyway, I'd like to give you something to eat. I've eaten and drunk at your house twice now."

I was very touched by Alexa's generosity and instantly regretted my cynicism about her tears. I wanted to hold her or at least give her money, but she declined both. "I get paid on Friday," she said, "and I can appeal the loan. I'll be okay. I'll be okay. Really. And I insist that you eat some of my soup. It's Campbell's Golden Mushroom, ninety percent salt."

I stayed and ate and we listened to music. She told me she had not left any messages for Janet Sainsbury recently and that Janet had not called. And after dinner, Alexa asked if I would spend the night. "Sleep with me," she said. "We can, you know, we can connect the snails." She was a lewd girl, that Alexa Stewart.

Late at night, when Alexa was asleep, I got up to go to the bathroom, then wandered into her kitchen to look outside. A Wednesday night, no one in sight. Someone had stuffed a mattress into the dumpster and on top of that what looked like a battered hockey net. On the window sill lay the firecrackers. I opened up a cupboard door to assess the food situation. A trapezoid of light cast from the street lamp fell into the shelves, illuminating a brown, wood-look vinyl interior. There sat the remaining non-perishables, those rectangles and cans reminding me of some distant past event. Oh yes, I thought, white gifts. I closed the cupboard door and went back to bed.

~

Only once did I sleep over at the Rochons'. The entire experience, after the fact, was interpreted in my mind as a type of field trip, immersion in an inaccessible other world, like the Indian village of Ste. Marie among the Hurons I had visited in grade five.

The invitation was extended at Graham's behest; Sylvie was inclined to withhold hospitality until she had secured her trip to the Pharmaceutical. "But when, Annie, when are we going to go?" Sylvie asked that day as the three of us sat, again, in the front row of the balcony. My response was to reiterate my father's standard reply: "It's a busy place. I can't make any guarantees."

"But can't he just make an appointment? Once he's made an appointment, then you can sleep over."

Graham finally brought an end to the negotiations by administering a skin-reddening snake bite to Sylvie's left forearm while hissing "Ask her!" between clenched teeth. Sylvie mumbled an invitation, which I eagerly accepted.

The evening of the sleep-over, Saturday night, was uneventful. Reverend Rochon went out in his jeans and white, short-sleeved shirt. He was busy, busy, busy, and had most certainly made a reputation for himself. The town was divided as to what they thought. One camp, composed mostly of unhappy women and, it seemed, men who favoured dark suits, judged the Reverend to have "a bit too much of the hippie in him." The other camp, being made up of happier women of all ages and sizes and the more exuberant men, those inclined to pastel fashion choices, had taken possession of Reverend Rochon. The latter group were often overheard referring to the minister as "our Reverend Rochon."

Nobody seemed to want to lay claim to Daphne, however. Even in her own home, she seemed removed. The night of my visit she rested on the couch with yet another headache. Because of her condition, silence was enforced. The television remained off. In complete contrast to my own home, no one yelled. So far away from my parents' house did I feel, in fact, that I was surprised to see Mesmer from Sylvie's bedroom window; even Mrs. Murdock out in her garden with a hoe struck me as unlikely. And in the evening light, from Sylvie's bedroom window, she did resemble a black-and-white photo from the terribly dated geography texts we used at school, the one captioned "Irkutsk woman works the soil."

Sylvie and I spent most of our time whispering in her bedroom, always aware of Daphne down below. Her occasional calls for ice or a damp cloth brought Sylvie down to the living room, into the kitchen, hammering ice, running water and always with the steady detachment of a paid servant. How alien it all seemed. My mother would no sooner have asked for ice packs or cloths for her forehead than she would have gone on a crying jag at the Pharmaceutical Christmas party. Mothers radically different from my own unnerved me; I found their food difficult to eat. Changing into my pyjamas that night, I decided I would probably not like breakfast.

As I passed by Graham's room with my toothbrush, he called me in. "Pssst," he said, "pssst, look at this." Graham began many interactions with an exhibit of some sort. In his hand he held a business card: Dr. Harold Zwirner, Psychiatrist — Children and Adults, it read. "They found me a new shrink," Graham said. "I thought that at least one good thing about Mesmer would be that it's too small for shrinks, lucky to have just a regular doctor. And I was right. But it seems they do have a couple in London. That's where I was this afternoon, on a little trip for Graham and his mommy. That's why she has a headache. Taking *me* to the shrink gives *her* a headache."

I studied Graham's head in much the same way I regarded Blodwen's abdomen with its logjam of babies: something improbable was housed in there.

"What does he say to you?" I asked.

"He says, 'Did you wet the bed? Play with your wienie? See your parents screwing?' As if *they* did that. That kind of thing. Mostly questions. Sometimes I wish he would just say something, get to the point.

"Anyway," Graham continued, "I'm doing a miniature drawing on the back of his card. Actually, I've done it. It's a present for you. Here," he said, "take it."

Needless to say, I was uncertain what to expect — a microscopic interpretation of God's big ass, a field of dots, who could know. What I saw was neither of these, but a bird's-eye view of two heads, one with hair parted on the side (his), the other with hair parted in the middle (mine), bent over a checkerboard. "I set it up to look like you're winning. See, you have four kings and I only have one. An unlikely situation, I admit," Graham said, "but nevertheless . . . Maybe you could play checkers with me sometime."

"It's nice," I said, "I like it." And I did. I held on to that drawing for a long time, used it as a bookmark until it was taken to the Mesmer Public Library in a book and vanished forever.

Sylvie was asleep by the time I returned to her room. I lay there in the designated twin bed, worrying that Daphne might call upon me to deliver her ice and her wet cloths. She did not, however; she must have gone to bed, Philip must have arrived home, some transformation must have occurred because the morning was another story altogether.

Miss Lynch came by before church for what the Rochons referred to as Sunday brunch. Philippa Lynch had had a composition — a solo for piano or organ — accepted for publication by a music publisher in Toronto; she was to perform her piece in church that morning. The brunch was in celebration of both events.

Miss Lynch and I were the only guests at this affair and were seated next to one another. I was extremely reluctant to eat Daphne Rochon's eggs and sausages, and my appetite was reduced even further by the proximity of those scars. Our bare arms brushed together at one point, sending an electrical storm from my head to my feet. Across the table, Sylvie's eyes bulged in genuine horror.

"Sylvie," Mr. Rochon said, "whatever you're up to you can cool it right now." Next to him Daphne sat, seeming to be watching Graham for signs of insanity. The muscles in her neck tensed and relaxed, tensed and relaxed, priming the migraine pump. I thought it best to eat everything on my plate, lest some terrible revenge befall me: psychiatric visits, wet cloths all over my face, white, white scars, like strands of bread dough woven into my skin.

Miss Lynch had no appetite. I think only I noticed that the one bite of sausage she took was spat into her paper napkin. Daphne urged her to eat in a way I found insensitive; the Rochons did not understand Miss Lynch's nerves. I felt an obligation to intervene on Miss Lynch's behalf. She was a sociological fact, like the Amish; she simply required some explanation.

"Miss Lynch," I began, but found myself at a loss as to how to proceed.

"Lost your train of thought, Annie?" Reverend Rochon said, trying for levity. "Got off at the wrong station?"

Brunch dragged on with Sylvie and Graham politely eating, appearing to be the dutiful children they were not. Never before or since have I felt the presence of two such muzzled minds, clattering and warm, just like the interior of the Pharmaceutical. No wonder Sylvie was so entranced by the place.

By the time we left for the church, Miss Lynch's nerves were undoubtedly completely shot. As we walked the short trip together, I watched for some indicator of her anxiety, thinking, I believe, that those nerves might perform some act, conform into patterns, erupt into new scar tissue upon the skin. Miss Lynch walked along in her beige and freckled body, however, with no sign of nervousness whatsoever, no tremor, no agitated chatter.

She performed early on in the service, the congregation listening breathlessly, anticipating a rare and perhaps ghastly display of human frailty. This did not occur. Miss Lynch played with apparent confidence, completed her piece, then stood and faced her audience. A moment of uncertain silence followed — to applaud or not? — settled quickly by the Reverend Rochon's enthusiastic clapping and shouts of "Bravo." The rest followed suit. That was the moment when Miss Lynch's face turned from beige to white, her knees buckled and she sank to the floor, reddish head knocking against the piano bench en route.

"She's dead," Sylvie said with the certainty of a coroner,

an opinion seeming within the realm of possibility to me. Reverend Rochon took control, calling upon a crew of church elders to carry Miss Lynch to the parlour, where the ladies of the UCW were dispatched to attend to her recovery. Reverend Rochon returned to his duties, and then the truly big surprise of the day occurred: Blodwen Scarfe raised her hand and volunteered to play the piano. "I'm sorry to say I've never studied the organ, but I could provide accompaniment on the piano."

Her offer was gratefully accepted.

And so, Blodwen moved to the piano bench, from which she could view the Reverend Rochon and upon which I could watch her, those high-heeled shoes on the pedals having a curious effect on me. Next to me sat Daphne Rochon, watching God knows who or what, those delicate ropes in her neck tightening and relaxing still. I'm sure a mathematician could have created some geometric design from the intersecting lines created by our watchful interests, some misshapen rhombus of love and suspicion in motion.

Oh the topsy-turvy world of church, I must have thought in the inarticulate chambers of my twelve-year-old mind. Where Blodwen Scarfe would find the courage of her vanity, the strength to parade her flat but crowded abdomen before the entire church body; where Miss Philippa Lynch would bounce, nerveless and at peace, onto the unyielding hardwood floor.

~

Edna and Isobel ate the lunch of spinach salad and cold chicken Edna had prepared. They sat outside on their deck, listening to the river, commenting on the breeze and the success of their tomato crop. Both women liked this time of day; they had worked enough years to appreciate its stolen quality, knowing most people were stuck in jobs or classrooms.

Isobel wanted to know if Edna had seen a specific brochure, one she had brought home from the pool. "It's a questionnaire and it gives you a score on your aerobic well-being. I thought I put it on the coffee table but it's not there. You haven't seen it?"

Edna pursed her lips, furrowed her brow, tried for an expression of concentration.

"Well, keep an eye out for it, will you?" Isobel said, pouring herself some iced tea and walking off toward the Bow. Edna stayed on the deck, then slipped inside a moment later to check the pocket of her big red sweater. There it was, the fitness questionnaire cut into strips, larger than the last because she had decided to include more information, her address and a description of the house — blue, white deck, potted tomatoes — the goal was to get back, after all.

No, no, Edna thought, give your head a shake. If she never found her way back, well, really, would that matter? The goal was to get there. The goal, Edna had decided on her most recent trial, the goal was to get to a place where she could stand on public land and blend in with all the others. Once she was on public land, her intention was to locate a bench, any old bench at all, and sit. It seemed to Edna that if she could only reach a bench on a bit of public land, she would have achieved a little victory over time. She would be able to feel herself, for a little while, firmly embedded in time once more, feel it actually ticking away inside her again, like her own heartbeat. Not like this, she thought, living with Isobel, hanging on for dear life, hanging on to one of time's fingers like a small child, like someone who will at any moment lose her hold.

Edna could hear Isobel out on the deck, moving the chairs around. Stuffing the strips of paper back into her sweater pocket, Edna thought, what I *really* want to do is just sit somewhere, out of the reach of Isobel, and hold on to myself. Preserve myself. Edna Plummer was an endangered species, she was vanishing. No one looked at her anymore, really, except in that slightly puzzled way; no one ever took her picture, that was for certain. Come to think of it, she was pretty sure no one had taken her picture, a picture of just Edna Plummer, since her husband had passed away. There was her son, of course, and the grandchildren, but that always involved a big crowd. Not that she was complaining. But, she thought, maybe I'll take a camera along with me and ask a friendly-looking stranger to take my picture. What the heck! Why not?

The back door opened; Isobel was coming inside. Edna quickly closed the hall closet door on her sweater and her pocketful of sliced brochures. She could not recall when she had felt this happy, this brimful of plans.

"I can't see that questionnaire anywhere," Edna called to Isobel from the hallway. "Maybe it's in with the magazines."

~

It was October when Martha and I saw one another again. I called to tell her I would not paint with her anymore, it was too stressful and I felt guilty about the two episodes, despite my as-yet-unfulfilled plans to impress Alexa with my unconventionality. Martha's response was, "Well, come over and talk to me anyway. I won't ask you to do anything in exchange. Just talk to me. I think I'm lonely, but I can't be sure about this. I get a kind of vague feeling sometimes, which I'm beginning to think is loneliness. I can't concentrate or make a decision. Although, maybe it's the heat."

She went on to tell me she was thinking of buying a new car; she wanted something with an air bag. "It's one of those things that just comes along," she said. "I've had the beetle for ten years now and all of a sudden I hate the sucker and I want something brand-new." Every so often Martha used the word "sucker," always in reference to an inanimate object. It was the closest I ever heard her come to vulgarity. "I can't afford a new car, of course, I'm a char lady after all. It would take all of my RRSPs but c'est la vie. I'm starting to like the idea of an air bag when I'm out driving around late at night with the drunks. I have a hard time with these big decisions, though, they make me feel vague and worried and before you know it, I'm missing Mac and feeling useless. Maybe you could come over for a while."

Memorial Drive was solid cars, metal and exhaust. *A stalled car in the inside eastbound lane,* I heard on the radio. Crawling along in my Tercel, I became aware of the weather not only as heat but as a presence, almost like Sylvie remained a presence in my house, a kind of stopped situation, reluctantly breathed into the lungs. "There's no wind," I said out loud, as if Sylvie might happen to be in the passenger's seat, "look at those flags. Nothing's moving. Maybe we're going to have a tornado."

Entering Martha's house after the hot drive was like entering a cave or what I imagined cliff dwellings might be like, outside the heat of a place like Durango. The white sewing machine sat in the midst of the living room clutter. Fabric and magazines lay about covering every inch of furniture. Despite this, the place had the look and feel of a cottage, long empty and awaiting us, the returning cottage-dwellers. From the roof came a skittering sound and Martha said, "Pine cones. They drop all the time. Those big white pines are too close to the house. Mac always used to say, 'Those trees are too close to the house.' Every other time we drove home together from some place, 'Those trees are much too close to the house, Martha,' he'd say in his serious voice."

I felt a certain skiff of joy when Martha mentioned Mac's name, as if a big cloud of pheromones had been released from her mouth and nostrils, maybe even her ears. And I was there to inhale them and follow this capable person to an involuntary, cellular understanding.

"Martha," I said, "do you know what? I brought some pictures of Sylvie. Would you look at them with me when you have a minute? Would you show me some pictures of Mac? You met Sylvie once, I think, at Ted and Maureen's."

"Yes, I did meet her. She was more gregarious than you, I seem to recall. Anyway, certainly I'll look at your pictures. I'll get some of Mac. We can sit at the table and have a little tea and have, I don't know, what would you call it?"

"I'd call it a wake," I said.

"Yes, a wake, of course. I've never been to one of those," Martha said.

She vanished down the hallway and I placed my pictures on the kitchen table. Outside was the breathless atmosphere. The leaves of Martha's lilac were motionless and appeared almost conscious of some timid intention, pressed against the window as if to watch us. Martha returned and filled the kettle. I watched the flame beneath the burner go from a generous and leaping yellow to a compressed and efficient blue.

"Want the light on?" asked Martha.

"It's getting dark out there, isn't it? No, I think we'll be fine here by the window."

"Okay, you go first," Martha said, sitting down across from me.

"Remember those flash cubes?" I began. "Well, this picture was taken with one of those in my parents' back yard. There's Sylvie. She was eleven and I was almost thirteen. That was 1967. She didn't really like to do the same things as me back then. There was this quarry outside of town that she loved and I didn't so much; I mean, it was old news to me. She was pretty bossy, really, in a quiet way, because when I think back I seemed to be following her around half the time."

We looked at Sylvie with the paper calf, Sylvie with the telescope, Sylvie with Graham the weekend he and the horrid Oona split up and he came to stay with us, Sylvie holding a blue pitcher she had bought at a junk store. I found I had nothing much to say.

"She was very pretty," was Martha's observation.

The inadequacy of this comment brought on a rather strange urge. I found I wanted to pick up my images of Sylvie and, one by one, insert them somehow into Martha's broad white forehead, slip them into that brain, bank-card-like. It seemed no less than an act of penetration was required to get Martha to truly understand all that had been lost with Sylvie. Instead, I said agreeably, "Yes, yes, she was."

"Well, here's a picture of Mac," Martha said. The tone of these introductory words, much like she had begun her talk on NAFTA, made me realize my turn was over. I stacked Sylvie's pictures next to my teacup. "It's black and white," Martha went on, "so I'll tell you he had reddish-blonde hair, kind of ruddy skin. Never grew a beard or mustache. Green eyes. Wore contacts, very myopic. But, it's not pictures so much with Mac as his things, his mementos. I've brought some to show you."

Maybe that's what I should have done, I thought. I should have brought along the blue pitcher, the calf, the map collection. That's what I should have done. Beyond my left shoulder, the fading green and brownish presence of the lilac leaves grew stronger; they seemed to have developed a clammy film in the moist air, an ability to attach themselves to glass. I had an uneasy feeling that lilacs might, if traced back far enough genealogically, bear some relationship to one or another of the more tentacled or adhesive sea creatures.

"He was an anthropologist," Martha said. "He loved all that social and cultural stuff, but, you know, I never really thought he was that much of an intellectual. He didn't finish his Ph.D. and was always somewhat less than permanently employed. Sessional this and sessional that. I don't think they liked him that much at the university. He'd get enraptured with a picture or an idea and try to build whole lectures around them. He'd see something in a book, an old textbook from the library, and he'd want that picture. Usually the book would be out of print so he'd look and look in used bookstores. Then, if he found it, the picture, he'd cut it out and stick in onto cardboard and write a quotation underneath. That's what he did to relax. See. Here's one. A photograph by Cecil Beaton and then in Mac's scrawl, 'One day I shall be happier looking back on this day . . . Virgil.' "

A row of Chinese girls, elongated by the perspective of a camera that must have been at about knee level, stared at me. They wore aprons over dresses and only those blurred by distance had bothered to smile for the photographer. "They worked in a cotton mill is all I know about them," Martha said.

"And this one, this guy with the painted face," she said,

"very alluring, isn't he? He was easy, simply cut from the *National Geographic*. And here we have a comment from Goethe . . . 'There is a delicate form of the empirical which identifies itself so intimately with its object that it thereby becomes theory.' I think that's kind of what Mac was striving for.

"But his favourites were the Bushmen, and Bushwomen of course. See these two girls he cut out of a book. 'Beautiful Ungka' he wrote here. Then, a quote from a Bushman who was dying: 'I would altogether talk to thee while my thinking strings still stand.' That was his favourite. He used to say that almost as much as he said the pines were too close to the house. Not exactly like in the quote. Before he fell asleep he'd say, 'Talk to me while my thinking strings are still standing.' And I'd talk and his strings would fall over; that's how it seemed to go. Until they got knocked over permanently. That's how I see it all. When you're alive, your thinking strings, they stand up, all those millions of them, electrified. And when you die, that's just what happens. Your thinking strings fall down. No more thoughts. Nothing."

"All those strings," I said.

"Yes indeed," Martha said, forming a deck with her pictures, tapping the lot of them conclusively on the table.

We both peered out the kitchen window to find the sun completely obscured by a bank of clouds rolling in from the west. An unnatural stillness seemed to have come over everything, even the traffic. Outside Martha's house, all of life appeared to be awaiting some strange and unbelievable announcement; I had a fleeting image of God in the form of Sam Yeats, clutching the microphone of a celestial public address system.

"Well, the sky is now turning green," Martha announced matter-of-factly. "Something's up."

Just then the first clatter of ice came from the roof. Then more and more. It was hail of the violent and roaring type. The kitchen window crackled then broke. A jagged piece of ice tore through the screen, followed by a little shower of shredded lilac leaves.

"Get away from the window," Martha shouted, "stand in the living room."

We pushed the sewing machine to the wall and then stood, shoulder to shoulder, watching. The crashing of the hail on the roof was deafening: no point even to attempt speech. From Martha's living room I watched the hail hit the street and grass with such force it bounced upward upon impact, creating a rather crazy impression, as if the earth were trying to rid itself of gravity, were trying to cough it out of a billion earthly throats.

～

During storms of any type Edna tended to remain calm whereas Isobel leaned toward agitation and compulsive action. The hailstorm was no exception. As the crashing and rattling began, Isobel's thoughts were of the tomatoes on the back deck. "They'll be ruined," she said. "I've got to go for them."

"Don't be ridiculous," Edna cautioned. "You'll be knocked

cold. We can buy tomatoes any day; your head, however, would not be so easily replaced."

"Buy tomatoes? You mean spend money on the sliceable cardboard available at the supermarket? I don't think so. I'll put on my old fur coat; everything just bounces off that old thing. Get me a cardboard box from the basement, will you Edna?"

Edna complied as she nearly always did and moments later Isobel stormed out onto the deck in gum boots, stockings and fox fur, one hand stabilizing the box on her head, the other carrying a paper bag. Deftly, she garnered more than forty tomatoes from the battered plants and returned victorious. "I haven't had an adventure like that for a while," she said, shaking a hand that bled from the cutting ice.

Showoff, Edna thought. To Isobel, she said, "Wash off your hand. I'll set the tomatoes on the counter."

In the kitchen, Edna stood for a moment in a curious state. If there could be an opposite of hail, she thought, I think I am it. All held back, all pushed in.

Stop now, she told herself sternly; she had made a promise with herself not to think about the future, should anything ever happen to Isobel. Outside the window, she saw Lucy, the wiener dog, racing across the lawn to her own territory. "There goes Lucy," Edna said. "I wonder where on earth she was."

~

Ted stood at the back door calling for Lucy, relieved when she finally appeared. "Where the hell have you been? Get in here before you get chopped into baloney," he said. Back in the living room, Ted resumed his excited pacing from window to window. What else needed to be done? he wondered. He had unplugged the appliances as he always did during inclement weather and was wishing there were other defensive tasks that needed doing. Lucky to be alone, he liked to be alone in storms; Maureen and the kids were at the pool — swimming lessons — or at least he hoped so, hoped they weren't on the road in this.

God, this was the best thing to happen in some time, he thought. Let it rip, he said to Lucy. Maybe Annie's at home, maybe I'll give her a call, be nice to talk briefly about this phenomenon. It was something else, after all, it was really something else, he wanted to say to Annie. Do you see the size of those hailstones? Can you buzz over for a drink without sustaining a concussion? But there was no answer. Well, shit anyway, Lucy, he said, unplugging the phone then plugging it in again; Maureen might want to call.

Flopping onto the couch then, Ted sat motionless, listening to the roar of the hail. He remembered a time back in Saskatchewan when he was maybe twelve or thirteen. A tornado had blown through and the effect on his dad had been transforming. This normally even-tempered man had come in from the fields and struck the house like a weather system himself. Up and down the stairs he had gone, calling to everyone, "Jesus Christ, take a look at that, it's a funnel cloud. Margaret! Margaret!" he had called to Ted's mother. "The oak tree's going to come down for sure." But the funny thing was, sometime in the midst of all his comings and goings, Ted's father, James R. Nixon, had gone into his closet, located some dress pants and a white shirt, the type of clothing he might have worn to a dance or card tournament in Milestone, and put them on. He *dressed* for the occasion. Diane, Ted's sister, had motioned him into the bathroom to share a nasty little laugh about this. Still, it had been the most life they had seen from him in years, just possibly since the barn fire at the Qually's.

Ted put a hand on Lucy's head. He noticed that the veins in his arms were rising up and arranging themselves in a familiar configuration, not unlike the late James R. Nixon's circulatory system in the latter part of his life. The phrase "phantom limbs" entered Ted's mind, then left it.

Time to move, he thought, take a look from an upstairs window. Climbing the steps with Lucy, aware of the lump of excitement in his abdomen — sourdough stomach, Ted called it, a case of sourdough stomach brought on by hail — he advised himself, half seriously, half jokingly, to stay away from his closet.

~

aturday afternoon and Alexa was at the mall selling toys. People stood at the entrances to the place, watching, waiting for an opportunity to make a run for their cars. In the toy store, the Rocking Horse, though, Alexa was unaware of the hail bouncing off the mall's roof. She continued working, within an enormous insulator of retail, goods and music, artificial light, food smells and a kind of dissonant hubbub — To spend or not to spend? For all Alexa knew, she might have been buried beneath fifty feet of styrofoam packing. Her thoughts were divided between Janet Sainsbury and the Nintendo game that, she was patiently explaining — "It's store policy" — could not be returned.

Meanwhile, Janet Sainsbury was enjoying a day off from work. She was at home, alone, sitting on her leather couch with Diva, fearful, very fearful actually, but composed. The hail clattering against her windows reminded her of one of Alexa's messages. Could Alexa have orchestrated this whole thing, she wondered, with an ice-making machine from the theatre? It had been more than six weeks now since Alexa moved out. Six weeks was the absolute minimum time she had designated to remain incommunicado. Time to call now, Janet thought, time at last to call the new number she had memorized two days after Alexa left.

As the answering machine played its response, images of Alexa as Malvolio, Alexa as Feste, Alexa as Sir Toby

Belch moved across the big screen in Janet's head.

The beeping, a long, long beep. "Hello Alexa. It's Janet here. How are you? I'm calling to say that I miss you. I miss you like crazy if you want to know the truth. I'm sure you're pleased to hear that. But what I miss even more is . . . the coffee bean grinder. Please return it. It was never yours, you know."

Janet hung up and returned to her couch. As the banging of the hail grew louder, she leaned over, picked up her video camera and held it very close.

~

I begged Sylvie to return to Blodwen's with me but she was not interested. Spring in the quarry had become her passion. With a hatchet, we chopped down small trees and lopped off branches for our raft, working on the gravelly shore. I had not yet learned to swim, did not do so in fact until my university days, but Sylvie paddled effortlessly to the centre of the pond and dove down, trying to get a reading of its depth, a sounding of the imaginary life she seemed to wish to create. No longer would her family of choice have been bank robbers, but gypsies, camped in the quarry, dependent upon her for their diet of fish. It seemed I was forever calling from the water's edge, "Will you just come with me one more time?"

"But you haven't taken me to the pill factory yet. Anyway, I don't want to go. It's boring there." On that afternoon, Sylvie's reflective blue-green bathing suit reminded me of the wings of a dragonfly. The bust was constructed of empty, conical mounds of foam which dented in, I noticed, where the nipples should have been and the rear of her bathing suit hung over her skinny backside. I don't think I altogether knew it then, but I loved the derelict look of Sylvie Rochon.

Eventually, I gave up on the notion of Sylvie coming with me and set off myself, on a Saturday I believe, because life was bustling in town. I suspected this meant Blodwen would be at home because her life did not at all conform to the social rhythms of Mesmer. She would not be seen in front of the IGA, holding a box of groceries and gossiping with one or another lady of the community. Edward maybe, but not Blodwen.

I did not plan my actions that day; I had no plans at all, really. I was simply drawn to the Scarfe house by some acoustic spell, those inaudible, humming waves of attraction, tuning forks held to the lower abdomen. I was almost thirteen years old and in some form of love, the form of love felt as unidentified excitement, like smashing eggs and causing splattering transformations of something hard and white and smooth to a pool of yellow slipperiness — that which cannot be picked up.

As I approached the house, all was quiet, as usual. Edward appeared to be gone: the car was nowhere to be seen. And there was the screen door again, wooden and grey with its sprung hinges, perfect, no childish finger-pokings to allow the passage of insects. I did not knock but stood outside in the sunlight looking through into that large kitchen with its potted plants and gleaming white appliances. To allow my eyes to accommodate to the inner darkness, I pressed my face against the screen. That's when I saw the highchair by the oak table, an old wooden highchair, and in this highchair, oh wonder of wonders, a plastic baby doll.

The door opened with hardly a creak and I stepped inside. From upstairs came the sound of Blodwen's type-writer. Apparently there was no child, no visiting niece from the city, who might provide an explanation for this doll. I came close to it, stared at its round and empty head, the plastic markings meant to be hair, dimpled arms held out in anticipation. Was it waiting for the arrival of all the cramped and crowded sisters and brothers plugged up inside Blodwen?

Wanting that which had died to return to life was familiar enough to me by then, through loss of pets, dead squirrels, birds found on the road side. But this was a different alchemy I had before me — wanting that which was not, never had been, rubber, plastic, stuffing, all of the inanimate and thud-ding syllables — this was exotically strange. Touching the doll's head, I said "Hi, dolly. Hi." Which is when Blodwen appeared in the doorway from the living room.

"Don't you know how to knock?" she asked angrily.

As a child, I was never fearful of adults. Oddly, adults cause me more difficulty now than then. Looking at the object of my affections, I said, "I'm sorry," although I did not mean it. I was more than glad to be there.

Blodwen yanked the doll into her arms then pushed the highchair against the wall, out of sight behind the elephant-eared plant. The doll she placed on its step in the hidden staircase, slamming the door so hard a fine spray of plaster fell from above the jamb. I thought briefly of retarded kids, kids hidden away, food slid under doors and so on. But when Blodwen turned around to face me, she was surprisingly all calmness and intimacy. "Don't suppose," she said, "that I'm so crazy I don't know this is crazy. I just catch her out of the corner of my eye. She sits in that chair and I catch her out of the corner of my eye as I go about my business. Don't think that I sit at the table offering her mashed bananas. I do not.

"I shouldn't have walked in like that," I said.

"Oh, that's all right, that's all right," Blodwen said wearily, sitting down. "Do you want some tea? You didn't bring your Sylvie friend. Thank goodness for that. We can't have the minister knowing I entertain dolls in my home. You won't tell anyone about this, will you?" she asked, leaning toward me, looking directly into my eyes. Being asked by an adult, for the first time, to keep a secret must be an important rite of passage. The way things appear is not necessarily the way they are: plastic dolls lurk in hidden staircases.

"No," I answered, "I won't tell anybody."

I wanted to leave then and put an end to Blodwen's discomfort, but thought she would be hurt if I darted away, seeming to have been disturbed by what I had seen. So I stayed and drank tea and she became bright and asked me about my parents and mentioned the Dominion Day party again. "And be sure to bring your friend again the next time," she said. Those were her final words to me as I stepped back onto the porch, into the sunlight, out of there.

~

On October ninth, I met Janet Sainsbury. Alexa had returned the coffee bean grinder as requested and spoken with Janet, who had allegedly been civil, even kind. She had extended an invitation to Alexa and me to attend a meeting of, what Alexa called, the bold loons. "She's curious about you. She'll have her camera so she can get you on video tape. You know she calls herself the Eye of the Eye of the Beholder. Anyway, there's supposed to be some kind of convergence happening out on a hill east of the city. The place is called Paradise Hill. See? They can't really rip themselves free of their Biblical roots. Anyway, Janet got permission from the farmer for them to meet there. She's like that. She's able to do such things, primarily, I think, because of her appearance, which most men seem to like. So what happens is, they all drive out there early in the morning to watch the sun rise and listen for some kind of humming sound which is the convergence. It's the great pitch pipe of the goddesses. They're all into matriarchs, you understand. Patriarchs are taboo. As far as I'm concerned, we don't need concepts of any type ending in the syllables 'i-arch,' but that's neither here nor there. After the pitch pipe sound, they eat and they have what they call a chanting cone and after that get into their Nissans and Datsuns and drive home again. It was a similar type of event that inspired the three-way with Brigitte and Henry. They won't be there; Janet assured me of that.

There's been a falling out. Actually, there's a pretty high turnover in the membership of the Eye; it's a bit like retail in that way. I said we'd come but we're under no obligation. My main interest is in the free food. It might be good if you two met. We could start to normalize relations."

We drove there in my car, leaving at four a.m. The Ativan in my pocket gave off a comforting warmth in the chilly fall morning. I moved it around with my index finger as we puffed up the side of Paradise Hill. A friendly woman named Annette informed us as we walked that we should be prepared to hear some spherical talk. "Nothing linear here," she said. "Leave your linear thinking at the fence."

"Yeah," Alexa said, "I'm pretty familiar with Janet's circular reasoning." Annette looked perplexed. I fell behind, broke the Ativan apart and popped half into my mouth.

Janet was already at the summit when we arrived, in the centre of a small clutch of what I assumed were the beholden. She was immediately identifiable by the video camera on her shoulder. "Wait here a minute," Alexa instructed, "I'll go get her." Standing there, I felt a bit like a lightning rod for materialism or free-wheeling doubt.

Moments later, Alexa said, "Annie, Annie, I want you to meet Janet. Janet, this is Annie."

Janet's camera lens gazed at me, as did Janet, with slightly less neutrality. "Nice to meet you. Hello," we said, shaking hands, hers cool, mine cold. Janet was luminescent, all in white and her hair, apparently still wet from the shower, was brushed straight back and tied, revealing the high, smooth forehead of the self-professed Eye of the

Eye. Her own eyes were very direct, under the control of a brain that would brook no timidity, nary a furtive glance. She was in a hurry. She would *connect* with us later. There was the daybreak oration to deliver.

The eastern sky was brightening with the new day, while in the west the dark behind of yesterday still covered the mountains. The Ativan had not yet taken hold and I was overcome by a tired longing to be taken somewhere, dragged along by the reins of the previous day, thus avoiding all daybreak orations, thus residing forever in the sleepy folds of the International Date Line. I looked around for Alexa, but she was nowhere in sight.

The thirty or so people on the hilltop formed a circle and Janet appeared with her camera. Apparently, she would video tape as she spoke. "Welcome all," she began, "to our convergence. Welcome. It is time once again to remind ourselves that we are all Eyes of the Beholder. We are children of the sun, which is in turn the child of the Great Beholder whose form we do not know until we pass from this dimension. Let us watch the great eye as it rises. The time is almost upon us. I'll pass to you the vision pieces as the voice-catchers come to the centre of the circle."

I looked in vain for Alexa as Janet travelled the circumference of the circle, handing each person a black strip. "It's film," Alexa said, appearing behind me out of thin air. "I used to cut this stuff up for Janet and her disciples. It's unprocessed film to look at the sun through."

I was reminded of viewing an eclipse as a child at my Uncle Albert's farm. We had used a double thickness of film to prevent retinal damage. I could remember being frightened, almost made sick, by the sudden loss of day for twilight. The birds and insects all seemed so convinced by the sun's disappearance. The ease with which they could be duped was disturbing.

Daybreak arrived. Sunlight rolled across the prairie to that band of people wearing rectangular blacknesses over their eyes. I wondered if one of the few men might be Wayne Abelard; I often wondered this at public gatherings. Only Janet moved, with her camera. Inside me, the Ativan reached my central nervous system like a very good piece of news. This is all quite temporary it said, in its always-convincing way. Next to me, Alexa watched without her protective film. "You'll hurt your eyes," I warned.

"It's the sky I'm looking at," she said, "not the sun."

Janet asked the voice-catchers to begin. I noticed Annette was one of the elect. "Absolute quiet, please," Janet intoned. With great solemnity, the voice-catchers held aloft what looked like reeds, tubes about four feet in length. They moved the reeds slowly this way and that, like weather vanes. All drew close. From where I stood, some resonance was audible. This was the music of the convergence! I almost laughed out loud. Audiologists should not attend convergences of any type. Perhaps, I thought, I should prepare a paper on this topic for the upcoming audiologists' conference.

"Alexa," I said, "I think I'll go for a walk."

"I'll stick it out until the food shows," she said.

About half a kilometer away I could see a huge stack of straw bales toward which I set off, fifty steps walking, fifty steps running. I was reluctant to look back. The entire scene had such a fantastical quality to it I feared I might, from that distance, see figures in more than living colour, Disney characters animated in lurid and dancing pixels.

Atop the straw mow, I sat against a bale with my back to them all. Very carefully, I smoked a cigarette, butting it in the foil wrap and storing it in my pocket. All around, the sunlit stubble shone. Paradise Hill might have been the huge unshaven chin of some sleeping blonde giant man. I had the feeling that possibility would not have pleased Janet Sainsbury.

Presently, Alexa appeared with two boiled eggs, some buns and coffee. "I knew it would pay off if I stuck around. There's always food at these hootenannies. This is way better than the food bank. It's almost, you know, living off the land. Let's eat."

We created a room arrangement by positioning bales, two deep, in a snug u-shape. There we sat, eating and watching the mountains. Afterward, we followed the base of the hill to my car, as the great cone of chanting got underway.

~

How does a person know when things are about to go wrong? Easy. Listen to the subtext. The subtext of all talk hangs in the very air as smelly as wet wool. It is often necessary to slap it out of the way, otherwise that subtext might get caught in our mouths, cover our eyes or smudge our glasses with its furry tracks. Always the same old practical messages, homely and direct. And yet, messages that must be stared at in silent disbelief. "It was doomed from the start," for example, or, "I could have told you this would happen." The subtext began to mutter these and other messages to me the moment Alexa arrived at the straw stack. She must have spoken with Janet, or maybe watched her closely, or perhaps remembered a past incident that turned the tables. I'm sure I'll never know. But when she came to me with the food and coffee, Alexa was humming with it, that barbaric language of blood, glands and heat. And as we were driving back, she said, "I think I'd better just go home now," even though it was a Sunday and we hadn't seen each other all week, and, "I have lots of work to do, that paper on Shaw is due this Wednesday." Something was being shouted at me, I knew that much.

"Sure," I said, "of course. I'll take you home."

Take a hammer, take a wedge, secure wedge along fault line of skull, tap with hammer. Crack. Skull pops open.

I have never been one to ignore the subtext completely. What I will do is hold out as long as possible for another interpretation. I am capable of a tense, yet foolish, optimism. Stretched like an elastic, this optimism will deflect all cues, all tacit messages and ricochet them elsewhere. With my grey brain open and exposed, I will await another meaning.

That Sunday morning, I dropped off Alexa and came home with my premonitions to an invitation from Edna and Isobel to join them for breakfast. They fed me scrambled eggs, and Isobel described her rescue of the tomatoes, showed off her cuts and said, "I was rather impressed with myself. You know, I think I inherited a good deal of my grandmother Lowry's character. She died when I was seven but I remember her for one thing, no, two things, no, make that three things. First off, she was deaf as a post. Secondly, she addressed me and all of my sisters and female cousins by one name, 'Sissy,' as in sister, I guess. I suppose the feminists nowadays would like that. But, anyway, most importantly, point number three is that she ran out into the hail once herself."

"I see," I said. "I was beginning to wonder what exactly the point was going to be, Isobel."

Shooting me the sort of look usually reserved for Edna, Isobel went on. "My sister Ruby and I were visiting her in her little house in Medicine Hat, and she had lilies in her garden, white ones that had just begun to bloom, and this hail came one afternoon and out she went wearing a big, black cape she had and some kind of hat and we stood and watched from the front veranda. I was certain she'd be killed. But, she came running back, and with the hail still clattering on the veranda roof, she pulled at least a dozen white lilies out from inside that cloak. I'll never forget that moment, unless of course something goes terribly wrong in the next few years and I lose my marbles. So, you see, Edna, I really could not help myself. I had to go out into the hail; it's a familial thing, a weakness I've inherited."

"Oh," said Edna, slightly annoyed at Isobel, "that's what so many of them used to say at the San. 'I can't help myself.' Now that would irritate Dr. Reid."

"Does it irritate you, Edna?" Isobel asked.

"Well, yes it does and no it does not. It's the way people

think, that's all. I can't help *myself*, but you can help *yourself*. Anyway, no I was not annoyed with you so much as worried. I worried about you getting knocked out and me having to drag you inside by the ankles, and that would not have been a pretty picture, I assure you.

"Did you get any damage, by the way, Annie, last Saturday?" Edna asked. "I know! Come upstairs and we can take a look at your roof. It's lower than ours. You'll know whether or not to call the adjuster."

Upstairs, from Isobel's bedroom window, we surveyed my grey asphalt interlocking shingles for hail damage. The roof seemed intact to me, but Edna insisted that appearances can be deceiving. Isobel concurred. Ray had called the adjuster immediately, first thing Monday morning. He would have a new roof in a matter of days. As for Edna and Isobel, their roof was constructed of cedar shakes; they had nothing to worry about, nothing at all to worry about.

And that was when the subtext of my morning began insinuating itself into my mind. As Edna and Isobel talked on about insurance and roofs, I had an irresistible urge to sink into Isobel's bed, or otherwise take up residence in her room. I liked the smell of it, the smell of an old body's room. I had an impression of time stacked up and shelved, a density of experience that caught each new moment and put it in its proper place. What Isobel seemed to have in her room was a taxonomy of instants: bags of time, boxes of time, cartons, ring containers, whatnots. Nothing disorganized to jar your preserves, as Edna occasionally said.

By way of contrast, the sight of my squat little bungalow, soon to be without Alexa, I was certain, was quite jarring. I was conscious of Sylvie's ashes in the midst of all my possession and terrors, exposed and hanging forth much like the heart of Jesus in Catholic artifacts. Surprising that the urn was not actually visible, glowing redly.

My life in that little house seemed to me all set to go haywire again. Pretty soon, there I would be, wandering mateless in the electric light of my rooms. I shuddered an invisible shudder and thought of my mother. In her view of female psychology, the two most telling signs of trouble were spells and crying jags. A spell was any behaviour or group of behaviours entirely out of character and brought on by strong emotion or prolonged stress. Thus, when Eve Desmarais threw a plate of tarts at her husband on the occasion of their twentieth wedding anniversary party at the Mesmer Community Hall, she was judged by my mother to have suffered a spell.

Crying jags involved sustained crying at a social function. My sister, Lorna, has always been prone to crying jags. My mother, of course, has never indulged in either spells or jags. She carries on bravely; in fact, that is her motto — "Well, carry on bravely!" I am capable of carrying on bravely, but only for a while. There is always the chance of a mild spell or a light flurry of lies.

Edna had asked me a question I had not heard. By way of responding, I smiled and said, "Why don't you two come over to my place for a while?" following what I knew would be my mother's advice. "I could show you my indoor clothesline. You haven't seen it, have you? I have a feeling they're going to be all the rage."

We drifted across the yard to my house, only to

encounter Ted wanting to pay me a call as well. He had had his cable television disconnected in a pique a couple of days earlier, incensed at the cable company's ever-escalating rates, then discovered that one of the thirty-odd networks he now no longer received was carrying a baseball game he wanted to see.

After a demonstration of my retractable clothesline, the four of us settled companionably into the living room to watch the Blue Jays play the White Sox. Deep inside of me, though, a curious and private event was occurring: I was making myself desperate in my need to know if my assumptions regarding Alexa were correct. I worked at this while Ted helped himself to a beer, scraping away at my own interior, hollowing myself out with an aluminum spoon, digging, digging, until at the bottom of the seventh inning I was compelled to take action and begin lying. I had not lied for a while, so felt I had it owing.

"I've just remembered I'm supposed to meet a friend," I announced unconvincingly, like a very poor actress. Ted eyed me suspiciously, I thought. "You can all stay," I said. "Just leave the place unlocked. It's my friend . . ." and here I actually paused to invent the name, so obvious was I, "Stella, from work." There is of course no such Stella.

They agreed to stay and I drove off, dramatically squealing my Tercel's balding tires on Bow Bottom Road. I was headed to Crowfoot Mall, where I knew the toy store was located, where I knew Alexa would be found. My intention was to simply and genuinely state my feelings and request some statement from her. I felt better already for having made the decision, I told myself. Certainly.

The mall was a short drive away. Enough time for me to begin to wish, wish, wish I had more than just one and a half remaining Ativan. God damn that Dr. Panesh anyway. So incredibly straight, so invariably buttoned right up to the neck. I wondered if she had ever contemplated audiology as a back-up career; it seemed a logical choice for one so stiff-upper-lip as she.

I arrived. Parked. Entered the mall. I had no idea of the layout of the place and consulted a map immediately upon entering. My greatest fear was that Alexa would surprise me, on a coffee break, and undo my strategy. As long as I could manage the pace and staging of events, I felt prepared for her.

The Rocking Horse was at the east end of the mall, directly across from Woolco. Good. I headed purposefully in that direction until the neon lighting of the store came into view. Then I automatically moved closer to the Woolco side of life, close to the glass walls. The place was crowded, thank God, overflowing with mall-hounds, as Alexa often referred to her patrons. Plenty of opportunity for camouflage existed, which was good, because with each step, my resolve to confront Alexa diminished.

The Woolco entrance was not directly across from the toy store. I could enter Woolco and spy on the Rocking Horse's counter and cash area from the infants' wear department. There, after a minute or two of examining a Jolly Jumper, I decided that it would be unfair to put Alexa on the spot at her workplace. Don't do it, a faint-hearted Ellen Nestle urged. And besides, what information was I acting on? A gut feeling, nothing more.

I decided to watch the place anyway. At first, I could see only another employee; then, from behind a display of Lego, Alexa appeared. There she was, with her black hair and her funny bobbing walk and her general aura of gregariousness. She was showing a customer the inner workings of a huge water gun. Only Alexa could pull this off in a manner both sincere and faintly self-mocking.

Maybe I'm wrong, I thought. Maybe. But that tentativ little word could not stem the tide of sadness that overcame me as I pawed mindlessly at a bin of babies' sleepers. I do not cry easily, as a rule, and therefore a crying jag at Woolco was out of the question. In public places, I often substitute coughing for crying, and that is what I did now. I began a fit of several deep and ripping coughs. I think I believed if I coughed hard enough I might tear off a piece of heart muscle, which might miraculously pass along the pulmonary artery and into my lungs, from where I could expel it. A little sugar cube of meat. I would have liked to cough it up into my hand, look at it, drop it noiselessly onto the department store's floor, and go home, a contented shopper.

~

The allure of Blodwen Scarfe had been intensified by my accidental glimpse of her secret life with the plastic baby. My next trip to the Scarfe farm was planned very carefully. Conditions had to be such that I would see the doll and Blodwen together again; that is, Edward would have to be out.

I had learned the basics of reproduction by then, although I cannot say I believed what I had been told. What seemed more likely to me was that the intensity of wanting a baby would in some way cause a birth to occur. And that, therefore, a woman like Blodwen should possess enough desire to leave behind a trail of babies, plop, plop, plopping out behind those pretty dresses and matching shoes. The fact remained, however, that Blodwen could not have children. It must have seemed to me back then that if I could catch Blodwen at home alone and spy on her and her plastic baby through a kitchen window, a fundamental riddle would be answered for me: the riddle of "What do adults do when stuck, alone, with the facts?"

I planned my outing well.

My father was a Rotarian. So was Edward Scarfe. In June they held their final meeting of the year in the Mesmer Rotary Park. The men barbecued steaks and drank a few beers while the Rotary wives and children sat at home eating the type of meal enjoyed when the men were out. In front of the television, Lorna, Grant, Mom and I ate roast beef sandwiches washed down with a glass of water. I ate especially fast, then told Mom I was going over to Sylvie's house. Instead, I rode my bike past the park to make sure Edward Scarfe was there. As I coasted past, I saw him light his pipe, standing in the midst of a group of men, talking.

Off to the laneway I sped, through the Van Epps' place to the fence, where I left my bike concealed among the chokecherry bushes. I followed the pathway to the bank of the Little Mud River. There, I sat and waited a while. I wanted to let the sun set. I wanted to allow Blodwen and her baby to get into the full swing of whatever it was they did. And I had plenty of time. The Rotary meeting went until all hours and it was a Friday night, so I was not expected home until ten. I would wait until dusk.

Dusk was a word and event familiar to me from drive-in movie advertisements. Every holiday weekend, the Mustang Drive-In staged dusk-to-dawn horror shows. Graham had tried to organize a trip to the drive-in for the May twenty-fourth show, but Philip Rochon had rejected the scheme, calling the entertainment "unsuitable for pre-teens."

"But I'm well into my teens," Graham had argued.

"You, maybe, but if you average your and Sylvie's and Annie's ages the result is only twelve and a bit. In other words, pre-teen. *Ergo*, dusk to dawn is inappropriate. *Ergo*, I am not taking you."

"*Ergo*," Graham said, "I'll just grow up to be one of those misfits they study in psychology courses. Or, *ergo*, maybe I'll be written up in *Life* after I've gone crazy and blown up a bridge or something. Somehow, people will find out I wasn't allowed to do anything when I was fourteen, ever, *ergo*, I was crippled by my father."

"Well, maybe I should get you an electric wheelchair, Graham, to make up for it. Would that make you happy?"

That was how they spoke to one another. Lying on decaying bark and leaves, picking at last year's empty beechnut shells, I weighed this in my mind against Grant and my dad's rare exchanges in front of the television, usually having to do with the issue of who had farted. "Skunk smells its own hole first," Grant always said. Dad liked to grunt disparagingly in response.

When dusk had truly come, I felt I could climb the hill and cross the yard without detection. Up the big hill I went, through the pasture, following a cow path. Edward's Holsteins stood about in groups, watching me, neither coming nor going. Cows' behaviour can at times convey a perfect ambivalence.

Upon my arrival at the crest of the hill, I was dismayed to see a car parked in the Scarfes' yard. Could Blodwen be entertaining a friend? I wondered. My hope of seeing the doll diminished, but having come that far, I had no intention of turning around. And besides, as I drew closer, the car became more and more recognizable as Daphne Rochon's Buick. I knew that car well, but could not be certain of its identity until I had scurried to the car's rear. On my haunches to avoid being seen, I peeked in to see the box of Kleenex Daphne kept in the rear window-well, alongside the ever-present and dusty pair of white kid gloves.

What the hell is Daphne doing visiting? I thought, conscious of using the word "hell" like an adult. Strengthened by my spontaneous and guiltless use of a curse-word, I sprinted across the driveway and yard to the cover of the lilacs. There, I crouched, listening intently, like the budding audiologist I was, to the sounds of worry and excitement created by my own heart.

The lilacs were past their prime and gave off a promiscuous scent, desperate in their attempts to attract agents of pollination. "Promiscuous" was a word I had learned from Graham and used from time to time in his and Sylvie's company. We might comment, for example, that Darlene Daley looked promiscuous in her red short shorts.

I crouched until my legs ached, then knelt beneath the kitchen window, contemplating how superior the human head's design would have been with eyes placed above the forehead. That way, spies and soldiers could peek out of hiding places without their enormous and shiny brows attracting bullets and other dangers. In the end, I just decided to look. I rose up, like a cobra, and there they were, Blodwen Scarfe and Reverend Philip Rochon, completely oblivious to my presence.

Blodwen was against the kitchen wall, her profile — head thrown back, mouth open — unlike any I had ever seen before, except maybe on one of the midway rides at the Canadian National Exhibition. My first thought was that Reverend Rochon was attempting to strangle her, but further observation revealed his hands to be nowhere near her neck. One hand seemed to have disappeared inside the dark spaces beneath Blodwen's blue floral dress. Her underpants were a wrinkled pool of blue nylon at her left ankle. I could see Reverend Rochon's bare elbow bobbing back and forth with the rhythm and regularity of some mechanical device, something with a job to be done, a crankshaft maybe. His clothing was all in order, nothing unbuttoned on him, no skin exposed except those arms in their short sleeves.

I have to admit, I watched with pleasure. Vaguely worded wishes entered my mind and were abruptly kicked out. If only Graham could have been there too; if only I could be right in the kitchen, invisible and listening. If only Reverend Rochon would take off all of Blodwen's clothes. Then I began to worry about Mrs. Scarfe. Her facial expression changed. She looked as if she were about to sneeze or yelp in pain; she appeared to experience a type of convulsion. All of the movement then ceased and I slumped out of sight.

"Evening In Paris" was all I could think then for a while, amongst the lurid lilacs, Evening In Paris. The dark blue bottle of cheap perfume that sat on my dresser appeared against the dark blue sky, and dancing white silhouettes, Sylvie and Graham Rochon. Regaining my senses, I scrambled across the unlit yard and down the hill, retrieved my bicycle from the chokecherries and was in bed by ten o'clock.

$\sim$

For the past week, Isobel's regular pool had been closed for repairs and she had foregone swimming, forcing Edna to change her routine as well. No matter. Isobel was a heavy sleeper and a night hawk; she could be counted on not to stir until eight or later. So, Tuesday morning Edna rose at five-thirty, long before Isobel and the sun. She was drawing closer to the park every day and more confident with each day's success. The strips of paper were now filled with information on both sides and included her full name and phone number, her social insurance number, Ted and Annie's work numbers (places to call in the event of an emergency) and a lengthy description of her own house. At times she threw in entirely gratuitous bits of information, such as her shoe size, seven and a half, or the title of her favourite novel, *The Woman in White*. Edna got a laugh out of this.

Today's notes were written on the remains of a brochure on low-fat diets. These Edna stuffed into her cardigan pocket before quietly stepping onto the deck and shutting the door. Just stand for a second and wait, she thought. If Isobel gets up, I'll hear her and go back in. I'll say I just couldn't sleep and thought I'd get a breath of fresh air. From the house came only silence. Good, Edna thought. Sleep tight, Izzy.

There had been a frost or two in late August, but since then nothing but mild weather. In the unseasonable warmth, Edna would leave no footprints. This morning she would get herself past the steep spot by the chain link fence. She had had to stop there on her last trip, wondering how she would ever descend that little bank without becoming one of those old women who languish forever in hospital with a broken hip and die weighing sixty-five pounds. Then she had hit upon the perfect solution. She would bring a cane, hook the end through the fence and ease herself down backward in a form of geriatric rappelling. On the return trip, she would use the same technique to hoist herself back up. Once over that little hurdle, Edna reckoned she would be more than three-quarters of the way there. The Eighty-Seventh Street Bridge would be visible around the next bend in the river, she was sure.

"I didn't realize she'd be up this early," Edna thought, passing by Annie's house. In the kitchen, Annie could be seen moving here and there, ducking occasionally beneath the articles on her clothesline. Edna increased her pace to avoid being seen.

It was necessary to detour around the one big willow

tree in Ted and Maureen's yard, either into the river a bit
or up onto the grass. Some instinct told Edna to stop
there, stop and hide for a bit. Bending low over her cane,
she hoped this instinct was not actually a sign of confu-
sion. No, it was not. Ted opened his back door to release
Lucy, who immediately flew diagonally across the yard,
yelping all the way, to the big willow and Edna.

"No, Lucy. Lucy, go. Lucy, shut up!" Edna whispered.
Then, "Oh, why bother. It's not possible to collaborate
with a dog," she muttered, stepping up the slope and into
Ted's view. "They just don't understand."

"Edna? Is that you? What are you doing?" Ted came
closer, wearing sweat pants and plaid slippers, no shirt.

"Don't worry, Ted, I'm perfectly fine. I am not in any
kind of state. I'm just out for a breath of fresh air. Nothing
to be alarmed about. As for you, what are you doing out
without a shirt? You'll freeze."

"Nah, it's hot. And I'm a tough kind of guy," said Ted
from what Edna saw as his perfectly functioning brain,
arms crossed, observant. He was not convinced she was all
there, that was clear from the look on his face.

"You're up awfully early," he added.

"Couldn't sleep."

"Well, come in for some coffee then. It's a while before
I'm off on my appointed rounds."

"I suppose I could, I suppose I could. As long as Isobel
doesn't wake up and find me gone. I suppose we'll hear the
alarms from here if that happens."

"Aaah, not to worry."

"No, not to worry, that's the goal," Edna agreed, taking

Ted's bare arm. She had come to realize that, because of her age and reputation as no longer entirely all there, no matter what the context, most people pretended to understand, or at least accept, everything she said. And she had begun to take advantage of this by saying whatever popped into her head.

"You know, Ted," she said, "they used to have some pinball machines at Bowness Park. I used to like to watch my son Robert play pinball. Back then, I sometimes thought it would be nice to be a pinball, just go where things took you, never make a decision. Of course, now I feel I've had a chance to be more like a pinball, you know, here, there, bounce, bounce, maybe it's not so great after all. Do you know what I mean?"

"Oh, I think so. Events. Things flapping at you. I think so," Ted said, as he closed the door behind them.

~

Well, I was right. I was right, God damn it. Four days went by without a word from Alexa. I could not sleep past five, so I went to work early and came home late. I read the paper and stayed inside. Edna and Isobel wandered into my yard but I ignored them. Sometimes I ducked down out of sight so I couldn't be seen through my back window. And, I could never be quite certain of this, but it seemed that when I opened the door to my closet, a vindictive little red light appeared to vanish from Sylvie's corner. The opposite of the hail-fellow-well-met of the refrigerator light, this was more a mean little "I told you so," always extinguished by the time the door was fully open. I was annoyed to the very roots of my teeth. I wanted to gnaw on things; I chewed gum furiously, even smoked eight cigarettes on Wednesday.

But by Thursday, through some miracle of adaptation, Alexa had begun to corkscrew herself out of my mind. I had lined up my aids to daily living, my five smokes, my one and a half remaining Ativan, a mid-week movie culled from the Academy Awards section of the video store, and was deciding that life was perhaps a reasonable bargain after all. That's when the phone rang and it was her, Alexa, the she-devil. What I heard first was the sound of ice cubes at the other end of the line. She had had a few drinks and was having another. The rapid-fire talk began.

"Annie, Annie, Annie," she said, "I'm in my cups here. I've had a few nips, as they say. How are things in Bowness? How's the calf? Is he on his feet? That's more than I can say for myself right now. I'm in my floor bed, kind of longing for a Sealy Posturepedic, levitating just above the lovely taupe-coloured floor tiles, and I wish you were here but I really must spend some time on my own."

"Uh, huh," I answered, throwing the half-moon of Ativan to the back of my throat and swallowing. The sensation was of Martha's seam ripper moving along my esophagus.

"There's something I must tell you," she said. "It's à propos of the moment. I must speak."

"That sounds ominous," I said.

"Now, don't say that. To me it would be best just to let things be, let them sort themselves out as they always will, or let them just get a direction like a compass needle. But it cannot be that way because I am part of [whispered] a therapy group [end of whispering]. Yes, it's true. Janet organized it all for me a year or more ago. Don't ask me why. Anyway, it seems that the main purpose of it is to shape my guilt, just keep shaping it and reshaping it like those little animals and figures made out of shrubs. What are they called?"

"Topiary," I answered.

"Right. Well, I can't seem to stop attending. Every Tuesday night, there I am with the others. And they are all adult children of all sorts of situations, alcoholics and abusers and so on. All of them except for me, that is. And they are all very big on honesty," Alexa said, taking a sip. "Telling it all and crying, of course. Maybe it's good for me, I don't know, but last night I kind of lost it. I gave a bit of a speech. I stood up and I said, 'You know, I've concluded that since my parents weren't alcoholics or horrible in any major way, I have decided that I must be the adult child of some other life form, something nasty, a wolverine, let us say. There's no other excuse for me, for the things I do, for the way I seem to be sitting back on my haunches and snarling at life and love. I think I'm the adult child of a fucking wolverine,' I told them. 'That's my excuse.'

"Well, that got them going. They jumped in, telling me I had anger, as if anger were a thing, an object one could have in the same way one has perhaps a blue, plush steering-wheel cover, for example. And then they questioned me about my love life and I told them about you. And they asked me about Janet, because of course they've heard all about her, and that's why they insisted, they insisted that I have more honesty. Again, note the verb of choice, *have*. So, I am complying in an effort to be less wolverine-like."

"Okay," she went on amidst a tinkling of ice, "the truth is, I am not totally finished with Janet. We have slept together a couple of times since I moved out. Actually, three times."

"Uh, huh," I said, "uh, huh. I thought maybe."

Something passed between us on the phone, not altogether bad; I pictured blocks falling through space and landing, tumbling acrobatically into a very specific shape. So this is how it was to be.

"I'm not entirely surprised," I said. "I've been wondering all this week. It's best to know; your little group is right." I was struggling to retain my composure, flailing about in a search for the correct words, words that would keep my mouth open and aggressive. It seems when my lips collide for certain sounds, the bilabials, *m*, *b*, tears are more readily formed. "I've never been involved in this type of thing," I said. "Do you want to go back to Janet?"

"No, I don't think so. I do not think so. I like being on my own. When I'm with Janet I feel like I'm living with a big blanket or a muffler. My self is muffled. Anyway, I've told you the truth and that's about all I can do for now. If you still want to see me, like you have been, let me know. Unless you know right now. Do you? Do you know right now?"

She actually sounded a little fearful and this strengthened me. Ellen Nestle's face appeared before me giving an instruction I could not quite make out.

"No, no, I don't know at this moment."

"Good. That's good," Alexa said.

"Good-bye then," I said.

"Yes, I guess good-bye would be the thing to say now. Good-bye, Annie."

The receivers clicked down simultaneously.

~

Martha came by the following evening, causing a bit of a reaction in me, comparable to, but not exactly, a spell. She was wearing a fedoralike hat and a pair of gloves with the fingers cut off at the first knuckle, even though the temperature was moderate. Martha was very concerned about preserving body heat, as if it could be stored like oil or potatoes. "Despise the approach of winter," she said. "Anyway, just out for a drive in my beetle, the car I'll probably be driving for the remainder of this millenium. Who am I kidding about this car plan? I can't afford a new car and I'm sure the Royal Bank of Canada would concur."

Frankly, I didn't care, but I pretended to. "Oh well," I said, "you don't have to decide immediately. Come in. Have a drink with me."

I had been using most of my energy hunkering around, beginning small projects and leaving them unfinished to begin another, bothered by a kind of migrating anger verging on hatred for Alexa. Migrating because it would start out directed at her, then quickly be deflected back onto myself for being so pathetic as to put up with such a situation. Then I would concentrate on abandoning all female conventions related to sex and simply enjoy what came along with Alexa. This had the effect, I believe, of causing my entire cardiovascular system to constrict, so much effort was involved. I felt like the Olympic weight-lifters. I could manage the jerk, a sudden snap based upon a decision, but I crumbled beneath the effort of slowly raising the weight above my head. It fell and I wanted to kick something in frustration. I had sent Sylvie's calf flying onto the couch moments before Martha's arrival. Then, I had taken out my final bit of Ativan to admire but, with the knock on the door, had returned my pill-friend to its vial.

Martha wanted to know if I had finished the sewing. This struck me as comically ludicrous, that I would undertake sewing in my circumstances, and I said, "No, of course not," testily, as if she had asked me if I had been telling lies of late.

"Well, get the material. I'll help you."

"No, you won't," I began. "No, no, no, no, no. I don't think so. Not today." Then weakening, I said, "Oh all right. But not without that preliminary drink."

"Oh, let's just get at it," Martha insisted. "You know I'm a controlling old hag. I never let other people have their way. But I'll concede we could have a drink while we're pinning on the pieces."

"Oh you will, will you? Well, I'm afraid I'm as stubborn

as you are controlling and I say no, we have a drink first."

Martha finally relented and I poured us both a Scotch. "Not made in Canada, I'm sorry to say."

"It's acceptable when only an inferior product is manufactured here," Martha said.

"Oh, I see. That pretty much opens up the floodgates, I'd say."

Martha looked hurt by this comment, as if I had made a critical remark about her slightly large ears or her bread-making capability.

"Listen," I said then, struck by the idea that had precipitated my near-spell. "I want to show you something. I hope I don't alarm you. I want you to see this," I went on, disappearing into the bedroom, the closet, where Sylvie's ashes sat in their urn, in their hallowed spot. I carried them into the living room.

"It's Sylvie. Here she is," I announced merrily, like a demented old kook, like my great aunt Agnes saying, "Well, *there* he is," about her husband Frank as he lay in his coffin.

"Sylvie still inhabits this house after a fashion," I said. "I like having her around, I must admit. But it's kind of unhealthy, don't you think? The whole North American *Zeitgeist*, as my friend Monica would say, summed up by this: clutching your dead girlfriend's ashes. I bet you didn't do this, did you? Did Mac even become ashes? Oh, I'm sure he did."

"Yes, you're right. He did," Martha said. "And you're correct in assuming that I didn't keep the ashes. Mac was very conventional, really. He always said he wanted a pleasant little grave with a headstone and that's what he got. A gravestone that says Malcolm Peter Lancaster, August 20, 1949–July 5, 1988. Once in a while I take roses or flowers from the yard. It's very sentimental, I know."

I looked hard at her, giving my thoughts time to ferment. "Would you like to see the ashes?" I asked.

"I don't mind looking at them, if that's what you want," Martha said, stretching out the *a* in "want," inflecting down a half-note. "They're really symbolic, you know. Just a scoop or two from the oven. Most of her is long gone."

"I know, Martha. I know. So look anyway."

She peered in, pulling at her fingerless gloves.

"Well, what do you think? What gives?" I asked.

Martha shrugged, took a sip of Scotch.

"Well?" I went on, and that was when the spell really got going. "What kind of chemical transformation is it that changes a person like this," I asked, poking her in the leg, "not exactly the same but with a similar carbon base, similar currents of electricity causing heart to beat, thoughts to occur on a continuous basis, eyes, ears containing a tympanic membrane and the ability to interpret complex sound messages, into this?" I shook the urn at her. "What process would that be, Martha? I mean, who could tell from a casual glance that these ashes weren't a two-by-four? What is your explanation for that? You must have one. Mac is as dead as Sylvie. It's not as if there are gradations; it's not a seven point scale. What do you have to say? I see no reason why you should scamper about so hearty and well-adjusted while I'm sitting here in my house, consorting with remains and an unfaithful drama student. I don't see how that is fair when I've gone out with you painting those messages in the dead of night."

That was the better part of my outburst. I stopped there, feeling a bit ridiculous and yet at the same time entertaining visions of going farther, chopping some willow branches from the river bank and whipping Martha until her secret was revealed, until her peace of mind bled out of her and onto my floor. I felt as if I might begin hyperventilating.

Martha said, "You look a little bit like my dad did just prior to his last heart attack. Maybe you should sit down."

"Okay. That sounds reasonable," I said.

"Now," Martha said, "I brought along my sewing scissors, the pinking shears, and they're a darn good pair if I do say so myself. Made in Quebec. You would be amazed at the cost of a pair of these. I'll pin on the pieces and you can cut."

I certainly cannot say I was placated by this diversion. More images of myself in a state of crazed secular disappointment, slashing away at Martha with willow branches, appeared before my eyes. But in the midst of it all, I did manage to ask, "Should I get us another drink?"

"Get yourself one. I'm fine," Martha instructed.

I returned the urn to its place and made myself another drink, and through some process of necessity and resignation calmed down and helped with the cutting up and pinning on of the pattern pieces. By the third drink, I was sewing and experiencing a kind of grace brought on by the combined effects of alcohol and concentration. By late afternoon I had a pair of grey, cotton track pants with elasticized waist and cuffs. They fit perfectly and were well-made. Martha had insisted on French seams, out of deference to one of Canada's founding peoples. I laughed. And we drank coffee and ate tomato-and-lettuce sandwiches before she left in her beetle, asking, "Who am I kidding, thinking I can afford a new car?"

"I'll buy one for you, Martha," I said. "Whatever you want. I'll pick it up for you tomorrow. The bank gives us audiologists loans. They know what kind of people we are."

And then she was gone, leaving me to sit in this back yard once again, a teeny bit tipsy. Almost seven o'clock it was. The sunlight slanted at me from the southwest. Soon it would be Thanksgiving. The sun was no longer so insistent on burning and growing and heating. On October evenings, perhaps it was able to concentrate more on its lesser tasks, algae, moss, the underwater creatures' needs. It brought forth life in refracted and indirect ways. I thought for a while about Alexa's fish, the green puffers with their transparent and skeletal tails. I could clearly see Sylvie's lovely, departed ears. So pleasant it was, at times, to contemplate the interiors of things, places vaguely illuminated, such as river bottoms and ear canals.

～

I spent much of the entire next week entertaining and tormenting myself with visions of Janet and Alexa in various carnal embraces, quick peepshows, very quick, the type another quarter could not really complete. Blink: Janet and Alexa. Blink: audiogram. Blink: Janet and Alexa.

In this state of uncertainty, jealousy likes to come and go. It is a bit like sound, little troughs of pressure followed by vague air, the pressure representing Alexa and Janet, the vague air, my interest in employment. Thursday and Friday, I called Alexa several times only to listen to the message and hang up. I no longer worried how this might be construed. And, to make matters worse, there was a new message on the machine, Shakespeare again. How I loathed Alexa's cavalier approach to life, her squandering of it on her alone. How dare she locate and record this new passage while I made fruitless trips to Woolco and made grey track pants, all on her account.

But then Alexa surprised me. She showed up at my office, late Friday afternoon. Individuals such as Alexa are not often seen in or near elementary schools, unless as members of a performing troupe. Too many layers of clothing, unusual footwear, slightly unruly hair: all are considered signs of danger to children and will cause alarms to sound in the minds of those situated in the front office. By the time of Alexa's arrival, though, the administrative people had left. It was Friday afternoon, after all; they had all stampeded out at three-thirty, and Alexa had wandered the building freely until finding my door. My heart melted.

"Somebody did see me," she said, "a science-teacher type. He looked at me as if he thought I might be drunk, which isn't all that inaccurate an assumption in light of my behaviour last week. But I told him in my best parental kind of voice, 'I'm here to see the audiologist. I have an appointment with her.' I knew you were still here. I saw your car."

"Well, you know the thinking of most schools," I said. "Unless you look like a close relative of Margaret Thatcher, you're likely a subversive."

Alexa wanted to know where we stood, now that I knew about Janet. And I, having developed some theatrical ability through the chronicity of my lying, pretended I had actually made a reasoned decision, that I had considered the option of aloneness again, of becoming the pair of eyes behind the venetian blinds once more. I had not for a moment done so, but I hinted that I had. I intimated that I had thought it through, had creased my brow, asked myself gravely civilized questions and arrived at an answer.

"Yes," I said, "I think we should carry on like this. I'm not looking for a full-time commitment anyway. This is fine, excellent, as a matter of fact." My legs were crossed and at the word "excellent" I began twitching my left foot in a manner I hoped would suggest mild indifference.

What I said was exactly what Alexa wanted to hear. Which is why I said it. I know ears. They are my business.

The air was cleared by my easy acquiescence. Alexa made herself comfortable in my examining chair, then assured me she could never return to Janet because of her escalating teleological needs. "I don't know how it came to be, but now everything represents something else. Nothing just is. It's all weirdly symbolic. And she's pretty preoccupied with you. You are a message. Last week you were a mere messenger; now you are the message. She woke up in the night and said to me, 'Annie Clemens is a message.' I think she just likes to say your name. It makes her feel as if she has some way of managing you."

"Well, I can think of a few messages I might be able to transmit for her benefit," I said. "And by the way, what night was it she woke you up with that insight? I'm interested to know what kind of schedule you have us on."

Alexa looked at me with disbelief. "Oh, come on," she said, "I thought you didn't take part in those female responses, jealousy and possessiveness and all that."

"I wouldn't say they're necessarily female. They seem to be pretty human responses if you ask me, maybe even mammalian. Dogs get jealous, female and male dogs."

"Okay, okay, okay. Let's drop it. Why don't you test my hearing? I think I'd like to have you probing around in my ears, just like a Q-tip. Don't you find Q-tips just a little bit exciting? My friend Martin once told me that he considered Q-tipping his ears was the closest he'd ever get to the female sexual experience."

I followed Alexa into the sound booth, acutely aware of the ease with which I could be roped in by her talk. Events in the sound booth, however, did not go as planned, or maybe they did. Impossible for me to remain the audiologist with Alexa running her hands up my legs and unbuttoning my shirt.

"Let me see who's still in the building," I said.

The classrooms on the third floor were empty. Only Armin, the custodian, posed a problem. Occasionally, he wandered up to my secluded office for a chat. Once I had even come across him in the sound booth, reading the newspaper. I opened the door onto the first floor, a point from which Armin's radio could be heard if he were still in the building.

The five o'clock news scattered into the lonely hallway. Damn. Still in. Some other time, Alexa, I thought. Maybe just as well.

But she was already undressed by the time I returned, sitting cross-legged on the floor of the sound booth. "I'm glad you're back," she said. "It's freezing in here. Do you have to keep it cold for the sound waves or what?"

I knew I was crazy to fall for her again but at that moment even her dishonesty attracted me. I imagined our bruised hearts rubbing shamelessly together. We made love noisily and maybe even passionately; I could always hope. And afterward as we lay together in the quiet, I had an impression of our sounds somewhere above us, trapped in that little room. And of those sounds tumbling back down upon us, like insects, falling upon our backs, our ribs, our legs, folding their wings and waiting because there was nowhere at all to go.

~

Out in the back yard, with my flashlight, I said, "What I find odd about the creation story, Sylvie, I'm talking to you now, is that nowhere in it is sound mentioned. Dominion is spoken of, as is fruitfulness, but no word of talk. No 'and God created chatter, he forced us to comment.' This was not part of the creation package.

"What I am beginning to think, Sylvie, is that at least a mid-sized bang occurred early on in the evolution of our

species when someone, somewhere, discovered that the
larynx and lips and tongue and sound waves could inter-
mingle with the mind to create a word, a moving thought.
And I don't imagine that the word was 'fire' or 'help' or anything meaning meat. I think the word probably had more
to do with someone's loved one dying — a child, a grandmother, whoever — and that someone, a hairy someone with a Neanderthal forehead screwed up that face with
just as much effort as was required to blow this original ball
of matter to bits, and uttered a monosyllabic wail-squawk.
I think it might have begun with an *m* or a *w*. I think we
both have some idea what it meant. But that wasn't the
biggest bang. That occurred when whomever, standing by
with an equally contorted Neanderthal face, heard and
understood.

"Don't you agree, Sylvie?"

∾

By the end of May, Sylvie and I had finished the raft.
Although I had helped, it was hers, her planning,
her design, her goal to have it done before the end of
the school year. And in the end it would support only her,
so small were many of the dead elm branches that both of
our weights would have sunk the thing. But Sylvie, the
swimmer, could lie down, distributing her bathing-suit-
clad body over the surface of the raft, and scull her way out
to the centre of the reservoir. Away she floated, hovering
effortlessly on the water, her breast cones squished. Once

out on the raft, she seemed to have migrated into another phylum. She did not speak, only dip, dip, dipped her way weightlessly here and there while I stood at the water's edge in my gum boots. She had no further need of me.

Standing on the bank of that lagoon, surrounded by mounds of gravel, through some process of decision-making peculiar to children's minds — involving not words but perhaps forces more like weather, bands of pressure and so on — I up and left. Where once I had wanted to spend time with Sylvie there was now a compulsion to see Graham. Sylvie was a child, floating on a pond in an ill-fitting bathing suit, whereas Graham seemed to be very close to some other pool, a warm pool of adult promise and delight and sin. I wanted to be near him, in the same way I wanted to see more of Blodwen Scarfe's secret life, but all of this wanting was diffused by the lack of knowing, really, what it was I wanted. Thus, I could only approach Graham with the same sort of excitement that compels the salmon upstream, leaping rocks and crashing skull-first into logs.

I went home and changed out of my boots and into flip-flops: barely attached footwear seemed right for the occasion. I knew where I would find Graham. He had not yet made many friends and would be in one of two places, the church or the manse.

"I don't know where he is," a bewildered Daphne said from inside the house, calling from the living room without getting up. "Isn't Sylvie with you?"

"No," I said, "she's still at the reservoir."

"Oh my."

I went next door, into the church, through the side

entrance, catching the door with my foot before it crashed shut. And there I stood in the foyer, steps going down into the parlour and Sunday school, and steps going up into the choir room, past the study and into the nave. The place seemed full of life, unlike how it felt of a Sunday. There was mischief afoot, Graham's presence could be felt. He was like a poltergeist, a quiet force that might turn into a sudden push.

He'll be in the study, I assumed, but I assumed wrong. From the study came adult voices, Reverend Rochon and a female, a familiar voice I did not wish to place. I hurried past, not wanting to eavesdrop, past the choir loft as well and into the nave. Everything in the place seemed to have been polished and silenced and all the more so to be filled with sound, or at least messages, like one's own skull under water. The place sat filled with waiting for Sunday.

"Graham," I whispered loudly. He could have been any-where. Standing near the base of the pulpit and scanning the balcony, I asked "Graham, are you here?"

Nothing. One of the light fixtures swayed in a cross-breeze. The windows were open. Secular noises entered — a dog barking, car doors slamming.

I moved down the centre aisle, checking between the pews, even looking underneath. No Graham. I turned and climbed up behind the pulpit so as to study the painting that hung there, eternally lit. Fat little angel boys and girls; their wings fascinated me, as did their genitals. Little penises, little vulva, little wings. Suddenly there occurred a thumping noise behind me, followed by laughter from above. Graham had dropped a hymnbook from the bal-cony and I was appropriately startled.

"Bad nerves, Annie Clemens. Very bad. Must have something on your conscience. I heard what you did to Miss Philippa Lynch, by the way. Not a nice thing. Not a nice thing at all."

"I'm coming up there," I said, conscious of Graham's need to shock, wanting to foil him.

"Be my guest."

The balcony was dark, as always. There were no windows, only the warmed and dusty air which had travelled up and over the pews. Graham had himself positioned in the back row by the time I had ascended the stairs. He had his paper with him; he had been drawing.

"What are you drawing?" I asked.

"Other galaxies," he said. "Not much sign of you-know-who in most of them. He's fallen right through Andromeda. He's started to shrivel up now, I imagine. Barely noticeable."

He showed me pages of dots, a style of pointillism he had developed. Densities of dots and scarcities of dots, patterns of dots forming shapes, forms I did not recognize. Of the six or seven pages of galactic drawings, only one contained an image of a body part, a little foot in the lower left-hand corner. "Actually," Graham said, "I'm getting bored with this concept. It's important for artists to keep moving on."

"I guess," was my response.

We sat together for a while, not saying much, hiding out it seemed. From where we were we could see through the doorway adjacent to the choir loft and into the little room the Reverend's study opened into.

"Do you want to know what I'm really doing here?" Graham asked.

I was unsure how to answer; this sort of question usually led to near-depraved disclosures. But I knew he wanted me to say yes, and I wanted him to draw me closer. "Okay, what?" I asked.

With this encouragement, he pulled a small plastic packet from his jeans pocket, flat and square with a raised circular formation, like a minute inner tube. "Sheik," it read.

"I'm spoiling my father's fun," Graham said.

I did not follow, but I indicated that I had by exhaling through my nostrils in a knowledgeable manner, like a mechanic might, looking under the hood of a car.

"I found this in his desk yesterday. It's how he operated in Burlington and I'm the one who had to go to a shrink. Boy, he sure works fast. We've only been here for five months. Anyway, he's got his guest in there now and things won't be going exactly as planned. Not this time," Graham said, returning the condom to his pocket. "I just want to see who she is. Do you want to wait here with me?"

"Sure," I said, feeling slightly faint. It was unlike Graham to ask like that. It was unlike me to know more than Graham.

We waited for some time, Graham making dots, me sitting, conscious of my shoulder touching his. I felt scandalously close to his smell and scandalously close to Blodwen. I remember daydreaming about swimming along the bottom of the reservoir, looking up at the floating

Sylvie, smiling, aware of an entirely other, weedy world, a place that pressed equally on every square inch of my body, even those inches between my legs.

"Okay, here we go," Graham said.

We heard the door open, the female voice, distant and muffled, his voice, then hers again, farewells. Then I saw nylons, shoes, the same dress Blodwen had been wearing the time I saw her with the doll.

"He's got good taste, I'll say that much for him," Graham said. And slipping his paper and pencil beneath the back pew, he said "I leave this stuff here. Anyway, do you want to come to my house and play checkers, maybe? I like to play checkers."

"Will your parents be there?"

"Well, not my dad, obviously. He's way too busy. And my mom will be lying down. We can play in the back porch. Mom will say, 'Is that you, dear?' when she hears the door and I'll say, 'Yes, it's me and I've got Annie Clemens with me. We're going to play checkers.' 'That's lovely,' she'll say, then she'll go back into her coma. And after that, nobody will bother us."

And Graham was right. That is exactly what happened.

≈

Alexa was talking. My bedroom was blue with talk. She was talking about last year's Thanksgiving, and about her brother, Andrew.

"It was a scene from hell," Alexa said, "several scenes

from hell, in fact. Janet was there, and my mother and Janet despise one another. Mom describes Janet as ghoulish. On Thanksgiving Day, Andrew was already drinking when I got up. He was tanked by noon, actually fell over in the kitchen at one point. He was laughing at the time, so it's not as bad as it sounds; he's a happy drunk. So he laughed himself horizontal and we put him to bed before dinner.

"Mom and Janet had three barely contained arguments about, let's see . . . they argued about fur, I believe, yes, the wearing of fur by humans with my mother for, of course, and Janet taking the opposing view. That led into a discussion of Greenpeace, which sent my mother into a fit. And finally it was diet, yes, cholesterol, fat, red meat versus dairy products, with Janet aligned with the eggs and cheeses, Mother with the tenderloin and bacon. Janet herself did not eat any turkey; she did sample the stuffing, however. And naturally my cousin George was there. No doubt he'll be there again this year. I talked to Andrew last night and he said that he had had a call from George. It bothers George that I'm a lesbian. He wanted to know if I'd be at Mom's again this year with Janet, and Andrew said, 'I don't know. Why don't you give her a call and ask?' And George, in his usual manner, sidestepped that question by posing yet another. 'Hey,' he said to Andrew, 'is it true that some lesbians have a clitoris the size of a jackknife?' 'Gee-o, I don't know,' Andrew said. 'Again, I would advise you to ask Alexa yourself. You could do that on Sunday, right after you say grace.' "

"What did he say when Andrew told him to ask you about the jackknife stuff?"

"George made his usual rejoinder, a snappy little retort he's been using since he was eight. He said, 'As if.' That's cousin Gee-o's response to any and all confrontation: 'As if.' He was a very unpleasant child. Much of his personality seems to stem from some inborn obnoxiousness. I can't explain it."

I had hoped Alexa would invite me to her family's Thanksgiving dinner, hoped that just once she would begin a sentence with, "I was wondering if you would like to," or, "Maybe we could." But I knew this was improbable, impossible, completely unthinkable. This talk was Alexa's preamble, her introduction to the announcement that she would be going with Janet. A long rambling set of particulars meant to form a picture into which one detail, hardly significant, would finally be placed.

"Alexa," I said, "tell me. Will Janet be going with you to Edmonton for Thanksgiving?"

"She hasn't decided."

"But you've asked her?"

"More out of habit than anything else. Believe me, you would hate it, with Gee-o, and Andrew drunk, and my sister and little Victoria and her gross motor shoes. And my mom would probably find some reason not to like you either. In actual fact, it's an act of malice on my part, inviting her, I mean Janet. I know you don't believe that, but it's at least partly true. You would hate it." Alexa paused before speaking the word "hate," exhaling on it as if it were burning the roof of her mouth with its intensity. "And then, it's partly because I feel sorry for her. She has no one else."

"What about all those Eyes of the Beholder?"

"They're not really friends. Not like you and Monica. You have Monica. You said you always have Thanksgiving with her, isn't that true?"

"Not always. Just the past five or six years." Yes, I had told Alexa about Monica, implied she still lived in Calgary, that I saw her often. Why, oh why?

"So, that's a tradition," Alexa said. "Why mess around with it?"

It was six-fifteen in the morning, but I decided to squander my first cigarette of the day, and to smoke it in bed. Alexa carried on. "Thanksgiving and so on, all of those holidays, can actually be pulled right out of the order of things. Let's face it. You nearly always have to drive somewhere so as to recreate the scene. It's this huge pilgrimage to the place called Convention. I know it sounds like a lot of rationalizing but it's not worth agonizing over some ritual turkey slaughter, believe me."

"It's okay," I said. "It's okay that she goes with you. I just wanted you to tell me." Alexa got out of bed, began to dress. "Not go on and on about Andrew and George. I just wanted you to tell me. I'm happy to go to Monica's. Happy. It's what I want to do."

Alexa had to go. She had to get home and check on her fish and then get to an eight o'clock class. That's Alexa. Her style was to skitter ahead of the moment, it seemed, always be slightly ahead, turning around from some distance to watch the rest of us plod onward.

"I've got to go," she said, then kissed me good-bye, a real kiss, and put on her watch and her shoes and her earrings. She had five bracelets to put on, and that took some time. I sat and smoked, feeling more alone than I had thought it possible to be. Alone like a fish, surrounded by a heavy, formless medium that made words impractical, gulped them up and carried them away, coming together with others of my kind only to copulate, carry out the most rudimentary of affiliations, then waft onward, blinking out of the sides of my head.

"Okay then," Alexa said, conclusively, "I'll call." And she was gone.

I listened to the front door close. Time to get up for work. Snow had fallen during the night, only a skiff but enough to discourage me from driving. I decided to take the bus to work, catch the seven-twenty with Ted, sit down with my fish head alongside my seal friend.

$\sim$

Thanksgiving Sunday arrived. I had declined invitations from both Ted and Isobel, alluding to a fictional cluster of friends and acquaintances living in Bragg Creek. I debated driving to the airport to investigate the possibility of a flight to Vancouver, but rejected that idea. Monica was doing her catering work; it would be a busy weekend for her.

One Ativan left. I decided to crush it with my mortar and pestle and use it as a seasoning in my scrambled eggs. Ativan for the welling up — I thought this would be a good slogan for the pharmaceutical ads.

At around two in the afternoon I left my house, not

even bothering to head west out of my driveway, but east instead, then around in circles. Because I had no direction, I was reminded of a time when I was a child on my uncle's farm, watching a rabid fox from a fencerow. The fox was standing in a field of oats, standing and intermittently jumping into the air as high as it possibly could, arching its back like circus dogs will in an attempt to achieve some state contrary to nature. This was the fox: it leapt and leapt, moving hardly an inch to the left or right, seeming to know that it could no longer reside on this earth. It had to hop off now, which it did. My uncle felled it with a single shot.

I was feeling a bit like that fox, until I settled upon a plan of action. I would walk along Bowness Road and visit the pawn shops; some might be open, and as for the others, I could peer inside the windows. Perhaps it was the Ativan, but I did not care if Ted or Maureen happened to drive by and see me caught up in my own contradictions. And after the tour of the shops, I would walk to Edworthy Park and lie on the grass for a while.

Sylvie used to love the pawn shops and the secondhand stores. They stoked her imagination in a way I could never really share. Whether it was miniature plastic farm animals, topographical maps, old Scrabble games or a piece of pastel blue Luray crockery, all these objects evoked pictures for her of previous owners. Sometimes she would even draw these images in sketches she called artist's conceptions. So many afternoons we spent strolling along and exploring what was behind those windows filled with old clarinets and accordions, knives, watches, rings. I told her once that it was easier for her to love those shops because she wasn't bothered by the smell. To me, they smelled of dust and dirt, bad memories and worse plans, so I usually waited outside.

Along Bowness Road, each store front was familiar to me in the way such places must be to dogs: the familiarity of the situation waited in. In the still October air, I felt as if I were entering and leaving small pockets of those past days. That was the sort of day it was: so calm that the atmosphere, like a mind, could call back specific moments, certain clusters of thought mingled with a breeze, possibly diesel fumes, and position them where they were before. This, then, was the store where Sylvie found the map of Iceland. Because it was a hot summer, we had talked about going there. And then Sylvie had found the map in a box of books, after a long search for whatever she had been hunting. I remember that day she had been in the store for a long time, Bud's it was called, while I waited and waited. At last, I pressed my face to the glass to see what was going on, and there at the front desk were Sylvie's shoulders, momentarily lighting up the dark interior. Her head and torso were not visible because of the stacks and shelves of debris, only the shoulders, those two half-moons of mine. Then I turned to watch the street and the passersby and their hips. I watched them approach and recede, hips of all sorts, crotches male and female. On such a hot day, I guess the inner life of the thighs and the spaces between them must have been of interest to me, all that slipping together of skin and hairiness. Eventually, though, I became impatient with Sylvie, anxious to see her emerge from that recessed doorway into the sun, cool from the interior, in her baggy shorts and undershirt.

I was hit then with a stark recollection of Sylvie's physical self, her body, her breasts, the taste and the smell of her, the taste and smell that walked this sidewalk so many times, like all of the others. Only hers, her taste and smell, were for me, I guess I thought, forever. With the sun on the back of my head, I stared into that pawn shop window, remembering again Sylvie's shoulders as I had seen them, two illuminated curves, skin, muscle, life now gone somewhere, while those abandoned objects, things chosen for their value and unnecessity, remained. An enormous ruby ring glinted its longevity at me.

All right. Nothing new here, I told myself. This thought has passed through me before, and turning around I wondered, why is there no actual weather today? No wind, no clouds, just light, the only prevailing element. Light that fell from so far and with such irradiation it landed upon my ears like two hands, clapping down on them. There is no Sylvie here, the light said, none, no Sylvie in this pawn shop. Remnants of her shadow will not be glimpsed around any of its cluttered shelves. Bits of her voice have not been held in the flaps of this canvas awning. No. Have you heard that word before? A short word, but at certain decibels it will cause quite a flattening of those hair cells. A bully of a word.

So be it, I said to myself. I knew this well enough. It would be best to walk to Edworthy Park now, anyway. Start walking, Ellen Nestle said to me. You'll get there. I could hear my own breathing coming from someplace below and behind my eyes. It was not that bad.

And it was not. I arrived at the park, sat down, checked my watch, coughed once or twice. The Ativan was wearing off, the last of my pharmaceutical pals. My nerves jangled. And although to any observer I no doubt seemed to be sitting peacefully in the shade, what I longed to do was spin, spin like a human-sized drill bit through the grass, the topsoil and the earth's mantle, keep spinning until I hit somewhere near the centre, where the pressure of the earth's weight, its tons and tons of muddy sense, would hold me still, hold me tight. It seemed no less restraint would do.

~

On 20 June 1967, I turned thirteen and decided I was old enough to be considered Graham's girl friend. This involved sitting in the sun porch playing checkers, or in the balcony watching Graham draw, or walking the streets of Mesmer. Sometimes Sylvie came with us.

A couple days after my birthday, all three of us were in the balcony watching Miss Lynch practice. She usually took over for the organist during the summer months. We made no attempts to frighten her, had even gone so far as to announce our presence and say hello. I remember whispering to Graham that her arms looked perfectly normal from that height, and Graham replying that he had heard her scalp got ripped right off during the accident and Miss Lynch now wore a wig. I later learned this was untrue.

Apocryphal tales tended to spring up around Miss Philippa Lynch; she was the sort to inspire them.

"I figured out how to get into the belfry, by the way," Graham announced in that ironic voice of his. "Dad tries to keep me out of the belfry, wherever we go. Maybe he thinks I'll jump or something, or maybe it's just the old bats-in-the-belfry thing. They both think I'm nuts, don't they, Sylvie?"

Sylvie remained silent.

"See? No answer. That says it all. It's Dad who should be going to the shrink, not me. He's the reason we're here in Mesmer, not me. I wasn't doing it with any of the United Church Women. And now he's at it again. I can't believe it. What place smaller than Mesmer can they send us to?"

"How do you get up into the belfry?" Sylvie wanted to know.

"There's a ladder behind that curtain," Graham said. "Come on, let's get it."

The ladder was heavy, and as we attempted to lift it from its hiding place behind the pointless balcony curtain, it clattered against a pew, causing Miss Lynch what internal horrors I do not know.

"Sorry," Graham called out, "my dad asked me to move this thing."

From then on it was easy. Within minutes we had entered the belfry and ascended into one of the highest vantage points in Mesmer.

"This place will never be as big as Burlington," Graham said, an observation I had heard from him and Sylvie at least a dozen times by then. I had no defence for this statement. Yes, Mesmer was, I supposed, an inferior place. But to me, on that afternoon, it spread out like a metropolis should, with its roofs and treetops and little cars. Tiny Mrs. Murdock in her garden. The eyes could move like airplanes, intentions could be seen, plans understood: oh yes, this street leads to the creamery, that pathway to the Scarfe farm. And if I looked hard enough, I could see the upstairs windows of Blodwen's house, could imagine her sitting at one of them. The pigeons stayed and showed no signs of fear. The belfry was not a human place to be.

Graham dug into his pocket and said, "You should read this. I found it in my dad's study, the latest in the 'Misc.' file." He pronounced the abbreviation for miscellaneous with a hard c sound.

"I don't know," I said, "I'd feel like I was snooping."

"Oh come on," Sylvie said.

"I'm the one who's doing the snooping," Graham added. "You're just an accessory, that's all. Come on, read it. It's from her, that one we saw, Mrs. Dish."

"You mean Mrs. Scarfe?"

"Yeah, her."

That ended the debate in my mind. A message from Blodwen — yes, of course I would read it.

Graham handed me the note and I moved from beneath the bell to read it, leaned out over the railing and into the suppertime sunlight. The sound and smell of pigeons hung over us, a tent of fecal odour and empty-headed warbling.

"Philip, Philip," the note began. "The next time we meet

you must tell me about the angels. Is there not some sort of hierarchy (as to their arrangement)? Are the seraphim not thought to be closest to God? And are they said to be ablaze with devotion? Their heads ablaze with devotion? Well, whatever . . . My feelings for you must equal the seraphims'. I am ablaze with devotion, burning up in the kind of contradiction that would be too intense, I imagine, even for Moses to look at directly. Philip, I am three days late. This never happens. I fear and yet hope that I am pregnant. Yours, Blodwen."

"She's pregnant," Graham said, when I finished reading. "That's good, isn't it? That's really great. It would appear that we will be leaving Mesmer soon, possibly for some fur trappers' outpost north of the Arctic Circle. Maybe Ellesmere Island. I was looking at the atlas just this afternoon during geography. I think that's about the farthest we could get from Mesmer."

"Give it to me," Sylvie said. And grabbing the letter, she folded it into a paper airplane and sailed it out of the belfry and across the street, into Mrs. Murdock's climbing peas. I was dumbfounded. Sylvie was capable of such meanness at times.

"There," she said, "the evidence is gone."

"No it isn't," I said. "Somebody will find it, Mrs. Murdock, and she'll read it and then everyone will know. What are you? Stupid? I'm going down to get it."

"No you're not," Sylvie said. "It'll blow away."

"Get out of my way," I said, and I pushed her aside, scrambled down the ladder and the stairs and out the front door of the church. I was thankful for my age and size, both of which had enabled me to shove Sylvie out of my way. Every so often she turned cruel like that.

Mrs. Murdock had gone around to the back yard, thank God, so I was able to pluck the letter from her peas.

"Bring it back," came Graham's voice from the belfry.

I made no reply. My cheeks were red with anger as I tramped home with Blodwen's note, through the evening cooking smells of Mesmer.

≈

Alexa wanted to meet me somewhere, outside, in the open air. "How about the park?" I suggested to the telephone receiver. "Bowness Park. The bench we sat on the first time we went there."

"All right. Sure. The bench would be fine. In maybe half an hour?"

I had a feeling about those words, *I want to meet you somewhere*, the way I sometimes did about specific sets of words. I pictured them as sounds worn clean, faded from a certain predestiny, as if the speaker and the listener would just as soon abandon the use of speech altogether and watch for some pale inevitability to float by. Message enough.

"Two more weeks and we turn the clocks back," I said heartily, sitting down on the bench, looking at my watch. I was determined to present a façade of heartiness; that was the theme word I had chosen for this encounter. "Five-thirty," I said. "Yes, in two weeks' time we'll practically be in the dark. How was Thanksgiving, by the way?"

"Well, Andrew didn't drink," Alexa said. "It was, I guess it was as I thought it would be, except for that one difference. His sobriety actually created more of a tizzy — could we say that? or can only one be in a tizzy? Let's say his not drinking created a stir in that we had to concentrate on the others, who are really kind of tedious compared to Andrew when he's loaded. How was the day with Monica?"

"It was good. I had a great time." Along with my efforts at heartiness, this was all the lying I felt capable of. My heart remained predominantly pink.

"Great. Great," Alexa said. "Well, Colleen and her husband split up the day before turkey day so she was there with Victoria, but no Calvin. Colleen was of course tense and sullen when she wasn't full-force crying, and every time Victoria went out of room Mom would make a comment about Calvin, who she never liked, of course. Mom doesn't really like anyone, although she will admit to a grudging admiration for Liz Taylor. In general, tensions were high. So you see, a drunken Andrew might have improved the situation. And George wanted to play Monopoly. Nobody else did but he kept insisting, so finally Andrew and I played with him, but it just wasn't a board games kind of day. George takes it all so seriously and a gloating Monopolist is hard to endure at family gatherings. Janet sat on the couch watching him with a look on her face that said, 'I'd like to photograph you and dip the images into hot bacon fat.'"

At this point in her monologue, I began to see something taking shape, a structure of some sort around Alexa.

It was a little house, a little bungalow of words for Alexa Stewart and Janet Sainsbury.

"So?" I said. "What did you want to talk to me about? It wasn't your cousin George, I don't think. Or your sister Colleen. I don't think you invited me here to talk about them."

"No, I didn't. You're right there. I didn't ask you here to discuss my Thanksgiving." She looked at me, then away. "Well, I guess I might as well say it. She, her, you know, the pronoun that dares not speak its name, she told me I have to make a decision."

"Ah yes, a decision."

"As to, you know . . . Who? You or her? Which? And I know I'm going backward in time here, I'm deteriorating before your very eyes, but I cannot go back to the food bank again. I can't seem to survive without her. She takes care of me. Pretty banal type of love, *n'est-ce pas?* I mean, she doesn't make my lunches or do my laundry, and I know her Eye of the Beholder stuff is bullshit, but at least she believes in something, which I can't say for myself. It makes for a complementarity I can't seem to leave behind. I'm sorry. I really am. But remember, we were going to be guys about this. Have fun, remember?"

"Oh, I remember," I said, "I remember that agreement. And I can't say I'm surprised. It's just that there was a complementarity for me too, having you in my bed. You complemented the empty space that's there right now, the same one that will be there tonight. It was lots more interesting with you in it."

"I'm sorry," she said again, in an irritatingly genuine

way. Her Thespian background stood her in good stead. "I truly am sorry."

"Yeah, well, I'm sorry too but of course it had to end. I knew that from the start. And you're right, we were going to be guys about it all. You're absolutely right. So, get lost now. I'm being a guy about this. Get out of my park. Get into your car and go. When are you moving back in with her, anyway?"

"End of October."

"Oh yes, how nice for you. Anyway, like I said, get out of my park. Shoo. Don't come back. See? I can be a guy. Get the hell out of here; this is my park. Go on. Go!" I pushed her shoulder hard, then glanced around anxiously, worried I might have been seen by a parent of a deaf child or anyone else who knew me as an audiologist.

"Okay, okay, I'm gone," Alexa said.

She could not tear off in her car, though, because the speed limit in the park is five kilometers per hour. She was not able to leave dramatically, had to jostle over the speed bumps, waiting for the mothers and children. Alexa was forced to leave slowly and with frustration, and this afforded me a moment of pleasure, but only just a moment, before I turned myself around to look at the river.

~

Alexa was required to brake one last and exasperating time, just before the bridge, to allow an elderly woman in a red cardigan to cross. It was Edna

Plummer, right hand deep in her pocket, clutching a handful of bright yellow strips of paper, left hand swinging a cane. She had arrived.

In a matter of minutes she passed over the green lawn behind Annie, walking, walking, walking toward the playground until she came to a bench that suited her and sat down. Her first thought was, "Well, the San looks a little different from here, doesn't it? To think I worked there for sixteen years. Came and went. Came and went. The way my feet used to move."

And her second thought was, "No one knows I'm here. I feel decidedly unhitched." She held herself tight and watched the people. This was very good, excellent in fact. There really was no need to have her picture taken, although the camera was in her pocket just in case.

~

It was the eve of Canada Day, 1967. The citizens of Mesmer and surroundings had walked or driven to the Scarfe farm. Cars lined the concession road the way they did when an auction sale was underway.

Edward Scarfe was very happy with the response. He had gone to a great deal of trouble and expense. An enormous pile of branches and wood sat in the pasture nearest the house, ready to feed the fire that was already burning when we arrived. There were sparklers for the kids and packages of firecrackers strung together. Children were even allowed to dip bulrushes from the creek into a bucket of gasoline, then ignite them in the fire — as long as we stayed in the pasture. It was a child's garden of delight, so much fire, noise and possible danger.

For the adults, there was a table of bottles, a tub of ice, food, plastic glasses and music from the speakers on the side porch. Edward and Blodwen seemed to be everywhere, especially Edward. He lit a package of firecrackers for me, then threw it. Rat, tat, tat, tat, tat they went, endless, like pictures from a war. "Wait till the fireworks," Edward said, tapping his watch. "Midnight."

Graham and Sylvie arrived and we ran around like little kids. We lit sparklers and ate and ate. And when it was truly dark, past eleven, we each claimed a reed, soaked it in gas, set it afire and walked down the pasture hill to the creek. "You kids be careful," somebody yelled.

"We'll put them out in the river," Graham shouted back.

And when we arrived at the Little Mud River, we did extinguish our torches because by then we wanted the black night, and with it, separation from the others. Half an hour until the fireworks. We would watch them from there. Graham held my hand.

"I am ablaze with devotion," he said, sounding almost sincere. "By the way, what did you do with the note?"

"I put it in my dresser."

"Girls always put things in their dressers. Everybody knows that's the first place to look."

Sylvie wondered aloud about the possibility of transporting the raft to the Scarfe farm.

"Better do it soon," Graham said. "We won't be in this town much longer."

That was when we saw the flame that was Blodwen's head coming toward us. A burning head travelling faster than was humanly possible. A Halloween vision.

"What the hell is that?" Graham asked.

As the rattling of the bicycle became audible, we knew it was someone, on fire, on wheels. Screams came from the hilltop: "Blodwen's on fire! Blodwen's on fire!"

Blodwen herself made not a sound, did not scream as she hurtled toward the creek. Arriving at the muddy river bed, she threw herself into the shallow water, head first, dousing the flame just like that. Like an apparition she rose up, then collapsed.

I ran to her. Others ran down the hill, Sylvie and Graham ran, but I ran first. And I held her head out of the water and smelled the smell of burnt hair and flesh and felt the heaviness of a human body. I had saved her, I felt certain, saved the most beautiful woman in Mesmer, and for a moment I felt completely stopped, held as in a photograph, as if I might not ever need to leave that waterside place. Then Edward arrived and I was pushed aside as others helped to lift her. I could hear Miss Lynch, of all people, yelling "Call an ambulance. Call an ambulance."

They climbed back up the hill, everyone, Edward and some other men carrying Blodwen, Sylvie and Graham and I lagging behind, astounded, astonished. So this was the sort of price the adults paid. The fireworks, needless to say, were never set off.

Blodwen was not seriously hurt; it seemed she knew exactly how much gasoline to dump onto her head before setting a match to it. Enough to create drama, confession, pathos. Edward loved her; he forgave her. Although I'm told she still has a bald spot from the burn.

Not long after, as Graham had predicted, the Rochons were moved again, this time to a small town in Manitoba. Sylvie and Graham soon became like a dream to me, a good dream which I believe I must have kept tucked away in a small, contemplative urn until that day at the Planetarium. I do believe the Reverend Rochon changed his ways, at least that is what Sylvie told me years later. He did wind up with one of the biggest churches in Vancouver, after all.

And early in March 1968, Aaron Edward Scarfe was born, Aaron Scarfe who is now a young man and, I believe, studying law. The last summer I went home to Mesmer, I saw him on the main street. Easy to recognize; Aaron has the same grey eyes Sylvie had.

~

It really was not a crisis: the inconstant lover departs. It was to be expected. Janet Sainsbury's image had hung over the affair from the start, like an enormous head projected onto a drive-in movie screen, moving its lips, barking out instructions. This was not an event even to be taken seriously, I told myself. It was not as if I would have to drive, like Martha, with a dead Alexa in the back seat of my car all the way to Edmonton. It was not at all like the irreversible sort of departure Sylvie had made. It was neither of those, really, one of the lesser types of loss but made difficult by the fact of actually watching it occur. Like a rabbit that's got loose tearing off in desperate zigzags, or a helium balloon that taps gently on the eaves, tap, tap, tap, before rising, lifting off into the blue sky out of reach. And you could run and slosh in your boots all you wanted, but you knew from the outset it was a hopeless pursuit.

Nighttime and I was in my house. Next door, Ted and Maureen and the children were in theirs, Edna and Isobel too. Several neighbourhoods away was Martha. Then there was Monica, over the mountains.

I imagined the sound field around and above each of these homes would include voices in the speech banana, whole bunches of fruit, maybe an iron clump, clumping as Ted pressed a shirt, or the whir of Martha's sewing machine. Even Monica's silence, her fifteenth-floor silence, would have a type of timbre missing above my house. In my sound field there would be the chattering of the river and above that, only pinpoints of noise like my patients heard in the sound booth, blips and bleeps listened for with the most vigilant ears. What next, for heaven's sake? What next? I'm ready and waiting.

Well, I thought, standing in my kitchen, reeling in my clothesline, I guess Miss Lynch is having the last laugh, wherever she is. At least her spinsterhood had dignity, an elegant frailty: one could forgive her her nerve pills. But not me, a big overgrown woman like me. Size nine feet. Ativan. It's a sad commentary, I could hear my brother saying.

I'll bet Miss Lynch used to make herself tea and listen to

recordings, probably took the train to Toronto and bought sheet music sometimes. No doubt she had a lady friend here and there. She read, went on trips. Seeming to be frayed at the edges, alone and nervous, she was in truth defying all of us, moving here and there just as she wanted.

My God, I thought, glancing outside, it's dark out there. The night seemed right outside my windows, leaning its back on them. But instead of going to bed, I decided to do something I had not done for a while. I put on my jacket and went out, picked up Spike, attached him to his silly leash and sat in my lawn chair down by the Bow.

I thought briefly of all the creatures floating by. Then, picking up Spike, I said, "Spike, you have no idea of the big picture here, do you? This river comes out of the mountains, out of a very clear, glacier-fed lake which I myself have seen, by night, in the moonlight. And by day. It's an unnatural shade of blue from the glacial deposits. You would not believe such a blue is possible. Your first instinct would be to think that the hotel owners had been mixing dyes into the water, but not so. It is a natural phenomenon.

"And then there is the hiking path, all along the river-side, in the valley. It's necessary to ford the river to reach it. Yes, Spike, ford the river. Something you would never be able to do. It's one side or the other for the rabbits of the world. You can walk along that trail for hours and not see a soul because most people don't want to ford the river to get to it. Well, the water goes right up to your crotch; you have to carry your pants and shoes across. When Sylvie and I hiked it we didn't see anyone for eight solid hours. And I never told Sylvie this, but I was terrified the entire time. I kept looking over my shoulder for bears, Spike. I kept imagining us being ripped to pieces, our blood dripping into the river, flowing by our very own house a few days later, followed by other bits and pieces, fingernails, teeth, glasses.

"No, I never told Sylvie that and I'm glad now that I didn't.

"Sylvie wasn't perfect, was she, Spike, but she wasn't afraid of much. It seemed as if she had seen it all up close, early on. The flesh rattling around in the church, the blood with the stories and the hymns, Graham amidst pictures of small, fat angels. Sylvie was never afraid of being alive. She thought it was enough, early on. She thought it was just right."

I placed Spike down on the grass and he began to nibble. The weather had turned cool at last; time to move on to autumn.

There was a half-moon and I said, just for something to say, "Spike, that is called a half-moon." From behind me came a rustling sound, the wind picking up, I thought, but no, it was Ted. He had come out to join me and I was overjoyed. He wanted to go out in the canoe for a while, upstream a bit.

"Do you want to come along?" he asked.

"Yes, yes, I'd love to. Just a minute and I'll put Spike away and, hold on for a second, Ted. I want to get something."

Ted flipped the canoe over and waited while I dashed inside to my bright kitchen and farther, into the dimly lit bedroom. It was the urn I wanted, the ashes.

"Let's dump these," I said when I was back outside. "I think it's time I did that."

"I can't argue with you there," Ted said and we lifted the canoe and carried it to the water's edge. Ted took the stern while I sat in the bow, talking. The water was very slow but even so it knocked against the canoe gently as we paddled upstream. Upstream, past the houses to the edge of the park, that is where I decided I would dump the remains of Sylvie so that later on her ashes would travel by my house, reflecting a bit of light or sound. In the meantime, I decided to tell Ted the story of Blodwen Scarfe and Philip Rochon, and later, maybe show him that note of Blodwen's. I still have it, packed away with all of Sylvie's maps.

~

~

About the Author

Marion Douglas lives and writes in Calgary, Alberta.
Her first novel, *The Doubtful Guests*, was short-listed for
an Alberta Book Award in 1993. She is currently
working on a third novel.

~

About the Artist

Originally from Toronto, Sheila Norgate now lives
and works in Vancouver, B.C., where she often
dreams of a larger studio space and believes
in her art with all of her heart.

~

Press Gang Publishers has been producing vital and
provocative books by women since 1975.

A free catalogue of our books in print is available from
Press Gang Publishers, #101-225 East 17th Avenue,
Vancouver, B.C. V5V 1A6 Canada